AUTUMN EMBERS

AUTUMN EMBERS

A Batavia-on-Hudson Mystery

TINA DEBELLEGARDE

For Mom and Dad
Who always told me I could do or be anything

For Alessandro and Wakana,
My real-life Ian and Aki,
For being as loving as you are
and
For making Kyoto a home for me

I love you all
Home is where our hearts are

Praise for Autumn Embers

"A beautiful novel that seamlessly embraces past and present, east and west, mystery and resolution, all the contradictions that make us human. This is the rare book that leaves its reader feeling balanced and whole."—Carol Goodman, two-time winner of the Mary Higgins Clark prize and author of *Return to Wyldcliffe Heights*

"A wonderfully constructed organic mystery, *Autumn Embers* moves back and forth from two charming locales—Bianca St. Denis's home in Batavia-on-Hudson, a village in Upstate New York, and Kyoto, the home of her son, Ian. Bianca travels to Kyoto to return an ancient Japanese artifact, only to find herself embroiled in a murder investigation that implicates Ian. Meanwhile, in Batavia-on-Hudson, a potential romantic interest, Sheriff Mike Riley, is fighting to keep his job while facing questions about his former NYPD partner's untimely death. Although more than an ocean apart, both Bianca and Mike lean on each other in solving their respective mysteries. Author Tina deBellegarde expertly captures the details of two very disparate worlds, reminding us that at the heart of these experiences is our shared humanity. I've become a new fan!"—Naomi Hirahara, Edgar Award-winning author of the Mas Arai mystery series and the Mary Higgins Clark Award-winning Clark and Division

"Get ready for another thrilling ride with Tina deBellegarde's mystery series, this time in our own Kyoto backyard."—Amy Chavez, author of *The Widow, the Priest and the Octopus Hunter*

"Fans of Louise Penny and *Crazy Rich Asians* will adore *Autumn Embers*, the third installment of the acclaimed Batavia-on-Hudson series. Heartful and human, an intriguing mystery, and filled to the brim with rich descriptions, this love letter to Japan is Tina de Bellegarde at her finest."—Jen Collins Moore, author of the captivating Roman Holiday Mysteries

"This is a scrumptious book. We expect a well-written, twisty plot, interesting, relatable characters, as well as a setting that charms from Tina de Bellegarde. In *Autumn Embers*, she delivers on all counts. But for me, the star of the show is Kyoto. As we work our way through this highly satisfying novel, rich in detail, we can taste the delectable Japanese noodles, smell the heady aroma of the brewing tea at the tea ceremony, and feel the fire at the festivals. The author's love for Kyoto comes through, and lucky readers can't help but share in the feeling. *Autumn Embers* will have you reaching for your passport and booking a ticket to 'the land of the rising sun.'"—Carol Pouliot, author of the Blackwell and Watson Time-Travel Mysteries

"Step into the world of Bianca St. Denis, small town librarian and amateur sleuth, as she arrives in Kyoto, Japan to visit her son. Like a richly woven tapestry, this immersive tale has it all: insights into Japanese culture, traditions and delicacies, as well as memorable characters, an intriguing mystery and… murder. With vivid descriptions and an unhurried writing style, *Autumn Embers* is thoroughly engrossing!"—Lida Sideris, author of the Southern California Mysteries

Batavia on Hudson
POOL HOUSE
BLANCHARDS
Ban Sawyer
Antiques
Olsen's HARDWARE
VAN PATTEN ST.
Lester Quink
V.F.W.
BOOKS
HIGHSCHOOL
Pharmacy
Library
CINEMA
STELLA'S
Rudy's
MARKET
Coffee
MAIN ST.
LUTZ
LIQUOR STORE
POST OFFICE
SHERIFFS OFFICE
BRIDGE ST.
COMMUNITY CENTER
TOWN HALL
CREEK
MILLER ST.
BENCH & MUG
Crossroads
Inn & Antiques
NEW TRAIN STATION
BATAVIA
AGATHA MILLER
OLD TRAIN STATION
ERNIE'S
Carriage House
OLD TANNERY
FISHER PARK
MILLER'S POINT
HUDSON RIVER

Olivia Last
Kenzo
McLoughlin's
PUB
STREAT REAL ESTATE
DAWSON'S
BETTY'S FLOWERS
FUNERAL HOME
MAIN STREET
Rectory
Church of St. James
LOIS LANES
GAZETTE
Bianca St. Denis
MILLER MANSION
DEKKER'S FARM
Claire Koop
GROENMEER INN
ROUTE 17
GROENMEER LAKE
ROUTE 17
BAIT & TACKLE
OLD MILLER TOWN COMPANY HOUSING
SOUTH MAIN STREET
Stewart Dekker
N
E
W
S

FUNA GATA
GOLDEN Pavilion
LEFT Daimonji
KITANO TENMANGU
KUABZI ST.
TORII GATA
IMADEGAWA ST.
Nishijin
Textile
District
Nijo Castle
Bamboo Grove
OIKE ST.
TENRYU-JI
SHIJO ST.
GOJO ST.
Togetsukyo Bridge
HORIKAWA ST.
MONKEY
PARK
KATSURA
RIVER
Kyoto
N
W E
S

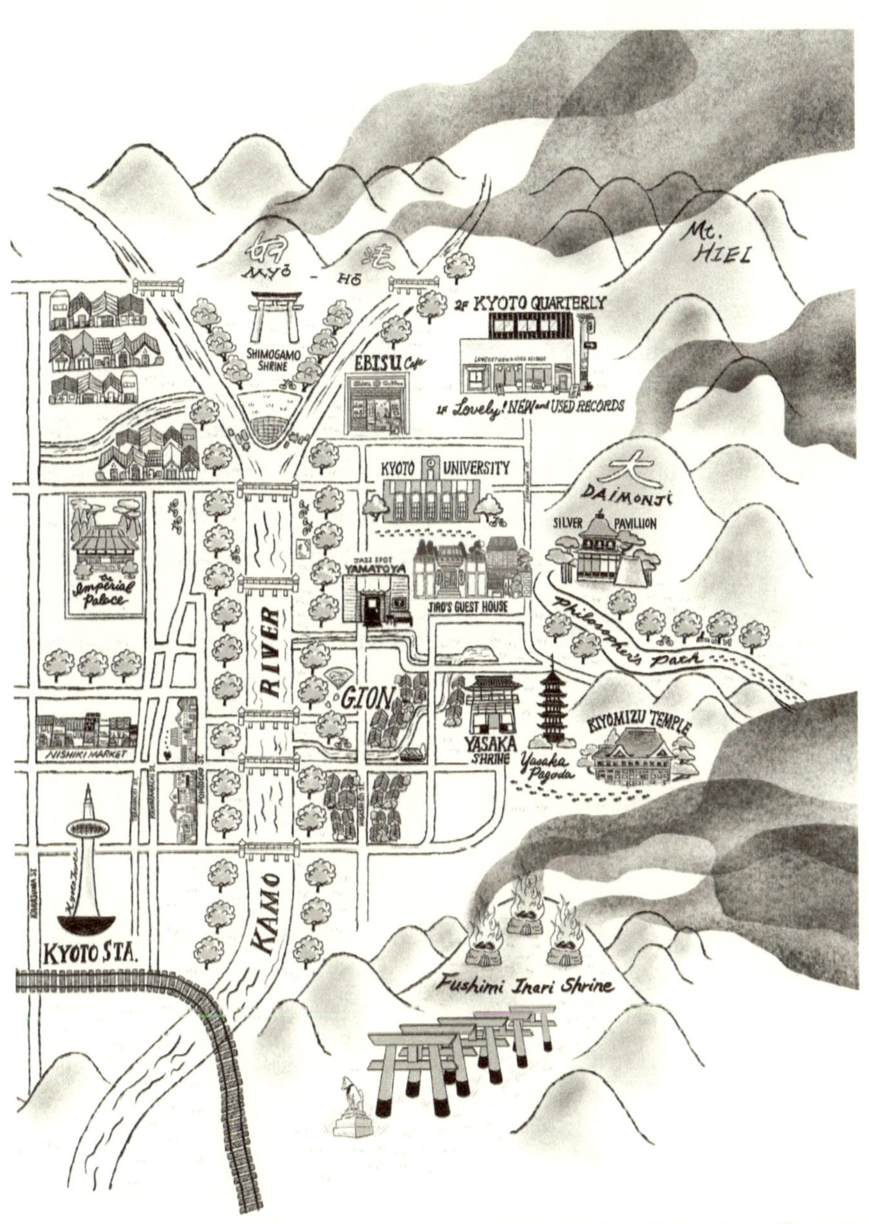
MYŌ - HŌ
Mt. HIEL
SHIMOGAMO SHRINE
EBISU Cafe
2F KYOTO QUARTERLY
1F Lovely! NEW and USED RECORDS
KYOTO UNIVERSITY
DAIMONJI
SILVER PAVILLION
YAMATOYA
JIRO'S GUEST HOUSE
Philosopher's Path
The Imperial Palace
RIVER
GION
YASAKA SHRINE
Yasaka Pagoda
KIYOMIZU TEMPLE
NISHIKI MARKET
KAMO
KYOTO STA.
Fushimi Inari Shrine

Principal Characters

Some of the Villagers of Batavia-on-Hudson

Bianca St. Denis: Not-so-reluctant amateur sleuth. Young widow. Recent transplant to Batavia-on-Hudson along with her cat Shelby, an orange tabby with cuddling issues. Writer, former high school history teacher. Works at the library and writes for the *Batavia Gazette*. Son Ian is studying in Japan.

Mike Riley: Sheriff, former NYPD. Moved to Batavia after his partner died on the job. City boy with a country heart.

Maggie Riley: Mike's wife, now living in New York City as they try a separation. Runs a literary agency. City girl through and through. Bianca's agent.

Olivia Last: Bianca's closest friend in town. *Batavia Gazette* editor. Known for her column "The Last Page."

Eugene Wilkins: Owner of Stella's Diner, the village hub. Still grieving his late wife Stella.

Kenzo Ishikawa: Lives a quiet life in the hills above the village with his dog, Tengo, a Shiba Inu. Escorts Bianca to Japan while addressing some of his own personal issues.

Vera Weber: Mike Riley's deputy who is running against him in the Sheriff's election.

Edward Angleton: Politician from Albany. Running for Sheriff against Mike Riley.

Lester Quirke: Village centenarian, not-so-retired lawyer, and owner of the bait and tackle shop with his rescue skunk, Dolly.

Characters in Kyoto:

Ian Grant: Bianca's son, studying and living in Kyoto, Japan.

Jiro Takeuchi: Ian's friend and owner of the guest house where Ian lives and works.

Daniel Wilson: Ian's friend, mentor, and father figure from England. One-man show at the *Kyoto Quarterly* Magazine.

J.C. Curtis a.k.a. Jay: One of Ian's former bandmates. Expat from the United States. Where J.C. goes, trouble follows.

Irvin Concannon: Another expat from the United States, J.C.'s friend, and Ian's former bandmate.

Riku Kawabata: Shady character with loose ties to organized crime.

Takeru Oba: A local police officer and Jiro's cousin.

Aki Hashimoto: Kenzo Ishikawa's granddaughter and Ian's love interest.

Prologue

"Every day is a journey, and the journey itself is home."
Matsuo Bashō
(1644-1694)

Kyoto, Japan

"Koji, let him know I'll have it all done for him by Friday." Riku Kawabata leaned in close to the barkeep, his breath a musky mixture of whiskey and cigarettes.

"I don't know, Riku. Can you really come through on this one? It's a tall order. Seems like more than you can handle." Koji struck a match and lit the cigarette dangling from Riku's lips.

"Let me decide what I can handle. You just deliver the message." The veins on Kawabata's neck throbbed as his pitch rose.

Koji turned up his hands to ward off Kawabata's unpredictable anger, but he still felt the need to caution him. After all, Koji would be the one delivering this message and he didn't want to be associated with another botched job. Messengers often got the short end of the stick. "I'm just worried for you. You fell short once before. Don't make promises you can't keep."

"Why can't you leave it alone? Just do what I ask."

"What do you want me to say—It's all going to be okay?"

"Yes. That's what I want to hear. I've got this under control, so stop worrying." Kawabata tapped his empty glass twice on the bar and pulled out his thick wallet.

Koji refilled it and poured a finger for himself. "This one's on me, Riku.

Just be careful. You know what happens to someone who doesn't come through."

"I know. I know all too well. I got a pass once before, and that's exactly why I must do this. I have to prove myself. You know that as well as I do."

J.C. Curtis sat at a rickety table with his friend Irvin Concannon. He strained to hear the conversation at the bar, but Kawabata's local *Kansai* accent was so thick that J.C.'s textbook Japanese couldn't penetrate it.

This whole ordeal had been frustrating from the beginning. Irvin had led him to a street off the beaten path and then downstairs to this dark and dingy bar. J.C. was in need of money, and Irvin had a scheme up his sleeve. He always had a scheme. This time, one of Irvin's infamous connections back in the States was going to help them. J.C. went along with all of Irvin's plans even when he didn't agree with them, because although some of his ideas fell flat, others had proven to be lucrative, and lucrative was what he needed right now.

J.C. knew and trusted the bartender who had introduced them to Kawabata. But Kawabata was another story. He seemed too desperate. He was a poser, pretending to be a tough guy, when in fact, as Koji had told them, he came from an elite local family. He had even attended business school at Berkeley. In reality, all Kawabata wanted was to break out of the strictures of his proper upbringing, and the best way to do that was to rub elbows with the underworld. He refused to follow in his brother's footsteps to become a lackey in his father's business empire. By fraternizing with the local mobsters, he was ensuring that his father would never allow him in the company. It would be too shameful.

J.C. tried to sit patiently, waiting for everything to be set in motion. He needed Irvin's plan to come together. It would earn them some quick cash and get them in good with someone who was well-connected. Irvin had assured him that it would come in handy later to have someone like Kawabata on their side.

He got tired of trying to eavesdrop, his eyes scanning the dreary club. The place was empty except for two scrawny old men half asleep at the back table. J.C. felt vulnerable sitting in the darkest corner of the place, but he didn't have enough time to regret his decision. Kawabata swayed to their table with his drink refreshed. He sat down with difficulty but clutched his glass so as not to spill a drop.

"Okay. It is all set. I will be heading out for Yokohama in the morning. You know what you need to do. I will be indebted to you both if you come through." As Kawabata's hands wrapped around his tumbler more tightly, J.C. could clearly see his pinky was missing above the knuckle. "Let me say that differently. You need to come through. Understood? Otherwise, get out now, and I will find someone who can."

Chapter One

Batavia-on-Hudson, N.Y.

Eugene Wilkins cleared his throat.

"Hey, listen up, everyone."

He raised his fingers to his lips and let out a shrill whistle over the clanging of forks on plates and the thuds of coffee cups on the diner counter. His gossiping neighbors froze in place, their forks laden with buttermilk pancakes dripping in maple syrup, their knives loaded with apricot preserves ready to slather on toast.

Silence. The only remaining sounds were the sizzle of bacon and Paul Desmond's saxophone emanating from the old turntable.

Eugene cleared his throat again and started reading from the *Albany Times Union*.

Local Batavian Solves Million Dollar Artifact Heist

Bianca St. Denis, 43, head librarian of the Batavia-on-Hudson Community Library, will be off to Japan today to receive her reward for being instrumental in the recovery of an 18th-century artifact, a hand-carved netsuke belonging to the noble family of Nakayama. Netsukes are tiny sculptures of wood or ivory. Since a kimono had no pockets, men suspended their tobacco pouches, pipes, or coin purses on a cord from their obi sash, along with the ornamental netsuke as a counterweight. Although they were designed to be functional, they were often beautifully carved. Over the centuries, some rare netsukes have become collector's items.

The Nakayama Family has spent the last eighty years trying to reassemble a netsuke set of the Seven Gods of Good Fortune hand-carved by the artist Kawakami Shinji. His works, and those of his students, have been collected the world over, but despite their best efforts, one piece eluded the family. The god Ebisu remained at large.

During the June 17th storm, Joel Stanton, an antique dealer from the firm of Stanton and Randall, was found dead at the foot of Dead Man's Leap in the outskirts of Batavia-on-Hudson in Onanda County. In his pocket was the carved figure of Ebisu, stolen from the Crossroads Inn as the owners prepared for the annual auction and rummage sale.

Bianca St. Denis, a resident of Batavia-on-Hudson, was the intended purchaser and was instrumental in solving the puzzle of the missing netsuke's value as she collaborated with Sheriff Mike Riley on this mystery. Of note, Ms. St. Denis worked closely with the Sheriff last year in solving the murders of two villagers of Batavia.

The Japanese Office of Cultural Affairs has reported that once the netsuke set is complete it will be taken under consideration as a national treasure. Quite a coup for Sheriff Riley and his right-hand sleuth, Bianca St. Denis. Perhaps Ms. St. Denis has missed her calling? The village of Batavia-on-Hudson must be proud of their newest villager.

"Well, look at that. Our girl has gone and gotten her name in the big Albany paper. Who'd'a thunk it. Pretty impressive for a local Batavian." These words came from Lester Quirke, newly turned centenarian, not-so-retired lawyer, and owner of Lester's Bait and Tackle. Lester winked at Bianca, then raised a coffee cup in her direction. He sat there in his pinstriped suit, grinning before an empty plate that once held a Lumberjack Special.

Eugene smiled to hear Bianca finally called their local girl. It must be true; even the Albany paper said so. He turned to find her sitting in her usual seat at the counter across from him and his grill, her ubiquitous notebook and pen beside her plate. She was beaming.

Bianca could feel her skin tingling as the blush formed on her cheeks. She wasn't usually a blusher, but that had more to do with the fact that she rarely put herself in situations of discomfort. She wasn't exactly a risk-taker. At least she wouldn't have thought so, except this last year had proven that impression wrong. What with being involved in solving some local murders and getting to the bottom of the stolen artifact soon to be returned to Japan.

She wondered about the blush. She was pleased to be called a local. That was certain. Everything she had done over the last year had been to find a niche for herself in this hamlet. Losing Richard two years ago had been unexpected, and after roaming around the house alone for almost a year, she had decided to get out and meet her new neighbors. It was a struggle for her, but with volunteering and her work at the library, she had finally started to feel like a local. The harder part was getting the Batavians to see her that way. But the cracks were showing.

The notoriety of this case had been fun, and seeing her name in the papers had been a new experience, certainly blush-worthy, but Bianca knew that this warm tingling on her cheeks had more to do with her name and Mike's name side by side once again.

The room returned to its usual clamor. Bianca heard the clatter of cups and plates, but something else as well. They were clapping. Eugene, tall and imposing, stood near the grill, his towel thrown over his shoulder, leading the applause.

Others joined in. Monica White slipped her order pad and pen into her apron and clapped. Lester grinned from ear to ear and elbowed Bert Henderson, the local handyman, who was whistling. Claire Koop was clapping and using this opportunity to tilt a little closer to Bert, the one who had, so far, gotten away. Bianca was pretty sure Claire was finally reeling him in, slow and steady as she does with the bass at the fishing tournament every year.

Gazing around the room, Bianca could see them all. The villagers. Difficult though some of them were, they were her friends. More like a family. They knew each other's best and worst qualities and tolerated them with grace.

Chapter Two

Bianca picked up the photo of Richard off the kitchen windowsill. It was one of many around the house, put there so Bianca could find him in any room at any time and chat. When he was alive, they would often share the same space rather than working in different areas of the house. They would crowd together on the same table, their papers out of order, not nearly as productive as they would have been had they chosen to work alone and separately. But that wasn't their way.

She swiped her sleeve across the glass to remove the dust that regularly accumulated because she insisted on open windows whenever possible. The kitchen breeze, together with Richard's image, made even dish washing pleasant. She loved it here in her old German farmhouse, their escape from the city. It had been run down, but some loving attention made it a home. When they weren't gardening or raising chickens, she wrote while he read and researched.

"Richard, here I go again. I'm finally going back to Japan. I wish you could be with me." She took the photo and tucked it into the carry-on bag she had prepared for the plane. She turned to the sofa where her suitcase remained open and found an orange ball of fur asleep on her clothes. She reached in and gently lifted him into her arms.

"Sorry, sweetheart. It's time to close up shop." Shelby yawned at her, baring his sharp teeth. Bianca kissed the top of his head, sad to leave him behind, but it made no sense to subject him to this trip. It was only a couple of weeks. Besides, he would get plenty of attention from Emily White. She would be cat sitting, plant sitting, and overall house sitting. Bianca had given Emily the final run-through yesterday. She had left her a key, although Bianca, like most villagers, rarely locked her door.

Bianca picked up her notepad. Neat little checks lined one side—she was done. All packed.

Just as the clock chimed three o'clock, there was a knock on the door. He was prompt.

She smoothed her sweater, tucked her short hair behind her ears, and walked to the door. Shelby beat her to it, trotting ahead and placing himself in the perfect spot to slip out when Bianca opened the door. She gently placed her foot in front of his furry orange belly to block his escape.

Bianca opened the door for Sheriff Mike Riley. Dressed in jeans and an Irish sweater, his eyes looked a deeper shade of gray against the ecru of the knit and the sharp autumn sky over his shoulder. He was youthful, out of uniform, and his salt and pepper hair didn't age him at all.

"Come on in. I'm just finishing up now."

Mike stepped across the threshold into the old farmhouse and followed her toward the luggage. He ducked his head at the low archway into the living room. Shelby intercepted his every step.

"Hey, little fella. You sure know how to get someone's attention."

"Sorry about that. He wants to be in the middle of everything we do. He was just napping in my suitcase."

"I see."

Bianca followed Mike's gaze to her open suitcase. Her black slacks, the last item she packed, now held a film of fur.

"Hold on." Bianca ran up the stairs to the linen closet and back down in a New York minute. She held up the lint brush like a trophy and tucked it into the carry-on bag. "Ta-da!"

"Smart move. Shall I load the car? Is this all you have?"

"All? That's a pretty big suitcase." She bent over, zipped it up and placed a lock on it.

Mike grabbed the handle and lifted. "Oh, I see what you mean. What do you have in here?"

"The usual. Clothes, gifts for Ian."

"Wow, feels more like bricks."

"Oh, yeah, that would be the books."

"Books? How many books? Aren't you going to be busy going to fancy dinners in your honor, visiting with Ian?"

"Well, yes, but there's always time to read. And Ian won't be free all the time. He goes to his classes; he's also tutoring English. A girl's got to have her books."

"Bianca St. Denis, you're an enigma. You're traveling all the way to Japan to read."

She blushed. She knew it wasn't exactly a compliment. In fact, she was pretty sure he was making fun of her, but in his unique way that made her feel special. Bianca always traveled with books, and she wasn't about to stop now. She knew that Japan offered many things. She would be sightseeing, but she would also have quiet moments in gardens and cafés where she could read and write for hours, and they would just let her be. It was one of her favorite things about Kyoto in particular, it was meditative. Last time she had visited, she had read so much that it had prompted her to return to writing. That, in turn, led to her retirement and their move to Batavia so she could write her first novel, and Richard could have the life on the farm he had always craved. It was a lovely domino effect that had changed her life completely. Last time she had been to Japan, the cherry blossoms graced the avenues. She wondered what secrets autumn in Kyoto might reveal.

Mike loaded the car while Bianca got her last few hugs from Shelby. He was tolerant for a few minutes but wanted down soon enough. She turned, walked out, and locked the door.

Shelby jumped up to the windowsill and watched her with that look. She hated that look. Usually, she was okay with leaving him, knowing she would be home soon, but this was going to be the longest time Shelby would be without her since Richard had died. Shelby was independent, but he was devoted to Bianca.

Mike closed the truck door for her. A nice touch, she thought. Men don't do that very much anymore. Richard had. He would always walk on the street side of the sidewalk, open the door for her. Always treated her as a lady. Bianca was a feminist, a very headstrong one at that, but she loved that he had treated her so kindly. He had been of an older generation. Twenty years older than she. It had suited her just fine. She was rather an old-fashioned person herself deep down. Mike shared that quality, he seemed to be of a different era. An older, wiser, gentler soul than his forty-five years.

As he closed the door, he bent to make sure she was tucked in properly, that nothing was dangling out the door, no fingers were getting smashed. He gently closed it, his face close to the glass. He glanced in her eyes, then looked away and walked around to let himself in.

"You okay?"

"Sure." Her eyes were a little teary, she knew, and he had caught that when he looked in her window. "Leaving my boy. He looks so forlorn at the window."

"Don't you worry. Emily will spoil him and play with him. Shelby will love it. He won't be lonely at all. And you're leaving one boy behind for another. Tomorrow at this time, you'll be having breakfast with Ian."

"Actually, dinner. Since they're fourteen hours ahead, I will be thrown into the future. Not to mention very jet-lagged." They laughed together. She was grateful for his comforting presence. A little awkwardness was still there but muted now. They had been through a lot together.

"Thank you for driving to the airport. Are you sure this is okay? That you have the time for this?"

"I told you, it's not a problem. I'm going to Albany anyway."

Bianca was pleased to have Mike do this airport run, but he seemed off and even a bit distracted.

"Is everything okay? Is it sheriff's business?"

"It's nothing. I have a meeting with my former commanding officer. He's now an Assistant Attorney General. Boy, has he got me guessing. I don't have any details... It's got me wondering, but I'm sure it's nothing."

He eased his truck down her long, winding driveway, the red and gold leaves forming a canopy for them. He turned toward town, and they drove along quietly. She appreciated the silence as she watched the village go by.

They passed Claire Koop, placing an envelope in her mailbox. She raised the red flag on the side of the box, then waved and raised her eyebrows. Even though everyone in the village knew exactly what Bianca was doing today, Claire would enjoy the nugget of gossip she had just acquired by seeing Mike driving Bianca. How serendipitous for Claire, who supposedly didn't like to gossip, but…gossiped plenty.

They passed Dekker Farm. Mike drove slowly around the curve to avoid any loose chickens wandering in the road. Frederika and Kurt Dekker would be out making deliveries about this time. The Dekkers were known for their fresh eggs, their wide variety of mushrooms, and Freddie's homemade jams. They were a couple, those two—Kurt with his long Rip van Winkle beard and Freddie with her soft features and jam-stained hands.

They reached the top of the hill and turned down Main Street. Bianca cracked her window to allow the breeze to ruffle her hair. She was used to seeing the village on foot. Now she looked out the car window to see the Church of St. James, Lois Lanes, and the *Gazette* on her left, Rudy's Market, and her library on the right.

Funny how she considered it her library now. How had it happened? She had come here with Richard to do things together. Now he was gone, but she was writing and had an agent. She hadn't sold a book yet, but still. And she was the librarian of the tiny community library, with one part-time helper. She loved it in there. When she wasn't writing, she was immersed in her books. She hadn't planned it, but sometimes things just work out. She was very happy, considering how much she missed Richard. She felt it was a second chance.

She stared off to the left and watched a barge lumbering down the Hudson. Slow as molasses.

The screech of brakes and the jolt of the truck sent her heart pounding. She jerked forward and back. At the sound of a whistle, she looked around and found Lester Quirke on the sidewalk in his brown pinstriped suit. He slowly bent over to watch as Dolly, his skunk, rushed across the street to meet him.

"That was close. I never saw Dolly until it was almost too late. What with the sun in my eyes."

Bianca wondered if it was more than the sun in Mike's eyes, especially since the sun was still slowly rising from the east over her right shoulder. Could he be that distracted about his trip to Albany?

Lester waved, oblivious to the close call. At the enormous Norway spruce in the square, Mike turned up Van Patten Street. Eugene Wilkins was sweeping the front of Stella's Diner. He stopped and leaned on his broom, and smiled as they drove by.

Bianca had the odd feeling she was on display.

"Looks like the town is cheering you on."

"I don't understand. I feel like I'm in a parade."

"What's not to understand? You helped solve an international crime; you're going to Japan to collect your reward. To Japan. A place most of us have never been to and probably will never go to. They are envious, they are proud of you, they are curious, but most of all, they're happy for you."

Mike and Bianca made their way up the hill overlooking the village, winding until they reached the long driveway leading to Kenzo Ishikawa's cabin.

"It's nice that you and Kenzo will be traveling together. I'm sure the whole trip will be easier for you as a result."

"I'm very lucky. Ian will be pretty busy with school and work, so having Kenzo around will be very helpful. And, of course, he's great company. Plus, he offered to translate for me whenever I needed it. His family lives on the outskirts of Kyoto. It seems he hasn't been back in a long while. So, this worked out for everyone."

They found Kenzo standing in front of his house, dressed in a suit, all ready to go, with his luggage by his side and Tengo, his Shiba Inu, on the other side. Ernie McCrae was just arriving in his old truck with the faded logo *Ernie's Landscaping and Plowing* on the sides.

Ernie, in his work overalls, opened the gate of his truck and loaded up Tengo's dog bed, a case of canned food, and a large bag of dry food, then slammed the gate closed. He shook Kenzo's hand, clapped for Tengo, and opened the passenger door. The dog hesitated, looking to Kenzo for approval. After a few words in Japanese from Kenzo, the Shiba Inu responded by jumping up on the seat to accept a treat. Without another word, Kenzo gave Tengo a pat on his head and closed the door.

Ernie started up the truck and waved as he left the driveway. Tengo stared out the window at the three of them. With that look. Oh, Bianca hated that look.

After adding his modest suitcase to the back, Kenzo squeezed into the cab of the truck next to Bianca. Mike picked up Route 17 as they headed north to the airport.

Chapter Three

Albany, N.Y.

After dropping off Bianca and Kenzo at Albany International Airport, Mike turned his truck around in the small parking lot, then headed toward the center of the city where he was expected at his meeting. He had forty-five minutes to get there. More than enough time.

He was still baffled by the call. Charlie Stephenson was not someone he had ever expected to hear on the other end of the line. His gravelly voice had thrown Mike back in time. It was reminiscent of so many good things in his past, but mostly, it was a reminder of all the bad he had left behind. The brotherhood at the NYPD had sustained him for years, and his relationship with his partner Sal, especially. But then it all fell apart, and Mike had needed out.

Sal had been like an older brother to him. They loved each other, would do anything for each other, and yet they couldn't mesh. Like oil and water, they didn't blend well.

When he was first assigned to Sal, he immediately planned to ask for a reassignment. Day after day, he worried that they were putting each other in harm's way. He was convinced that it was just a matter of time before they ended up in a dangerous situation as a result of their different approaches. Then, at a routine traffic stop, everything changed.

That hot and humid summer day, they pulled a car over and slowly came to a stop behind it.

Sal opened his door and stepped out, "I've got this."

Mike waved him off. "Don't worry. I'll take care of it. I know you still have a couple of reports to finish up. I'll be quick. Two minutes, and we'll be out of here."

Mike walked over to the parked car, then tilted his head into the driver's side window. He went through the usual questions and waited for the driver's license and registration. Mike was anxious to finish up for the day. Maggie was home early for a change, and they had a date night planned. They had been trying for a baby for months and tonight was a fertile time for her.

Like the rest of them, the driver was sweaty and grumpy. He fiddled with his wallet, then opened and closed the glove compartment, mumbling something.

Mike daydreamed of Maggie's soft curls, the way they surrounded her face on her pillow.

A shot rang out and Mike was jolted from his thoughts as the driver's head fell forward onto the wheel. Blood splattered the windshield. It had all happened so fast, he had never sized up the danger.

His senses awakened slowly. Sal standing next to him, then the iron smell of blood, the blaring car horn where the driver's head had landed, and finally, Sal's voice yelling for him to call an ambulance.

Pushing Mike aside, Sal yanked the door open, grabbed the gun from the driver's hand, and passed it to Mike. A gurgle came from the driver's throat as he gasped for air. Sal grabbed a jacket lying on the car seat and applied pressure to the wound.

"I said, call for an ambulance."

Sal saved two lives that night, Mike's and the driver's.

Without Sal's clear thinking, Mike would have been a dead man. After that, Mike never questioned him again. They were bound together by blood and brotherhood from that day forward.

That is, until they found Sal's crumpled body on the sidewalk at the foot of a five-story building just off Central Park.

Chapter Four

Osaka, Japan

When they landed in Japan, the efficiency of the airport in Osaka startled Bianca. One minute, she and Kenzo were gathering their belongings on the plane; the next minute, she was answering a few quick questions at passport clearance, and then her luggage was waiting for her at the carousel. In the blink of an eye, she and Kenzo were out on the sidewalk. She turned to the left and then to the right. *Hidari* then *migi.* No Ian. She looked again while practicing her Japanese. Left then right.

And then there he was. His dark curls bouncing as he rushed toward her. He hugged her so tight it reminded her of when he was a child and came home from school so eager to share his day with her. After a long minute of holding him, she finally allowed him to step back and bow to Kenzo.

"*Ishikawa-san, Hajimemashite. Ian desu.* It is so nice to finally meet you. Thank you for escorting my mother."

"It has been my pleasure. Your mother is a delightful companion."

Through glassy eyes, Bianca watched in amazement at her American boy as he seamlessly fulfilled all the necessary courtesies required of the Japanese: the bow, deeper than his elder's, the honorific added to the end of Kenzo's surname. And then Ian produced the requisite *omiyage* gift of thanks to Kenzo. He presented the modest parcel with both hands. It was a small box of Kyoto specialty cookies made with green tea and white chocolate. Cha no Ka Matcha cookies were her favorites. She secretly hoped he had gotten her a box as well. If not, she would plan to get them for herself very soon.

Kenzo responded in kind with a shallower bow. With two outstretched hands, he presented Ian with maple sugar sweets from Freddie Dekker's own maple trees.

"*Arigatou gozaimasu.*" They both thanked each other and turned back to Bianca, the reason they were now connected.

Ian bent sideways, an arm around his mother's shoulder, gave her a quick kiss on top of her head, and whispered, "Your cookies are at home. Don't worry." Then, a little louder, "I'll get the bus tickets. We should be boarding soon."

Kenzo held up his hand. "You two have a nice trip home and catch up. I will take care of some business in Osaka and meet up with you again in the morning in Kyoto. I have the address of your guest house. Thank you for hosting me, Ian."

Kenzo left them just as the bus driver stowed their luggage. Ian and Bianca found comfortable seats in the back of the nearly empty bus. Ian opened up his backpack and handed her a bottle of cold green tea and an *onigiri.*

"You remembered." She peeled off the ingenious little origami-like wrapper, revealing the rice snack. She took her first bite of the little triangle, the center oozing just enough tuna and mayo to be delicious but not messy. "I'm so hungry, thank you."

She sipped her tea and took little bites to savor the *onigiri* as Ian rambled on and on about his plans for her visit. The gardens, the festivals, the coffee shops, the picnics along the river, and the noodles. Oh, so many noodle shops she would need to try—*ramen, soba,* and *udon.* He tripped over his words as he broke off into tangents about his experiences at these same places. She listened, but mostly she watched him and his enthusiasm, his exuberance for a culture so different from his own, yet where he felt so at home. Her eyes filled up as she realized that he may never return home. That this place may be his place.

The bus pulled into Kyoto Station. After Ian retrieved her suitcase, he dragged it behind him as they walked the remainder of the trip to his place.

They eventually turned down a quiet lane off a main street and turned again, and then she realized that they were in a time machine. Here, behind the busy streets, was a lane that could barely accommodate cars that had existed for centuries. The wooden structures on each side were closed off to the public, each with a tiny potted garden on the street and a pail of water at the ready for the bucket brigade in case of fire.

Ian had moved out of the dorm when his friend Jiro Takeuchi offered him a job at his traditional guest house. Ian was living in this historic neighborhood in exchange for helping with the guests. The arrangement suited Ian and gave him enough space for his visiting mom as well as for Kenzo.

Ian and Bianca stopped before a door with wooden slats. Ian slid the door open and waved his mom in.

"*Tadaima*," he said to the empty entryway. Bianca recognized it as the announcement one made when returning home. Ian's home.

"*Okaeri.*" The disembodied response came from the other room. Jiro came out with a pen still in his hand. He bowed to Bianca and then returned to his full height. He was at least two inches taller than Ian, which surprised Bianca.

After the introductions, Bianca reached for her suitcase to take to her room and settle in. All she could think of was a pillow. She had lost a day crossing time zones. To her body, it was 2:30 in the morning, and all she wanted was some sleep. She could feel it coming over her now that she knew the bed was so close.

"Mom, it's 4:30. It's still early. You haven't even had dinner yet. If you go upstairs now, you will hit the bed, and you will be up by midnight. Leave the luggage where it is. We're going out."

"Out?"

"Yep, trust me on this. You'll thank me later. You'll sleep well tonight, and before you know it, you'll conquer your jet lag. If you go to sleep now, it'll take your entire trip to readjust."

"Ian, I don't think I can take one more step—"

"Oh, yes, you can. I know you, Mom. Let's go, you'll love it."

Chapter Five

Mike grabbed a beer out of the near-empty fridge, pried the top off, and let it clatter as it dropped on the counter. He took his first pull, standing there, the cold easing the fever he felt. Not a true fever but something vague burning from inside.

He held the cold bottle to his temple and decided to keep the lights off, hoping that would help. He also knew the dark room would allow him to ignore the framed photo of him and Sal on their last ski trip. More than a co-worker, more than someone to run ideas by, they had protected each other in the most dangerous of situations while they were on the force together.

But then something went wrong. One evening, after an uneventful day on the job, he was about to head home when he received a call from Charlie asking Mike to join him at a crime scene. He said he would explain when Mike arrived.

Mike left right away, but not before calling Sal, who was home on a personal day off. He left a message on his partner's machine, then headed out.

As he drove, he ran through the possible reasons for the call. Why was he needed at this particular call? Why the secrecy? Could it be a break in the big case they were working on? Or maybe something more nefarious or scandalous? He remembered how a few years prior there had been a scandal when the union attorney had been found mishandling funds. He ended up losing his license, serving time in a white-collar cell, and bringing down some of the union leadership with him. It had taken a long time for the NYPD to live that down. Could it be more of the same?

He soon discovered that it was worse. Far worse. It was Sal.

Sal had jumped. His body had been found at the foot of an apartment building off Central Park, the sweltering heat forming ripples in the air around his body, as if it were a mirage.

Mike knew Sal was in a precarious state of mind—the job had been getting to him. And his marriage had been broken beyond repair, shattered due to Sal's constant infidelities. It was a subject Mike and Sal had fought about regularly. Sal thought Mike was a prude, and Mike thought Sal had a fatal flaw that would catch up with him and hurt Elizabeth, his wife. Mike had been right on both counts.

Sal had been off his game for some time, and it had gotten dangerous. He had been disciplined a few times, and almost relieved of his badge, but Mike had come to his defense and had even taken some of the blame. Now Mike realized that maybe he had made a mistake. Maybe Sal had been sending messages, and Mike had missed them. Without Elizabeth around, Mike was the only one left who could have seen the signs, who could have helped.

It had started that day while Mike was staring at the hot pavement—the pounding heart, the dizziness, the blurry eyesight, and short, rapid breaths Mike couldn't control. His head spinning, his heart pounding out of his chest. The ragged breaths. It was the first of many panic attacks to come. He had had some anxiety before—who wouldn't after handling the brutal cases he had in Gotham. Still, he had been able to stay in control. Now, he realized he couldn't manage this at all. Like Sal, he had been losing his grip. The loss of Sal put Mike over the edge too.

Tonight, all these years later, safe in his old armchair, he stretched his legs out on the coffee table. The breeze wafting in the window cooled him and he closed his eyes a moment. Until the vision of Sal on the pavement reappeared.

He switched on the television for distraction. He flipped channels but couldn't concentrate. Today's Albany meeting was on his mind.

Today, the world he had come to understand, the world he left the city for, the world that decided he couldn't make it in New York City any longer, had shifted again.

He had walked into the Albany office and found himself face-to-face with Charlie Stephenson, the current Assistant Attorney General and his old supervisor from the force. Alongside Charlie stood two Internal Affairs agents.

The partnership Mike thought he had with Sal, the person he thought Sal was, had all gone down the drain in two sentences.

Chapter Six

Kyoto, Japan

Bianca followed Ian from the hidden alleyway to the center of a bustling yet somehow quiet city. They started at Teramachi Street, a covered shopping arcade. So much looked the same as the first time she had seen it, and yet so much had changed. She lingered at a boutique window displaying traditional fans and then wandered into a second-hand bookshop. Her frustration at being in an ancient bookstore and not being able to read a word did not dampen her attraction to the books.

Once she confessed to Ian that her feet were aching, they stopped at a corner kiosk for *karaage*, piping hot fried chicken pieces—glistening nuggets of delicacy. They claimed two seats on a bench nearby to enjoy their snacks along with two cold green teas.

They each picked up a nugget. In unison, they recited the words giving thanks for their food, "*Itadakimasu.*"

Her first bite of chicken almost burnt her tongue, but she knew it tasted best at that temperature. She savored the simple flavors, a repeat of her first Kyoto meal with Ian three years earlier.

Bianca looked around the bustling market. So full of activity and yet so calm. One of the joys of visiting Japan was to witness how such large numbers of people could live together in a serene and considerate way. No pushing, no yelling, no cutting lines. She was not surprised Ian loved it.

When they were done with their snack, they continued their meandering through the market. She admired the paradox of the modern and traditional side by side. The shops showcased colorful displays, from exquisitely crafted kimonos to a full-size Colonel Sanders. Along the edges of the modern market were old shops that had been there for centuries. Incense, wooden sandals, knives. More old books. Then there were novelty shops selling remote control toys, Hello Kitty merchandise, and even a pet shop. There was a *kaiten* sushi bar where the plates rotated around the restaurant on a conveyor belt, like a Lionel train set.

The pachinko parlor was packed with players of all ages, the noise magically enclosed within its sliding doors. Ian stepped into the sensor to allow the doors to open so she could hear the riotous clanging of the machines. Then he stepped back, and all was silent again.

As they left the covered market at Teramachi, they were met with a light drizzle. They stopped at the convenience store on the corner and purchased two identical clear umbrellas with white handles. The same umbrellas everyone carried all the time.

Slowly, arm in arm, they made their way through the dwindling late afternoon crowds at the Nishiki food market. They stopped to buy soy donuts, hot out of the oil. Then they headed toward the river for a slow walk north through town.

After about twenty minutes, Ian hailed a cab. Despite her throbbing feet, Bianca enjoyed the view. She rested her head on his shoulders and watched the city pass them by.

The taxi stopped before a two-story building, and the door magically opened for her.

At the door of the *Kyoto Quarterly*, a fairly modern building above a second-hand record shop, Ian paused a moment to peek in the store window, then guided his mom up the steps. At the top, Ian knocked and walked in.

"I let myself in. Daniel? Are you here?"

"Aye, it's Ian, my boy. Come on in." Daniel Wilson's voice called from the back office. His British accent had a sing-song quality that made Bianca happy to meet him even before he entered the room.

The building had large windows overlooking the street and a full view of the mountains to the east. The furniture was a mishmash of styles, colors, and shapes. Probably pieces Daniel had cadged from his friends or pulled together from his home to get the office up and running years ago.

"Daniel, I've brought my mom to meet you."

"Ah, yes, I remember you said her flight was coming in today. She should be sleeping by now. If my calculations are correct, it must be 5:00 a.m. her time." Daniel came around the door, squinting at his watch. He offered his hand. He was about Bianca's age, and a happy person, that much was obvious to her. This was someone who smiled all the time. Daniel reminded her of Ernie McCrae from Batavia. In fact, he was attractive in the same way—dark hair with some specks of gray, clean-shaven, and sparkling light eyes.

Ian and Daniel were very close. It made her happy to know that Ian had a father figure here and one so pleasant at that.

"So nice to meet the lovely lady who brought us this fine young fella."

Bianca shook hands and smiled back. "Ian says so many wonderful things about you. Now I know why."

"Welcome to my humble *Kyoto Quarterly*. We—." Daniel tilted his head as if in confidence. "We, as in I, hope to produce all the news that's fit to print for the tiny Kyoto expat community as well as local events and news. Culture, fiction, poetry, photography. You name it; if it has to do with Kyoto, we print it."

"Ian has sent me several issues. I really enjoy taking my time reading them."

"Well, thank you, M'lady." Daniel made a show of bowing. "Ian tells me you have a dispatch to send. Another journalist, we should get along splendidly."

Bianca reached into her tote and produced a crumpled page. "I apologize. It's been a long day. Or two, by now, I guess. I want to thank you for taking an interest in my dispatches. I'm looking forward to seeing them in print in your journal."

"I should be thanking you. It'll be an interesting perspective to see Kyoto through a newcomer's eyes again. I'll put this dispatch in the queue for the next issue, and I'll also have it sent over to the *Batavia Gazette* in no time. Are you reporting on anything in particular?"

"Not really, just my impressions. The only parameter my editor gave me was a required report from the gala event for the *netsuke* collection held by the Nakayama family."

"Whoa, Ian told me about your detective skills. Very impressive. How in the world did that tiny sculpture ever find its way to New York, I wonder? And how did you figure out it was so valuable? Obviously, Ian got his looks and his brains from you. How's his dad? A dunce, eh?"

Bianca laughed with him. She always appreciated when her brains were recognized. She had spent far too many years as a younger woman not secure enough to assert herself. She'd moved past that insecure young woman. She still surprised herself at how much she had grown in the years since her divorce from Malcolm. She had had to redefine who she was. She had needed to start fresh, needed to see herself more clearly, and she couldn't do that within the confines of their marriage. After the divorce, she continued to grow. She liked who she saw now. In fact, while some of her friends had always bemoaned the passing of the years, wistfully wishing back their younger days, she had always rushed toward aging, sure that as she matured, she would get better.

Daniel sniffed and then sniffed again. "If my senses do not deceive me, do I smell soy donuts?"

Ian rummaged in his backpack, pulled out a greasy bag, and handed it to him. "Oh, yes. I forgot. I know how much you love them."

"Righty mate, you're the best!" Daniel uncurled the bag, offering them to Bianca first.

"I had so many on the way. They are even better than I remember them."

Daniel put his hand into the bag and pulled out six little donuts, all scrunched into a mound of greasy fried dough.

Ian blushed. "Oops."

Daniel made a funny face as he figured out how to fit it in his mouth, but he succeeded. "Not a problem, mate. Taste just as good all together as they do one at a time."

Chapter Seven

Kyoto, Japan

Bianca removed her shoes and found a pair of slippers approximately her size. She tucked her shoes in a cubby and followed Ian up the stairs of the ramen house. They settled into a spot at the counter in the far corner. She looked at the menu out of habit, but knew she couldn't read it, nor did she need to. This was her favorite noodle place, and she knew exactly what she wanted. In fact, tired or not, this place had been on her mind all day. If she couldn't sleep, she could at least have her black sesame ramen.

Across the counter, the server brought them each a small beer and took their orders. Bianca looked around and realized that nothing had changed at all. It was as if she had never left. She wondered what it must be like to live in a world where the movement of change could be at once imperceptible and monumental. Kyoto was remarkable in its ability to modernize dramatically while remaining steadfastly traditional.

Bianca's mouth watered as a steaming bowl was placed before her. The handmade noodles beckoned, submerged in a rich, dark broth of spicy black sesame.

"*Itadakimasu,*" they said before they started their meal.

She took a slurp of broth first, the spice clearing her sinuses immediately, then with her chopsticks, she gathered up some long strands of ramen and did her best not to make a mess.

They barely spoke as they ate. The food was too delicious and demanding of their attention, and they had talked for hours already. They were content in the sounds of their eating and the sounds of the fellow diners having a fun night out.

When Ian excused himself to find the men's room, Bianca continued spooning the last of her broth, then was surprised by a nudge. She opened her eyes and slowly realized that she had nodded off to sleep at the counter with her spoon still resting in her hands. The last strands of noodles had never made it to her mouth.

"Time to go, Mom."

Bianca used all her energy to stand up with some dignity and followed him back to the shoe cubby and then out the door, but not before they called out to the ramen chefs to thank them for the meal.

"*Gochisousamadeshita!*"

Once outside, they lingered briefly at the window, watching as the chefs rolled and cut the fresh noodles. Bianca was mesmerized by their actions. They worked so effortlessly, as if they had no need to think about these motions.

Bianca leaned on Ian as they made their way through the alley known as Ponto-chō, the traditional bar district. Too small for cars, the cobblestone walkways were lined with tiny restaurants and clubs, their entrances illuminated by glowing paper lanterns. A different aroma escaped each establishment. Some scents Bianca could identify: ginger, garlic, grilling meats. Other delectable fragrances she couldn't. Despite having eaten enough, her appetite was reawakened.

They walked slowly, enjoying the cool autumn night. Just as they were leaving the quiet street, they saw a geisha walking beside a businessman. The rich fabric of her amber kimono shimmered in the light of the lanterns and her hair was perfectly coiffed with a burgundy hairpin. As the lovely girl passed them, Bianca turned to catch a better look. She admired the elaborate knot of the brocade *obi* belt and the delicate end points of the white makeup on the young woman's neck.

Bianca considered it a good omen to spot a geisha on her first day in Kyoto.

They were a rare sight. Some tourists could spend their entire vacation in Kyoto and never see one.

Arriving at the apartment close to 9:30, Ian unlocked the gate and led her to the front door of the guest house. As he opened the door to the darkened room, he whispered, "*Tadaima.*" I'm home.

He showed Bianca to her room, where Jiro had already deposited her bags. She hugged Ian, turned to her futon, and crawled into it without changing into pajamas. Ian turned to close the door.

"Ian, wait."

He turned back.

"You're happy here."

He nodded.

"You feel at home, don't you?"

He closed his eyes briefly, then opened them. He nodded again.

She closed her eyes and fell asleep.

Chapter Eight

Kyoto, Japan

J.C. slammed the phone so hard the desk shook.

"Damn that Irvin!" He punched the wall and instantly regretted it. The landlord lived next door and before J.C. could catch his breath, there was a knock at his door.

Taking a moment to compose himself, he answered the door. "*Sumimasen, Tanaka-san,*" he said, excusing himself as soon as the door was opened to reveal his landlord's frown. Mr. Tanaka didn't need to say much to be understood. J.C. had heard it all before. In fact, he was surprised he hadn't been asked to vacate. Especially after Kawabata had come around last week looking for him. Mr. Tanaka had been furious. He told J.C. to make sure that kind of person never came around again.

Once Tanaka left, J.C. lifted the receiver again. He knew it was no use. He had tried that same number ten times tonight, but always got the same result: an endless ringing. J.C. wasn't even sure if it was still a good number. Several times this week he had tried stopping by Irvin's last apartment, but no one ever answered.

J.C. liked to think that he didn't make bad choices, that instead, he was saddled with more than his fair share of bad luck. In reality, he was a type of gambler. He was attracted to schemes, to easy money, and to people who could promise him a quick return with the least amount of effort on his part. The problem, of course, was that when things didn't work out (and they frequently didn't, despite his optimistic attitude), they often led to disastrous consequences. It was a result of one of these schemes gone bad that he found himself in Japan.

But he was in a real bind this time. He blamed it all on Irvin. It had been Irvin who'd set them up to do a job for Riku Kawabata. He had arranged the plan. But they hadn't been able to close the deal on their end. Irvin had been M.I.A. for days, and J.C. was all alone dealing with Kawabata and his unseemly cohorts.

J.C. wished he had left the bar that first night when his instincts had told him to run. Before the deal had been struck. Or at least once Kawabata had given them the opportunity when he had told them to get out if they couldn't come through. Kawabata had warned them. Actually, it had been more of a threat.

J.C.'s biggest warning that night was Kawabata's missing pinky finger. As far as J.C. knew, missing pinkies meant *yakuza*. It couldn't be a coincidence. It's not like Kawabata was a farmer or a factory worker who had an accident. It was a bad sign. J.C. had lost his nerve right there and then, but he didn't get up. He had stayed at that table, and now he was going to pay the price.

Chapter Nine

Batavia-on-Hudson, N.Y.

Mike had guzzled the first beer and was halfway through the second before he was willing to think back to his Albany trip this morning—to his surprise at seeing two Internal Affairs agents with his old boss, Charlie Stephenson.

Before he was ushered into the office, he had already started having misgivings.

Once he walked in, Mike had stared at Charlie, his gut churning. He used to have the same feeling back on the job when he knew he was being misled during his interrogations.

His instincts told him there was more to the story than met the eye, and he hated that his instincts were always right.

He looked at Charlie now, the same imposing frame, the same sharp black eyes. The only differences were a softer middle and thinner, grayer hair.

Charlie had been a great supervisor, but he was a reminder of all that Mike had chosen to leave behind. After shaking hands and asking after Charlie's wife and kids, Mike took a seat.

"Look, Mike, I don't want to pretend we're here to catch up on old times. We have something we need to discuss with you." Charlie fiddled so long with his paperclips that Mike wanted to slam his fist on the desk to get his attention. But he pretended it didn't bother him and waited.

Then the waiting paid off, and Mike wished Charlie had played with those clips forever.

"It seems Sal may not have jumped."

"What do you mean? We know he jumped. We—"

"Mike, we only knew what we saw. What we know now is that Sal was… Sal was on the take."

Mike stood up, no longer willing to listen. "Sal was not on the take. You don't know what you're saying. You didn't know him like I knew him. You—"

"Mike, of course you knew him better, and since that's true, then you know what I'm saying is not far-fetched. Be honest with yourself."

Of course he knew it wasn't far-fetched, but he felt a loyalty to Sal that needed him to say it was a crazy theory. That Sal could never.

But Mike knew that Sal could. He could make bad choices. He often took the easier way out of a problem, or at least what first appeared as the easy way out. Sal was not good at seeing consequences, at anticipating. He was a devoted cop, or at least wanted to be, but his judgment often hurt him and sometimes hurt Mike too. How many times had Mike covered for him?

Sal was on the take. What did that mean? Why would he complicate his life that way?

Mike paced and took a deep breath to ward off the palpitations. The last thing he wanted was to have an anxiety attack in front of these guys.

Then Mike froze in place. Stopped dead in his tracks. He had focused on one thing and dismissed what else Charlie had said. "If he didn't jump, you're saying he was pushed? Is that what you're saying? That someone killed my partner?"

Chapter Ten

Kyoto, Japan

A creak disturbed Bianca. She awoke with a start, unsure where she was, unable to make things out in the dark.

She fumbled for her watch, still on her wrist. 3:00 p.m. How was that possible? It was pitch dark outside her window. As her mind cleared, she looked around, and the room came into focus. The *tatami* mat floor, with its distinct fresh fragrance of bamboo cane matting. A single purple cosmos in a bud vase by the window.

She settled back on her futon, pulled the quilt up to her chin, and smiled. 3:00 p.m. meant it was 5:00 a.m. here in Kyoto. Ian was right; if she hadn't chased after him all over Kyoto yesterday afternoon, she would have fallen asleep by 6:00 p.m. and would have spent the entire night staring at the ceiling. This way, she was up too early, but at least it was almost morning.

It took her an hour to get ready for the day. Sleeping in her clothes had been an unwelcome end to a long trip, but now, after a restful sleep, she showered and unpacked a few things. She was wide awake by 5:00. She sat at the small desk by the window and pulled out her notebook.

Ohayou from Kyoto,

Good morning, Batavians! I am speaking to you from the future. My morning is your yesterday afternoon, and my yesterday was a whirlwind. Ian refused to let me sleep upon arrival, knowing that early sleep would feed my jet lag. So, we rushed around the city and visited all my favorite places.

Bianca went on to detail her first afternoon in Kyoto, with all the sights and smells, as best she could. She knew that no matter how hard she tried, Kyoto could not be captured completely by words alone. It was a city needing a close personal encounter. One where you could witness the paradox of antiquity and modernity living peacefully side-by-side. One that needed to be done on foot where you could see all the tiny details, because Kyoto was nothing if not a detail-oriented city. Where every bloom, every pastry, every fold of paper was intentional. Her hope was to bring her new friends in Batavia along for the ride as much as possible.

Once she was satisfied with her dispatch, she folded it neatly and placed it in her backpack. She tiptoed down the stairs, then along the hallway to the entrance, where she slipped into her shoes and stepped out into the quiet city.

The crisp autumn air was welcoming. The sun was just peeking over the horizon as she left the house. She wandered down the street. The neighboring shops were just opening, the owners sweeping or splashing water on the pavement in front of their shops to ward off evil spirits and welcome their patrons.

Ohayou gozaimasu.

Ohayou gozaimasu.

Bianca happily greeted the shopkeepers, and they all gave a slight bow and greeting in return. With some rest behind her she found herself restless with enthusiasm to explore the city. She had been too tired yesterday, but today, her senses were alive.

She started down *Shijo-dori*, what Bianca considered the Fifth Avenue of Kyoto, with store after store of fine boutiques as well as the Daimaru department store. The shop windows displayed rich autumn colors and themes. She spotted a sweater that Olivia would love and a scarf that would suit Mike. Eugene would want some of the special cookies from the gourmet shop below the department store. She could hardly wait for the department store to open, but for now, she took in the quiet morning rituals of the vendors opening their traditional shops.

She could smell chestnuts roasting but couldn't see them. She followed the aroma and wandered into Nishiki market. Some stalls were just rolling up their gates, but many were already busy. Fish, pickled vegetables, bento boxes, and pastries. Fruits and produce. And then she spotted the *kuri* vendor with baskets of the largest chestnuts she'd ever seen. Their shells shone like freshly polished furniture.

"Kuri wa ikura desu ka?" She pointed and asked after the price of the biggest chestnuts. They were expensive but would make a wonderful gift for Freddie and Kurt Dekker. She would make a point of buying some before she left.

For now, she bought a small bag of roasted chestnuts. She whispered, *"itadakimasu,"* then peeled and ate one there where she could throw the shells in the little basket they had reserved for that purpose. She savored the smoky creaminess, then tucked the rest in her backpack as a breakfast snack for Ian and Jiro.

She continued to wander the market. She spotted bright orange persimmons and bought two of the plumpest ones as treats for Kenzo. Last autumn, he had told her how much he missed the large, juicy persimmons from Japan. The vendor packed the ripe fruit carefully for her, and she placed them in a snug spot in her bag beside the chestnuts.

On the other side of the market, she headed north along the river on the path that led to Lovely Record Shop and the *Kyoto Quarterly* offices upstairs. It was early, and she had plenty of time, so she decided to take the long walk rather than try her hand at the buses.

When she arrived, she admired the colorful leaves painted on the record shop window. Then she found Daniel's mailbox and deposited her morning dispatch for him to send along to the *Batavia Gazette* later that morning. Olivia would receive it yesterday evening, and it would be added to the morning paper. In the meantime, Daniel would publish it in this week's issue of the *Kyoto Quarterly*.

Satisfied with her early morning, Bianca wandered back toward home, Ian's home.

Bianca spent the early afternoon unpacking and getting herself settled while

Ian went to his classes. Kenzo had picked up two bento box lunches nearby and they ate overlooking the internal garden. She was glad Kenzo had returned from his business in Osaka so quickly. She enjoyed his company, and he was a link to her home in Batavia. Jiro had been a wonderful host, making rooms available for both Bianca and Kenzo at the guest house.

After lunch, Kenzo left to run errands. She decided to stay home since Ian and Jiro were throwing her a welcome party later, and she wanted to conserve her energy.

She settled into a comfortable chair with her book. As she read, her thoughts overflowed with ideas for her own writing. She reluctantly put her book down to jot some notes when she heard the front door buzzer. She hoped the person would go away. She had no idea how to make herself understood. Her heart raced when she heard the buzzer again, but realized she couldn't ignore it. She had to at least try. What if it was important?

She carefully slid the door aside to find a gentleman standing there. She started with a greeting. *"Konnichiwa,"* she said hesitantly.

"Good afternoon. I am looking for Jiro or Ian. May I speak to them?" His English was very understandable.

"Good afternoon. I'm sorry, but you have missed them both."

"May I ask when might I find them at home?"

"They will not be home until this evening. But they will be busy with an event. Then Jiro is here tomorrow all day and Ian in the morning. Can I give them a message for you?"

"Thank you. Just tell them I will come back. My name is Kawabata. Riku Kawabata."

She closed the door behind him and wondered what this man could have wanted with Ian. He didn't state his business, and despite his courteous dialogue, there was an edge, an impatience to him.

The phone rang at that moment, and Bianca was more than happy to think about something else. Jiro had told her that there was no need for her to answer the phone, but if she were inclined to do so, most of his business was conducted with English speakers. To be helpful, she took the chance and picked up the receiver. *"Moshi, moshi."*

"Buon pomeriggio, Lei parla italiano?"

Jiro had never said anything about Italian clients. Luckily, Bianca was in her element. This could be fun, she decided, as she dug right in to offer her Italian services. *"Sì, sì. Prego."*

Chapter Eleven

Batavia-on-Hudson, N.Y.

Eugene flipped through the *Batavia Gazette*, enjoying the hum of the diner patrons, the clinking plates, and most of all, Chet Baker's trumpet. Local news was never new for him since most of the gossip made its way to the diner before the *Gazette* ever scooped it up, but he liked to fill in any gaps.

He read the latest on the sheriff's election. Mike was up against an out-of-towner. Edward Angleton from Albany had decided to give it a shot. Eugene knew Eddie had a keen political sense. Eugene was confident that Mike was the better candidate, he just wasn't sure that everyone else agreed.

Mike had lost his edge recently. His separation from Maggie had deflated him; the last few big cases, too, had taken their toll. It all seemed to take the wind out of Mike's sails.

Then, yesterday, Mike stopped in for a coffee, and he was even more out of sorts than usual. At first, Eugene assumed it had to do with Bianca leaving for Japan. Those two had chemistry, whether they wanted to admit it or not. But then Eugene realized that Mike was off, really off, more than could be explained by Bianca's leaving.

Eugene prided himself in being discreet, but he was concerned that he might have witnessed Mike having a panic attack at the evacuation center during the storm last June. Eugene had been about to run over and offer his help when he realized Maggie was there and that she had it under control.

Eugene recognized the symptoms from his wife's attacks. Stella had them less and less frequently over the years, but when she was younger, they were common. The shortness of breath, the dizziness, the flush in the face from her accelerated heart rate. He remembered them with dread.

As if on cue, Mike walked in again, setting off the chime above the door.

"Hey, Mike, what'll it be?"

"Afternoon, Gene. Just a coffee. Thanks."

Eugene put the paper aside and placed the coffee with a slice of Mike's favorite homemade apple pie on the red Formica counter.

Mike drank the coffee distractedly and nibbled at the pie.

Eugene turned back to the paper. Monica White had everything running smoothly with the patrons, so he relaxed and enjoyed himself. First, he read the recaps of world news, and then on the second to last page, he found what he was looking for.

"Listen up, everyone." The diners quieted down but not completely; Claire Koop was still whispering to Trudy Bauer with her most recent gossip.

"Listen up, or I'll whistle." The room quieted down some more. Monica gave Claire a nudge, and the silence was complete.

"Okay, everyone, I've got our first dispatch from Bianca in Japan."

"*Ohayou from Kyoto,*" Eugene started.

"Ohayo's the name of the mountain on the other side of the river. Could it be Japanese?"

"Bert, shhh," Ernie scolded.

"*Good morning, Batavians! I am speaking to you from the future. My morning is your yesterday afternoon.*"

"That's the darndest thing, it is. Makes my brain hurt just to think about it."

"Bert, please," Big Ben chimed in.

My yesterday was a whirlwind. Ian refused to let me sleep upon arrival, knowing that early sleep would feed my jet lag. So, we rushed around the city and visited all of my favorite places.

I am pinching myself. I am finally back in Japan. As you may know, I have not been here since Richard died. In the meantime, Ian's life has progressed. He has formed a band, played the small clubs. He has dated a few girls, some of them Japanese, a couple were expats. I never met any of them. He is keeping a journal, creating a memoir of sorts—the foreigner making his way in a new city. There seems to be a market for those. In fact, the local expat newspaper, The Kyoto Quarterly, has hired him to write a weekly column. He embraces this city and tries to stay aware of the cultural expectations. Consideration for others is highly prized here. It fosters harmony in this densely populated and intricately interconnected community. I am proud that he works hard to understand the nuances of this culture and fits in so well.

But I'm here now. Nothing compares to being in his orbit, on his turf, where he calls the shots, where I can see the world through his eyes.

I will absorb it all and pass it along. The sights, sounds, and textures are unique in this ancient city, and I will do my best to report them back for you all.

Eugene read the dispatch with no more interruptions. He enjoyed their rapt attention. Mike was pretty worldly, the Blanchards up on the hill were too, but they weren't typical Batavians, they were transplants. Most villagers had never left the area, let alone visited a country so foreign as Japan. It wasn't that they weren't interested in travel, some didn't have the means, but others had lives and businesses that demanded constant attention. The Dekkers and the Streats ran farms. They had the means, but not the time. Big Ben Sawyer ran a business and ran the town. He took that very seriously. Bert Henderson never had two coins to scrape together. Ernie McCrae had had enough of the world in his past. All he wanted now was to immerse himself in a quiet village life.

Eugene himself never thought to leave the diner. He opened it seven days a week. What would he do with time off? He would only spend it with the same people who came into the diner every day. The only native Batavians who had traveled were the van Pattens. They had moved in high society for generations. Politicians, all of them, they needed to keep up with the Joneses.

The bell above the door chimed as Olivia Last walked in. Eugene had just finished reading Bianca's letter but knew that Olivia had the inside scoop since the dispatches originated at the *Gazette* with her.

Eugene waved to her, and she waved back. He watched as she stopped at each table to greet everyone. With her fit physique, she carried her pregnancy well. She had allowed the beginnings of her gray hair to come through naturally, so there was no way to ignore that she was well into her forties.

She could run for governor, if she wanted, and win handily, Eugene mused. She was smart as a whip, incorruptible, and well-loved. While she had always been wholesome looking, now she glowed with her pregnancy. She wasn't just healthy; she was happy. And it rubbed off on everyone she encountered.

Chapter Twelve

Kyoto, Japan

Bianca threw a shawl over her shoulders. The chrysanthemum pattern was a traditional Japanese motif, but what she loved most about the fabric was the deep plum and emerald color. A welcome back gift from Ian, it was from his favorite clothing shop in Kyoto which fused old and new designs to make something young and fresh but with a feel of the traditional.

The wrap was the perfect finishing touch to her outfit. It would keep the autumn chill off her shoulders at tonight's garden party in her honor.

She was happy and nervous for tonight's event. She would be meeting Ian's circle—his chosen family. Bianca hoped they accepted her, and even more, she hoped that she could feel comfortable with them. It would go a long way in putting her mind at ease. It didn't matter to her that Ian was an adult. She would always be his mother, he would always be her son, and she wouldn't feel comfortable across the globe if she didn't think he was with good people, that his chosen family was a healthy happy group. What if she discovered that they weren't the kind and supportive people Ian thought they were? Was he too young and naïve to see it? She would find out soon enough.

Wanting to make a good impression, Bianca took a last look at her appearance. She ran her fingers through her short hair one last time and gently pinched her cheeks and bit her lip. She was youthful looking for someone with a young adult son. More youthful than most people expected when they heard she was a widow.

She took the stairs carefully, the wooden steps in the traditional *machiya* house were a bit steep and narrow, not to mention slippery from use. As she made her way down, she could hear voices. Mostly, she heard Ian's energized banter as he rushed around to finish the preparations. He was talking to Jiro, but there was a third voice. A young woman's voice. And then another young man's voice. When Bianca turned the corner, Ian rushed over to embrace her and turned to introduce them all.

"Mom, these are my friends from Germany I told you about. They are in their *wanderjahr* of traveling after college. This is their third stop and we are hoping they love it enough to stay."

Daniel from the *Kyoto Quarterly* walked in with two six-packs.

"Mate, thanks for the invite." He added the beer to the fridge, obviously comfortable in the space. "Bianca, so lovely to see you again." He bent to kiss her cheek. She noticed the scent of beer on his breath, but also a clean and refreshing fragrance.

Behind Daniel, two young men appeared. Daniel turned and introduced them to Bianca. "More musicians. A friend of my daughter from uni and his brother."

Kenzo walked in with a carefully wrapped bottle, which he presented to Jiro. "My contribution to the party."

Jiro unwrapped it to find a bottle of Yamazaki whiskey. Jiro's face lit up. "This is quite a gift, Kenzo, thank you. You know my weakness."

"I thought you might enjoy it." Kenzo pointed behind Jiro to his collection of fine whiskeys.

Ian walked over, accompanied by a young couple.

"Mom, here are my neighbors, Andrew and Akane. Andrew's a drummer, and Akane is a terrific cook."

"I am so happy to meet Ian's mother. I will only stay a little bit. The baby is at home with my mother. She has been with him all day. So, I need to relieve her soon." Bianca wondered if her Japanese would ever be as fluent as this young woman's English.

Bianca met each of the guests as they arrived. Two young English artists, twin sisters who first moved up north to Hokkaido, then came to live in Kyoto for a change of scenery. A Canadian couple who moved here to teach English. An Australian who was here on an expired visa, hoping to find a way to remain. And an Irishman who owned a pub on the other side of town. She met them all.

They were all ages, all nationalities. A true expat community. It appeared to Bianca that what they had in common was the distance from their respective homes. No one would have had occasion to be friends if they had never left the protection of their hometowns and home languages. But the various versions of the English language and their homesickness bound them to each other. Like in Batavia, the incomers were in Kyoto for different reasons. Some because it was beautiful, some because it was peaceful, some for the novelty, and others as an escape. Bianca had always suspected that Ian had left the States to gain some distance from his parents' divorce. To seek a fresh direction. He didn't want to follow in his father's footsteps and needed some distance to work out his own talent. Malcolm was a hard act to follow. In literal terms.

Bianca stared at her son with his friends congregating around him. He was holding an audience with his storytelling. Making them laugh. His comfortable demeanor pleased her because she knew that it had never been easy for Ian to have a famous father. Shortly after she and Malcolm had divorced, Malcolm's talent took off. He no longer taught music and was performing more and more. Within a few years, he had made a name for himself. Eventually, he had become the most sought-after jazz pianist in the States and traveled a great deal of the time.

Ian had his own musical talent. What had started as a gift from his father had become a burden. Once Malcolm became famous and started traveling, he ignored his son's music. Ian never saw him, but he worked and worked on his compositions hoping to please his father once he returned. But Malcolm was either too critical or too busy to listen. Ian stopped trying to share his music with him. They grew apart. Bianca felt guilty to this day. If she and Malcolm had remained married, she could have helped bridge the differences, but apart, she had no way to inject herself. She would calm Ian when he grew frustrated with his dad. She would remind him how much Malcolm loved him and that he was busy. He was a perfectionist; he wasn't being critical, he was trying to guide him. On and on, she would try to help Ian see only the good.

Richard, Ian's stepfather, had shown an interest in Ian's music, but Richard wasn't a world-class musician, and he wasn't Ian's dad. Ian loved Richard and was pleased with his stepfather's approval and guidance, but it was his father's attention he craved. And it was his father's attention that was lacking.

Now that Ian was so far away, she knew that he and Malcolm rarely talked. But she did notice that without his father's harsh judgment, Ian was thriving. This place was good for him. Maybe in the long run, even if he had come here to get away, she felt that he had found something very positive here. She very much approved of the Japanese version of Ian. She hoped he was composing and playing again. He never talked about it, but she planned to find out.

Chapter Thirteen

Batavia-on-Hudson, N.Y.

Sal murdered? Mike couldn't face it. What he had seen that day was a suicide. That's what they had deemed it. How could he have been so naïve to accept it blindly? Had he suspected it was murder? Had his eyes really deceived him?

Mike stood in the middle of his office, comforted by his surroundings and by the quiet serenity of Batavia. The walls were adorned with faded newspaper clippings and framed accolades collected over the years. The afternoon sun poured through the window, casting a warm glow across the room. But today, none of that mattered. His thoughts were in another place, another time.

He picked up the photo of him and Sal on the fishing boat. Twelve years had passed since that photo was taken and nine since Sal's death, but the memories came flooding back like a tidal wave. The two of them holding a bass so large they needed all four hands. It made him smile, but then it caused him to stop and wonder. Was it all real? Had he really known Sal? The thought haunted him, and it took him back to that life-changing moment.

He was transported to that stifling New York City evening. The shrill scream of sirens cut through the humidity, and the distant hum of traffic was a constant reminder of the city that never slept.

He recalled the radio crackle as the dispatcher's voice rang out, directing cars to the scene. The air was thick with tension as he pulled up to a building on the east side of Manhattan, where the flashing red and blue lights reflected off the windows of the towering buildings. His heart pounded in his chest. He steeled himself for the moment as he approached.

Nothing could prepare him for what he saw that day. Sal's broken body lay sprawled on the sidewalk; a crimson pool of blood expanded beneath him. Mike looked up at the tall building, unbelieving that his friend had fallen from that unforgiving height.

The NYPD had concluded it was suicide. They said Sal had jumped, unable to cope with the pressures of the job, his failed marriage, his ruined finances. At the time, Mike had accepted the explanation, as painful as it was.

As the years passed, he'd left the big city behind, seeking solace in the quiet life of a small-town sheriff. But he couldn't shake the nagging feeling that something wasn't right. Today, as the memories came rushing back, he allowed himself to face the truth he'd kept locked away for so long.

He remembered how broken up everyone was, but no one was surprised. Sal fit the profile of a jumper. His marriage, his finances. All a mess. He lived in a motel room. He had stopped fishing, stopped skiing. He canceled most of his visits with his kids because he was too ashamed to see them. He even relinquished his vacation days because he had nowhere he wanted to go. He was required by their precinct to seek counseling. And he did. Why hadn't they seen it coming?

And the most chilling detail of all: no witnesses. Not until he landed. A passerby had called 911. People gathered in the aftermath, but they never found anyone who said they saw him jump or heard anything but the thud. No one witnessed it. The lack of sound, the lack of visual certainty had nagged Mike for years. Now he knew why. Sal was probably dead before he was sent over the edge. He never made a sound.

The anger boiled inside him. How could he have missed it? His partner, his brother, had been murdered, and he'd let the killer slip through his fingers. He hadn't wanted to believe it, but now, there was no denying the truth.

Tears welled up in his eyes as he stood in his office, the photograph trembling in his hands. Sal had been the most important person in his life. Now, all he had left were memories and the burning need for retribution.

He owed it to Sal to find the truth, to bring his killer to justice. He wouldn't let his partner's memory be tarnished by the lie of suicide.

He wiped the tears from his eyes, his resolve hardening.

There was work to be done.

Chapter Fourteen

Batavia-on-Hudson, N.Y.

Mike stared at the phone on his desk. He desperately needed to talk to someone.

Normally, he would go to Vera, his deputy, when he needed advice. But not this time. Besides, more and more, he had been relying on Bianca's good sense, and he noticed he also missed her company.

This time, in particular, he needed Bianca.

He looked down at his desk at the *Batavia Gazette*. There, on the first page under the fold, was the news that rankled him. Under the fold. One would think it wasn't important enough to make it above the fold, but to Mike, it was the most important piece of news in the paper.

Vera Weber Throws Her Deputy's Hat into the Sheriff's Ring, the headline read.

Vera was running for sheriff.

He knew there were rumblings in the village about the election. He knew many of his neighbors believed he wasn't up to the job. Hell, *he* wasn't sure he was up to the job. His panic attacks, the ones that started after Sal had died, had not relented. Sometimes, he thought they were getting worse. He wouldn't be surprised. What with the murder cases in the last year. He had handled homicides before in New York City, but the local murders had been different. Here, in Batavia, he had friends whose lives were on the line. He had needed to dig deep and investigate the people he considered family. He had been wrung dry by these suspicions and outcomes.

Then there was Maggie, a woman he had loved for so much of his adult life that he never had a backup plan for a separation. Never suspected that they could ever be apart or want to be apart. But the tensions over the last year had been too much on their marriage. And now, here he was, living the life of a bachelor again, wondering if they would make another go of it or if this was the end.

So, no, he wasn't surprised that some of his neighbors might vote for someone else. For Edward Angleton. He was a sly politician and had connections in town, or at least his family did.

Mike wasn't a fool. He knew that he was considered an outsider by many, and they would rush to put a local back in the sheriff's seat, but he never thought that Vera would turn on him. He was blindsided.

It was his own fault. Although he knew she was capable, he always treated her as his right-hand person, not as an equal. He never thought of her as sheriff material. And he was wrong. She certainly was qualified to do the job and do it well. Maybe he had just seen what he had wanted to see—a loyal and competent assistant. He had shortchanged her, and now she was staking a claim. She knew he was vulnerable. Everyone knew he was vulnerable.

If he wasn't fully up to his task before, this news about Sal had really taken him off the rails. Was he running for sheriff again because he wanted the job? Because he honestly believed he was the best person for the job? Because it was expected of him?

Maybe his time was up. No longer able to cope in the city, he had come to what he thought was a sleepy town just to discover that evil and desperation live everywhere. This town was no exception.

He may not be up to the job of policing at all anymore. Maybe it was time to hang up his hat.

Chapter Fifteen

Kyoto, Japan

"Bianca. Bianca."

She turned to face Daniel; her thoughts interrupted.

"Bianca, is it true that Ian used to play the flute? The flute, of all things? I know he is a fine jazz guitarist, but a flautist? I just can't picture it."

Bianca caught Ian's eye and smiled at him.

"Well, I'm not sure I would say that he played the flute exactly. He took it up in third grade and tried his best, but he gave it up for the guitar."

"Not any good at it, aye Mate?" Daniel turned to Ian and cuffed him on the back. "Not to worry, boyo. We can't all be good at everything."

"He didn't really have a chance to be bad at it. He gave it up because his arms were too short…" Bianca excused herself and left Ian to handle all the raucous ribbing her last statement provoked.

He had taken up the flute at school, Bianca suspected, because it was an instrument his father didn't play. Every instrument Malcolm played, he played well, even if piano was his passion. Eventually, Ian had to concede that his short eight-year-old arms were never going to play the flute, at least not for a few years.

She could hear them teasing Ian, but mostly, she could see how good-natured it was. Ian took it in stride, even enjoyed it.

At that moment, a strange hush came over the room. It hadn't gone silent. There was still a little chatter from the garden, the music on the stereo, and

Jiro shaking a drink at the counter.

Bianca turned to follow the gazes. Walking in the door was a young man about Ian's age, maybe a few years older. He wore jeans and a t-shirt that Bianca considered too light for the weather, and an orange cap with an anchor logo. Scruff darkened his face, but what she noticed most of all was an unsteadiness to his gait. He wasn't drunk, but certainly not completely sober.

The conversations picked up again, one at a time. The young man joined Ian's group and seemed unaware of the discomfort he had caused with his entrance. Daniel sidled up to Bianca.

"He's a piece of work, that one."

"I gather that. But who is he?"

"That scoundrel is Jay Curtis, more commonly known as J.C." Daniel took an angry gulp of his beer. "And that damn hat. Must he wear it everywhere?" He added more beer to his glass. "He has no idea, no clue. He was not invited, I can assure you, and he never gets it."

"Everyone here seems so kind and warm. Why isn't this guy welcome?" They both watched as the group where J.C. had settled disbanded one at a time to join other conversations. Eventually, the last person excused himself and headed to the bathroom.

J.C. sat at the counter alone and drank his beer. He approached Ian again, but this time, Jiro walked up to him and cut off his view of Ian.

"J.C., it's time to hit the road. You need to leave Ian alone. Can't you see he doesn't want to talk to you? Have some respect. It's his mom's welcome party."

"Let me welcome her then. Where is she?" Jiro moved to block him. "Come on, Jiro. I just want to have a word with him." J.C. tried to push his way past Jiro, but Jiro pushed back.

"Hey, man, that's enough. This is my place. If I tell you to leave, you leave." They were locked in what could have been mistaken for an embrace. Something that could escalate easily.

No one had noticed a man walk into the guest house. Overdressed for this casual gathering, he was a short but muscular-looking Japanese man.

He approached J.C. and put a firm hand on his upper arm. "Do not worry, everyone. It seems J.C. has been drinking. I will escort him out, and you can go back to your party. I hope you will excuse his bad manners." As J.C. walked out with the stranger, it seemed to Bianca he was leaving more out of fear than anything else. This man was not a welcome sight for J.C. When they passed her, Bianca got a good look at the man and recognized Riku Kawabata from earlier in the afternoon.

Once they left the room, Bianca could feel the tension lift. Even though no one said or did anything differently, she knew that order had been restored.

Ian joined her and Daniel.

"Well, I'm glad he left. He never seems to understand he is no longer wanted around here." Ian fiddled with his bottle. He rarely drank much alcohol, but tonight he was enjoying a mildly alcoholic lemon *chuhai*.

"Mate, I have to hand it to you. You were cool under pressure. I would have thrown him out on his duff, right out that gate as soon as he walked in. But it wasn't my place to do it. Cool as a cucumber, you were."

"Maybe if my mother wasn't here, I might have done that, but this evening is not about J.C. or me. It's about my mom. He got the message just the same, it seems."

"I have to say, no one looked happy when he walked in." Bianca wondered what could cause a room full of people to be so turned off. "And that man who walked him out—"

"That was Riku Kawabata. J.C. has a habit of fraternizing with the wrong people." Daniel shook his head in disgust.

"He does have an unsavory look about him. I thought so earlier when he came by. Ian, I forgot to mention that Mr. Kawabata stopped by today."

"When was that? What did he want?"

"It was just an hour or two before the party. I'm sorry, those Italian guests called just as he was leaving, and I forgot to mention it. He didn't say much, just that he was looking for you or Jiro."

Ian looked surprised. "I don't really know this guy, Kawabata. Maybe Jiro does. He must have been looking for J.C. and figured we could lead him in the right direction. When J.C. doesn't want to be found, he can make himself pretty scarce."

They stood in silence for a few moments, the music and the chatter around them enough of a distraction. Daniel tucked in a little closer to Bianca. "Kawabata is not a gangster per se. He just hangs with them. He's mostly a wannabe." Daniel twirled his bottle in his hands, thinking. "J.C. should watch himself with that guy. Then again, I take that back. What goes around, comes around, they say, don't they? Well, J.C. has damaged his relationship with probably everyone in this room for one reason or another. He owes everyone money, and then he leaves town to go on vacation. He's hit on most of the girlfriends or wives of the guys here, and then there's that thing with Ian and the band."

"What thing is that?"

"Mom, it's nothing. We can talk about it another time. Let's have a toast."

Ian got everyone's attention, and with one arm around his mother's shoulders, he made a toast to her and her arrival. Bianca was happy to change the subject and enjoy her son's attention. She had missed him so much over these last two difficult years.

They all clinked their glasses after toasting *kanpai*.

Bianca turned to Ian, tapped her glass against his bottle, and said in Italian, "*Cin, cin.*"

The group broke out in hilarious laughs all around her. After a very modest explanation from Daniel and a deep red blush, Bianca decided to learn more Japanese.

Chapter Sixteen

Kyoto, Japan

"Takoyaki time!"

A cheer broke out as Jiro came out of the pantry with an electric skillet.

Bianca had no idea what to expect next. She watched as everyone gathered around the table. Daniel plugged in the odd griddle that had eighteen golf-ball-sized depressions. He passed around one bamboo skewer to each person while Jiro whipped up some sort of batter. Kenzo's smile was evidence enough that she was in for a treat.

Ian walked around the table and dipped to reach his mother's ear.

"You'll love this. I just know it."

Bianca smiled up at him. Daniel reached over the table and grasped Bianca's hand.

"Are you sure you know what you're getting yourself into? *Takoyaki* isn't for everyone."

"Oh, but it's definitely for my mom. You'll see."

Ian walked over to the fridge, took out a bowl, and set it on the table. Jiro poured a bit of batter into each of the eighteen cups in the skillet. He gave his hands a careful washing as the batter started to cook, then he picked up the other bowl and added two pieces of octopus to each little mound.

"Octopus balls," Daniel said. "The Japanese really know how to have a party, don't they? I bet you've never had octopus balls before." He winked at Bianca, knowing his pun was on the edge of respectability as long as everyone left it at that.

"No, I must admit, this is new to me."

"Don't worry, you won't be the first foreigner to refuse them. No one will be offended. They do grow on you, though."

"There's no need to worry. I love octopus. I'm sure I'll love these."

Daniel looked impressed. In the meantime, Jiro had poured the remaining batter on top of the octopus. After a couple of minutes, the sizzling had settled down and everyone reached over with their skewers to help gently roll over each dough-filled ball. The rich golden-brown bottoms were now on top while the other side browned. The aroma was similar to Italian zeppole. Bianca's mouth watered.

Bianca looked around the table at the happy faces. Everyone seemed relaxed again. As if J.C. had never been there.

The skewers clacked into each other as everyone did their best to keep the balls browning evenly. Daniel started to scoop out the one closest to him, and everyone yelled at him.

"Too soon. You always take them out too soon."

"You need patience to make good *takoyaki*. It seems like simple street food, but it takes finesse. If they undercook, the batter is runny. If they overcook, they dry out," Ian explained to his mom.

Daniel pulled back and winked at Bianca. "What does this bloke know about octopus balls, anyway?" Then he leaned closer and whispered, "I do it every time just to get them riled up."

Jiro turned the octopus balls one more time to make sure they were ready, then he squeezed two thin lines of Kewpie mayonnaise across the tops, followed by pink shavings, which curled from the heat.

"Fish flakes," Ian said. "Just wait, you're going to love this. Just one more step, and they're done. My favorite part. The *negi*." They all watched as Jiro finished them off with thinly sliced scallions.

Jiro started scooping out the perfectly golden orbs and presented Bianca with the first plate of two.

"*Itadakimasu.*" She devoured them in no time. Two bites each, but not before she burned her tongue.

Daniel handed her his freshly poured cold beer as he reached for a plate. "It's a rite of passage. Everyone burns their tongue the first time. And it's a dilemma because they taste best very hot, and you can't help yourself. My rule of thumb is to recite a limerick and then bite. It seems like the perfect amount of time." Jiro handed Daniel his plate. "There once was a lady from Westgate—"

Bianca was relieved that the groaning drowned out the rest of his ditty. When he was done with his recitation, he popped his first *takoyaki* in his mouth with a big grin. Bianca handed him his beer, and he finished with a large swig to the applause of the group.

Chapter Seventeen

Batavia-on-Hudson, N.Y.

Mike balled up the sheet of paper, took another shot at the trash, and missed again. The crumpled mass sat beside all the others on the worn linoleum floor. The sun streaming through the window threw a spotlight on them as if to call attention to his failures.

He would normally dictate something to Shelley, his dispatcher and all-round office assistant. Always efficient, she would suggest appropriate words or phrases whenever he got stuck. Things would move along swimmingly. But he had to compose two things, and both were private. He had given up on the first—a note to Maggie to review a few logistics regarding expenses and details about the house. The insurance was due, and she usually took care of those things. She was organized; he had to give her that. It should have been an easy letter, but it was the sub-text that made it difficult. He couldn't seem to strike the right note. Since the separation, he had no idea how to talk to her. Too casual sounded like they hadn't just made one of the biggest decisions of their lives to separate. Too serious, and he ran the risk of sounding petulant. An all-business approach denied the personal gravity of their situation. He just didn't know how to be "Mike, not attached to Maggie."

So, he had pushed that note aside and had started on the second. A speech for the upcoming debate. Since he was not running for sheriff unopposed as usual, there would be a debate. Not one, but two opponents. And one was his deputy. How had all this happened?

When he had realized he would need to debate both Vera and Eddie Angleton, he had almost resigned. He had been ready to step aside and let them duke it out. But Shelley had talked him out of being rash. She had convinced him that he could not just take his ball and go home. She had not minced words—Angleton was just an arrogant SOB and should not be sheriff. Not in her town. Not if she could help it.

On the other hand, Shelley and Vera were close friends, and Shelley could easily work with Vera. But she had made it clear to Mike that she wasn't sure Vera was quite ready. She was certainly capable, but in Shelley's opinion, still a bit too young, without sufficient experience to run the sheriff's office.

"A year ago, before the murders, I might have felt differently," Vera had said. Mike remembered how yesterday Shelley had made herself comfortable in his office on her lunch break. Propped her feet against his wooden desk, leaned the chair on its two back legs, and munched on a grilled ham and cheese croissant from The Bench and Mug café. "Vera is my friend, and she is a great deputy. I think she has only been kept down by circumstances." Shelley had extended the other half of her sandwich to him as an offer, but he had refused. Shrugging, she'd taken a big bite. "Anyway, I was saying, last year I might have voted for Vera. Then we were confronted with those murders a few months back, and Mike, I must admit, I was comforted knowing you were at the helm with all your experience. So, be grateful the election is this year and not last year."

Now, he stared at the blank page again. He had not wanted anyone else to suggest the words for his opening remarks on stage this weekend. Shelley was sweet and helpful, but he didn't want to sound scripted. There would be enough of that with Eddie on stage. He needed to come across exactly as he was. The Mike everyone knew. If he had any chance of being re-elected, he needed to appeal to that sense of comfort and experience Shelley had mentioned.

He knew that his expertise had helped diffuse some bad situations last year. His expertise, and Bianca's curiosity and persistence.

He clicked his pen and started to write.

Chapter Eighteen

Kyoto, Japan

When the album finished playing, Jiro didn't replace it with something new. Instead, he turned to Ian. "Time to take out your guitar."

Everyone agreed and the encouragement wouldn't let up. Ian hesitated but finally gave in when Andrew agreed to accompany him.

"Hold on, I'll run next door and get my cajón. I'll be right back."

Bianca turned to Daniel. "What's a cajón? I've never heard of it."

"It's his drum. He's the first person I met who plays one. He likes it because it's portable. He sits on it. You'll see. I've tried it. It's fun and has a great sound."

"It took you long enough," Daniel called out when Andrew returned.

Andrew held up a bag with his free hand. It was stuffed with snacks. "Needed to shore up the refreshments."

Ian and Andrew played together for about an hour. Bianca reveled in it. Of all the things she missed about Ian being away, she missed this most. She watched the crowd and witnessed how his music was appreciated. Everyone was tapping toes and clapping hands. Some were singing. Even Kenzo, much older than most of the rest of the group, seemed to enjoy himself.

After a while, despite her best attempts, she found herself nodding off.

Bianca's head jerked at the sound of the music changing gears. Next to her, Daniel was clapping and singing. She looked around and was relieved that no one had seen her nod off. She shifted position in the hopes of keeping awake.

Daniel nudged her. She simply couldn't stay awake. "Psst. I think it's time you surrendered to sleep."

"I can't. Ian went through so much trouble to do this for me. I can't just leave the party early."

"Ian will understand. You've been a great sport, but I think Morpheus is now winning the battle."

"Oh no. Was it that obvious?"

Bianca's gaze darted from left to right, embarrassed that she had been found out.

"No, not at all. I have a front-row seat. I'm sure no one else noticed."

"I hope you're right."

"We can hold up your end of the drinking. Don't worry. We've got your back." Daniel winked and held up his newly filled beer mug as a sendoff.

Bianca decided Daniel was right. She couldn't keep her eyes open any longer. She had thought standing at the bar would have helped, but she had managed to drop off to sleep just the same.

Ian slipped the strap of his guitar over his shoulder for a break. He headed toward her and asked Jiro for a soda.

"What do you think, Mom? I wrote that last piece."

"I'm embarrassed to say I only heard a few bars and then fell asleep."

"At the bar? You fell asleep standing up?"

"I did, but what I heard was great. Maybe you'll play it for me again tomorrow? In the meantime…"

Daniel inserted himself. "Look, mate, you gotta let her go to sleep. Poor lass has been holding up the bar, but she needs a bed."

"Mom, I'm so sorry. I guess I should have made this party another night."

"No. This has been wonderful. I had a great time. Everyone has welcomed me, and now I see what you love about this community. You're a real family. Although, you will need to catch me up on the subject of J.C."

Ian's jaw muscle clenched at the mention of J.C., and Bianca quickly added, "Your guitar skills are even better than I remember them. You've been playing, and that makes me happy."

"Yeah, I stopped for a while. Long story. But I'm back in the saddle, and I'm glad. I had a few gigs in the neighborhood recently, too. Sold some CDs. It's been good."

Andrew stepped off the stage to the sound of booing from their friends. "Ian, thanks for a terrific party, but I need to get home to the wife and kid."

Ian looked at his watch. "It's only 10:30. Stay for another set."

"I would if I could. I'm up early tomorrow. You know how it is for us working slobs." He turned to Bianca. "Looking forward to spending more time while you're here. Maybe dinner at our place. My wife makes a mean hot pot."

"Thank you, that would be nice. I'll ask Ian to coordinate something with you and Akane."

"Daniel, she's all yours." Andrew pointed to his cajón on stage.

"Andrew, you're sure you don't want an *ichi for the michi?*"

Andrew shook his head, waved, and was on his way.

Bianca shrugged at Ian. He smiled and explained. "It's a Danielism. He loves a good play on words. It's his Japanglish of *one for the road.*"

Daniel swilled the last of his beer and rubbed his hands together in anticipation. "I'm going to make a quick phone call. I'll meet you onstage in a few minutes, mate."

Ian finished off his soda to the sounds of his friend tapping the mic. The guests were getting restless for more music.

"Mom, I understand if you need to sleep. It's already late under normal circumstances. Go on upstairs. Do you want me to go with you?"

"No. I'm all set. I've had a lovely time. Go back to your guitar and enjoy your friends. They're waiting for you." Bianca's voice cracked. She couldn't believe her good fortune to be standing here with her boy, in this beautiful place, gazing at his wide smile, surrounded by good friends. As a mother, all she needed was to know he was happy and a part of something. She pecked him on his cheek when he bent for his kiss. Then he kissed the top of her head, held up his bottle to his friends, clamoring for him to resume playing, and swigged the rest of his drink.

Bianca lingered just long enough to watch him get his back slapped as he got to the mic. His friends gave him a round of applause as he strummed the first chord.

Bianca wended her way through the small crowd, looking for Jiro. She didn't feel right going up to sleep without saying a proper thank you and goodnight to Jiro. He seemed like the glue that held this group together. As she had listened to everyone's expat story, she realized that Jiro appeared in all the stories in one way or another. Everyone seemed indebted to him. She wondered how it was that he was able to help so many.

Bianca said casual goodnights to everyone as she made her rounds and was pulled into a few conversations until she finally gave up searching for Jiro. She would see him in the morning.

She needed to pass through the garden to get to her room. Once she reached the crisp autumn air, she felt even more relaxed. The doors facing the garden had been open all evening and the guests had been floating in and out, but once the music started, they had all moved inside. The Japanese prized community over the individual, so the unwritten rule was to not infringe on others in any way, to make yourself small and quiet. The loud music, by necessity, was enjoyed indoors.

Now that she was back outside, she could appreciate the slight flutter of a breeze, the maple in the center of the garden swaying delicately. The fragrance of the black pine wafted from the corner of the garden. She debated sitting on the stone bench next to the quiet drips of the fountain. It called to her. She was mesmerized, as she had found herself so many times on her last trip. Amazed by how easily she could go from busy and boisterous to calm and pensive in this city. But she knew that if she sat now, even on a cold, hard boulder, that Ian would find her here asleep in the early hours of the morning. She resisted the temptation and decided to go straight to bed.

The breeze picked up and climaxed with a gust that shook the leaves off the tree and pulled her shawl off her shoulders. She shivered, fixed her shawl, and turned to the gate.

Out of the corner of her eyes, a glint of light flashed. She turned to see a shuffle of movement. Maybe there was someone behind the pine tree and hydrangea bushes in the far corner of the garden. She called out. And at her voice, the movement became larger. It was definitely a person, two people. Scuffling. In a fight? The glint again of something bright, maybe silver. A knife?

Bianca called out again, and one of them looked up. This time, she definitely saw part of a face and then heard a groan. She was paralyzed in her spot. She couldn't move forward or back, but she knew she was witnessing something. Something terrible. She heard another muffled cry and a thump.

Her feet unstuck and she ran back inside.

"Ian. Ian." Bianca ran up to him on the stage. He smiled at her as she urgently motioned to him to stop playing. His smile turned quizzical, then a look of concern crossed his face. He removed the guitar to complaints from his friends.

Ian pulled Bianca aside.

"Mom, are you sick? What's wrong?"

"I don't know. I…I saw something."

"What did you see?"

"I'm not sure, but I think I just saw someone get stabbed," she whispered, embarrassed.

"What do you mean? Here? In the garden? That's not possible. Japan is the safest place in the world."

"Please, Ian. Just come with me." She ran ahead. This was no time to discuss things. She just needed to show him.

Ian had no choice but to follow her into the garden. She ran to the center and then slowly approached the east corner. He caught up with her.

"Where? What?"

"There, behind the hydrangea. I saw a glint of metal. A struggle." Her voice cracked as she went on. "I heard a thump." She stopped and pointed.

"Mom, I am sure you're just seeing the leaves moving in the breeze or the moon reflected in the fountain."

But Ian followed her pointed finger and walked around to the other side of the bush.

Bianca held her breath, hoping upon hope that she was wrong. When Ian returned, she couldn't read his face. She started to tremble. She knew it.

"Mom, I don't see anything there. I told you. You're just tired."

"What do you mean there's nothing there?"

"I mean, there is no one and nothing here. Come take a look."

"But I don't understand. I know what I saw. I know I saw something."

"Mom, I thought you'd be relieved."

"I am relieved, but I'm also baffled. I saw something. There was a scuffle back here. I know it."

Ian put his hands on her shoulder and turned her around. He guided her to the stone bench where he sat and made room for her to join him.

"You've been through a lot lately. Richard's passing. I know you're not over that. The murders in Batavia. Losing your friend Agatha. The storm last season. It's a lot for one person."

"What are you saying? That I'm losing it? That I'm not coherent?"

Bianca immediately felt ashamed for snapping at him. It wasn't Ian's fault that there was no proof of what she had seen. "I'm sorry."

"No, I'm sorry. I didn't mean to hurt your feelings. I just think you're tired. You can't underestimate jet lag. You said yourself that you were falling asleep standing up."

"You're right. I'm tired. Obviously, there's nothing there. I'm sorry I took you off the stage."

"Come on. Why don't you get some rest? I'll walk you to your room." Bianca started to protest but decided that she wouldn't mind the company. Despite what she told Ian, she knew that there was more here than met the eye.

She knew she had witnessed something. But what?

Chapter Nineteen

Kyoto, Japan

Bianca opened her eyes and turned over. The grassy, clean scent of the *tatami* mat under her futon was refreshing. A unique fragrance to Japan.

For a moment, her mind wandered to the events of last night. She had slept badly and dreamt badly too. The glint of steel, the flailing arms, the thump. It all repeated in her dreams, over and over again. She decided to try to put it behind her today.

The perfect sky flooded the room with cool light, while the golden sunrise offered a balance of warmth. Autumn in Kyoto was a paradox of too cold and too warm. All of it, lovely.

Today, she was finally going to try her hand at *ikebana*, the art of Japanese flower arranging. She had tried to find an instructor back home, but there wasn't anyone near Batavia who could teach her. As a first step, she had helped Betty at the flower shop last Mother's Day. And she had taken a flower arranging class at the community college two summers ago, but she had never finished.

That was the year Richard had died. Unexpectedly. His death had stunned her, and she had never returned to her class. Or to anything for that matter. Ian had begged her to get back out in the world, and finally, she had, but it had taken all her strength to do so. She was glad that she had ventured into the community. She now had a circle of friends she could rely on.

Olivia had given her freelance work at the *Gazette*. Eugene was a great friend who understood the grief of losing a spouse; she spent many hours chatting with him at his diner. Big Ben Sawyer had given her the library job. Part-time work was perfect while she was writing. Mike, well, then there was Mike. Thanks to him, she had an agent and a great editor, even if it was his estranged wife. At first, it was awkward, but since Maggie had moved back to the city, it had been less of an issue. On the other hand, it made Mike more available, and that was something she wasn't ready to deal with. This trip to Japan had come at the right time. A chance to clear her head and move on. Make a fresh start without Mike as a distraction.

She hurriedly washed up and chose an outfit of layers to combat the dramatic weather changes. Cool now, warm later, and then cool, maybe even cold, tonight. She tied a scarf to her backpack just to play it safe.

As she descended the stairs, she could smell the unmistakable scent of bread toasting. She found Ian brewing two cups of tea. He seemed tense. She was sure it was from the energy it took to avoid the topic of what she thought she saw last night. They both pretended nothing had happened.

They ate their breakfast as they talked about each of his friends in turn. The toast was delectable. She had forgotten how wonderful the bread could be in a country that only recently adopted it. Thick slices of full-bodied white bread that made perfect toast. She indulged herself and topped her toast with soft butter and tart *yuzu* marmalade and almost succeeded in forgetting about last night's events.

They both struggled to avoid the topic as long as possible. Bianca played with the crumbs on the table as she looked around the traditional home that Jiro had made into a guest house. His family owned two of these *machiyas* side by side, and he had managed to make eight lovely rooms to rent, along with a common area for a kitchen and dining room that opened into the shared lounge space and gardens. The house retained the traditional feel with the dark wood beams and an internal garden—even a *tokonoma* alcove where a seasonal scroll and a flower arrangement were on display. Yet, Jiro also managed to give the space a young, modern flair. The furniture had sharp, clean lines, and modern art was displayed on the walls—something for everyone. Most of all, it was peaceful. The garden was the most tranquil space of all and took center stage, the early morning drizzle darkening the greens to a deep emerald.

Bianca and Ian cleared off the breakfast dishes, then washed them. Ian did a quick once over to make sure everything was in order before they left the house.

When they headed outside, Bianca did her best to avoid the east corner of the garden. But as she walked the path, she caught her foot on a small statue almost hidden under the maple. Ian reached out and steadied her.

"Watch out for the *kitsune*. They're shapeshifters." He pointed to several statues hidden in the garden.

"That's a fox, right?"

"Yes. They are tricksters. And certain ones, the *yako,* are known for possessing humans to make them do their bidding. They cajole humans into making foolish choices and seeking revenge on others."

She thought the statue was very attractive and feminine in a feline sort of way. She remembered the foxes at the Fushimi Inari shrine from her last visit to Kyoto. She had even bought one of the pretty white fox masks which now hung in her living room. But she hadn't known of their trickster powers.

"Mom, you aren't still worried, are you? I promise you're safe here."

"I know I am. But still. It makes me uneasy. I can't shake it. I saw something, but what?"

"Look, there's nothing here." Ian took her by the hand as they walked near the hydrangea bush. He swept his hand in a motion to encompass the area. "See, I told you."

Bianca watched as the breeze lifted his curls, and he looked ten years younger—just a boy before his parents had divorced, before his relationship with his father had become difficult, before Richard, his stepfather, had died. Before he moved to Japan.

Her thoughts were broken when his eyebrows lifted, and he knelt down. He rummaged around under the bush.

When he stood up, he held an orange cap in his hand. An orange cap with an anchor insignia.

Bianca and Ian looked at each other. Each trying to stifle a concerned look and neither succeeding.

"I told you!"

"Mom, it's just a hat."

"Yes, but doesn't that belong to your friend?"

"He's not my friend," Ian snapped.

"But why is his hat here in the garden? Maybe something happened to him. You said nobody liked him. What if someone actually did something about it?"

"Even if that were the case, Mom, look for yourself. There is nothing here."

"Yes, there is. His hat is here. Maybe he lost it in a struggle."

"It was the wind. It's no big deal. Look at all the leaves that have fallen since yesterday. It was windy last night. And he lost his hat."

Bianca looked around. She had to admit that the entire garden was covered in red maple leaves. The moss and the stones were all hidden, unlike the night before.

"But I thought you said he never takes it off."

"It's just a figure of speech. He wears it a lot, and everyone notices because it's ratty. We don't understand why he likes it so much. We tease him about it, that's all. But he *does* take it off." Ian shoved the hat into his back pocket.

Chapter Twenty

Kyoto, Japan

"Hajimemashite. Oba Takeru desu." Jiro's cousin, Inspector Takeru Oba, introduced himself. Taller than the average Japanese man, Takeru was an imposing figure, at least for someone as short as Bianca.

He bowed and handed her his card. Bianca accepted it with a slight bow in return, then realized she couldn't read it. Friend or no friend, she found it nerve-racking to be talking to a police officer in a foreign country.

"It is very nice to meet Ian's mother. He talks about you often."

"Thank you for coming." Bianca shook hands with him. "And thank you for speaking English."

"Hi, Takeru, good to see you." Ian put out his hand for a shake.

"Jiro tells me you had a problem?" Takeru shook his hand and then reached into his pocket for a notebook.

"Yes. My mother thinks she saw a struggle last night behind those bushes." Ian pointed to the hydrangea, and the group followed behind Takeru as he made his way to the corner.

Bianca interrupted to clarify. "Yes, I mostly heard what I thought was a struggle. When I looked in the direction of the noise, I saw a glint of metal. Possibly a knife."

"Who was involved?" He looked over at Bianca with concern. "Were you…ah…I'm sorry. My English teacher, she always said I need to study more. Damaged? Hurt? Are you hurt?"

"No, I was not hurt, but I am worried. Because I know I saw something." She broke eye contact. "I'm just not sure what."

"The metal could have been other things. Maybe keys? Jewelry? I am sure it was not a gun."

Bianca shook her head. "I suppose that's possible. Like I said, I don't know what I saw." She did know that citizens did not own guns in Japan, so the likelihood it was a gun was minuscule. But that did not rule out a knife. She didn't believe what she saw were keys or jewelry.

"Did anyone else see anything?"

"No, no one else saw anything last night. *Demo*...but..." Ian faltered and then grabbed the hat off the bench and handed it to him. "We found this hat this morning, and we thought we should let you know."

Takeru's eyebrows shot up. "Is that J.C.'s hat? I thought he never took it off."

"Yeah, he dropped by the welcome party we had here for my mom last night."

"You invited him?" The confusion was evident on Takeru's face.

Bianca could see that there was no love lost between J.C. and pretty much anyone. How could someone create such a large swath of damage, she wondered.

"No, he wasn't invited. He just showed up. When no one paid him any attention, he finally left."

"So, you think someone followed him out, and there was a struggle?"

"We don't know what to think. No one saw anything except my mom, and she's not sure what she saw. That's why we asked you to come over. We didn't feel like we had enough reason to call the police officially."

"You are right. There is nothing here to report. I think they say in America, 'No body, no crime.' At least, that is what I have heard on television. It is the same here. We have nothing yet to...to pursue."

"What about the hat?" Bianca jumped in, worried that this would be the end of it.

"I am sorry. But I cannot bring a hat to my superior and tell him that this is evidence of a crime. He would think me crazy. I will let you know if we hear anything that could be useful." He pulled out a pack of cigarettes and offered them around, though no one accepted. "Do you mind if I smoke?"

Jiro shook his head. "Not in my garden. You can smoke yourself to death somewhere else. You know the rules."

Takeru put the cigarette back in the pack and returned it to his shirt pocket. "I forgot you don't smoke anymore. Did anyone try to call J.C.? It is a simple matter."

When no one responded, he realized his error. No one wanted anything to do with J.C.

"I see. Of course. It is not a simple matter. I will call myself, and I will let you know."

As Takeru left, he reached into his shirt pocket and pulled out his pack of cigarettes.

Chapter Twenty-One

Kyoto, Japan

Ian stared at the orange cap. He knew when he had bent to pick it up that it would have an anchor logo on it.

The hat was unmistakable. The visor was frayed from overuse; the orange faded to coral; the threads of the anchor design coming loose at the edges.

He wandered back to the hydrangea bush and looked around. He wasn't sure what he was looking for. More proof that something happened to J.C.? Or proof that nothing happened to him? He wasn't sure.

He pushed a pile of red leaves aside with his right foot, then his left. This time, under the red, he saw a hint of white. He bent to pick it up.

It was a business card—that in itself wasn't so unusual. The culture of exchanging cards was so ingrained in Japan that even he, as a musician, needed a card.

The business card was not the issue. The name on the card was. Riku Kawabata's name.

Ian didn't like it at all that he kept popping up. First, he came by the guest house when his mother was alone. Then he showed up unannounced at the party, and now this card. Ian didn't know him, but Riku Kawabata was a name he had heard through the grapevine. Kawabata wasn't a member of a *yakuza* clan of organized crime, but he was too close for comfort as far as Ian was concerned.

Looking more closely at the card, he noticed that J.C.'s initials were scribbled on it. The card must have fallen out of J.C.'s hat. He had the habit of wedging slips of paper or business cards, mostly with phone numbers of girls he picked up, into the liner of his cap. What connection did J.C. have with Kawabata? It had to be strong enough for this guy to come looking for him in person. And more importantly, why was J.C.'s hat in the corner of the garden where his mother thought she had seen a knifing? Despite what he had told his mother, J.C. never took it off. Never.

Ian looked at his watch. He had two hours free while his mother was at her flower arranging class. He grabbed his bike and Bianca's dispatch and headed out. He arrived at Lovely Record Shop in no time. He saw Natsumi sweeping up the leaves that had blown into the entryway. He waved and headed up the stairs hidden in the alcove directly next door. He took the stairs quickly, knocked, and walked in without waiting.

"Hey, Mate! Good to see you. Where's the mum?"

Daniel shook Ian's hand, then handed him a stack of papers. "Here, hold these while I clear off the table."

Daniel looked perplexed at the mess of files on his old metal desk. He took his whole upper body and pushed everything to one side, then gave Ian a flourish with his hands to place the new pile on the table.

"She's at an *ikebana* class this morning."

"Oh, she will enjoy that. With Akane's mom? I've seen her arrangements. She's a pro."

"Yes, she is, and she speaks English. So, mom is all set."

Daniel hit the power button on an electric teapot. Care for a cuppa?"

"Yes, in fact, I would, thanks."

In no time, the pot clicked off. Daniel dropped a scoop of matcha green tea powder in two cups and poured the water. He whisked each tea quickly into a froth and passed one to Ian. "You're awfully quiet. Very uncharacteristic, if I might say so."

"Yeah, I know. I'm still thinking about J.C. stopping by yesterday. Why do you suppose he did that? How did he even know we were having a party?"

Daniel sipped and shook his head. "I can give you the answers to those questions. One—he heard about the party because this is a small community. Everybody knows everything in the expat community. I know you think you only told your good friends, but we all talk. Tell me you don't know Tyler is having an early graduation get-together Saturday at Rub-a-Dub?"

"You're right." Ian took a sip, lingering over the pleasantly bitter tea, and then switched the steaming cup to his other hand.

"And as far as why he came, that's even easier. J.C. has no idea he isn't welcome. His brain just doesn't work that way. He keeps inserting himself into our lives and has no idea that screwing people over, not paying debts, not delivering on promises, stealing someone's girl…"

"Oh God, Daniel. I should never have brought up J.C. around you. I'm sorry."

"Hey Mate, that's water under the bridge."

Ian put his hand on Daniel's shoulder in solidarity, but he didn't believe Daniel when he said he was over it. J.C. had managed to wrong the nicest expat Ian knew by having an affair with his wife. To be fair, Daniel's wife had had more than one affair. And they were no longer married as a result, but J.C. didn't need to do it. There are so many women in this country; why your mentor's wife? Daniel had helped J.C. in so many ways. He had given him work when he lost his job, and he had let him stay at his house for over a month when he was between apartments. Ian had his own gripes with J.C., but the hurt he had imposed on Daniel was unforgivable.

They continued drinking their tea. Ian regretted putting the usually jovial Daniel into a pensive mood. Ian was sure he was only pretending to be calm. If he were Daniel, the mere mention of J.C.'s name would have sent him into a fit of rage. He was surprised that Daniel had never confronted J.C., had never given him his due. Daniel could have done some damage if he wanted. He was a martial artist and was in good shape despite being twenty years older than Ian and J.C.

Ian sipped his tea. Then it hit him. He remembered that years ago, Daniel had taught *tantojutsu*. He was a master knife fighter.

Chapter Twenty-Two

Batavia-on-Hudson, N.Y.

Mike turned his truck onto Main Street and headed toward Town Hall. He wasn't happy about tonight's debate. He felt he was in for the fight of his life.

He was a law enforcement officer. He didn't know what it meant not to be one. He wasn't sure how he would handle losing Maggie, losing this election, and losing his memories of Sal all in the span of a few months. His entire identity was wrapped up in these three things, and he felt unmoored. He had made a decision. He needed to fight for this job. If only to preserve who he thought he was. Who he knew he was.

He was nervous. Heck, he was damn nervous. He was reminded of his anxiety before speaking in front of his high school class all those years ago. He thought he'd never need to do that again.

Every parking spot on the street was taken. People were leaving their cars up the road and walking to the debate. When he arrived at the parking lot of the town hall, he pulled right up front where he would normally park in an emergency or on county business.

As he turned off the ignition, he thought better of it. Parking his truck in the *No Parking* zone would not endear him to those who had walked the extra quarter mile. He was in a bind. He had dreaded this moment so much that he had waited until the last minute to arrive. He had wanted to avoid the chit-chat. He wandered up and down the lanes, but no spot was available. He should have realized why they were parking along Main Street. If he doubled back now, he'd have to park almost at his office, but he didn't see a choice. He drove out of the lot to the confused stares of his neighbors.

Trying not to speed, he arrived back at his office and screeched to a halt. He jumped out of his truck and rushed down Main while buttoning up his jacket and tightening his scarf.

Seeing the Blanchards across the street, he waved to them, and they waved back. Then he slowed his pace so as not to look as disorganized and harried as he truly was. But he made no attempt to cross the street, because then he would be late for sure.

He wished he could enjoy the autumn air and the twinkle of the Hudson under the moonlight, but it was beyond his reach tonight.

As soon as he was out of sight of the Blanchards, he picked up his pace and rounded the corner to the Town Hall parking lot. There were only a few stragglers making their way to the entrance.

He checked his watch. 7:56. How had he cut it so close?

When he got to the door, Sister Patricia Ann was slowly, very slowly, reaching for the handle. He waited. Then he grabbed the handle before she did.

She was startled. "Mike, such a gentleman. Thank you. But don't think you can butter me up with your charm. I am here to listen to what everyone has to say. Then I'll make my decision. Don't try to sway me. No politicking."

Now Mike was startled. How had he been accused of politicking when he was in this mess because he hadn't wanted to shake hands and sound insincere? It's true what they say—no good deed goes unpunished.

"Sister, I assure you, I was not trying to sway you. I just thought I'd open the door for you."

"Well, thank you. But I'll be the judge of that."

He followed her inside and heard Big Ben Sawyer's booming voice over the mic as he announced the debates were about to begin. Mike didn't have a moment to run to the men's room or to catch his breath. He was sweating through his shirt and probably his jacket, the nice Harris tweed Maggie bought him last year. Now he wished he had taken Shelley's advice to wear his uniform. She thought it would be a good reminder to the public that he had been watching over them all these years. He thought it gave him an unfair advantage. But right now, he needed any advantage he could get.

He walked into the room and stopped dead in his tracks. It was standing room only. Eugene Wilkins was holding up the wall at the entrance on his right. Mike rarely saw him without his diner apron. He had a coffee in his right hand, but he quickly switched it to his left so he could reach out for a shake. Big Ben saw him and leaned into the mic. "Well, here he is. We were wondering what happened to you, Mike. Come on up here, and let's get started."

Mike took advantage of the handshaking to catch his breath. He knew Big Ben wanted to get things underway, but he needed to compose himself. Once he turned away from Eugene, other villagers started to lean over for a handshake. Mike slowed down and said hello to each of them and shook everyone's hand. By the time a dozen of these encounters had come and gone, Mike felt better.

"Hey Mike, nice way to make an entrance. No last-minute campaigning." Then Ben turned to the audience and winked. "Those city folks, they think they're so slick."

Mike knew Ben was teasing. He was good at playing a crowd, but Mike wasn't sure how the rest of the audience thought about it. He stopped shaking hands and just waved to the others. He motioned to the stage and shrugged his shoulders. Everyone laughed.

He made his way to the stage, and just before he stepped up, he caught Sister Patricia Ann's gaze. He wasn't sure, but he thought he heard her tsking.

Chapter Twenty-Three

Kyoto, Japan

Bianca considered her flower arrangement. One of the tenets of *ikebana*, and many of the Japanese arts for that matter, was the careful use of negative space or *ma*. The space is as important as the flowers and plants themselves, with harmony and balance being the goal. Using what wasn't there as a way to emphasize what was there. It made her think about last night. What was there, and what wasn't.

She had searched the garden before leaving for her class and, once again, had found nothing. She was shocked and disappointed. Not that she wanted anyone hurt. Yet, how could she be so sure she had witnessed something if there was nothing concrete to prove it? Bianca didn't like second-guessing herself.

But she had to. How could she persist in believing there had been something there when there clearly wasn't? She had spent the night tossing and turning on her futon, tangled in her covers, dream after dream. Restless from all that she had experienced yesterday.

Today, Bianca wanted to focus on the positive and on her flowers. She wanted to clear her mind and let go of her worries so she could enjoy her visit. What better place to practice mindfulness than in Kyoto?

This was a city where Zen could creep in at any time. She could certainly access it here in the silence with her *ikebana* and each deliberate movement. She also noticed it in the nature throughout the city, in the serene temples, and even on the buses where everyone whispered.

Zen had a strong presence by the riverbank and in all the gardens at every establishment, big or small. She especially liked the tiny gardens before each home. Even if it meant only one pot of flowers or a tiny tree, it seemed that every home had something resembling a garden. She had even found three red maple leaves floating in a fire brigade bucket outside someone's home. It was as if mindfulness had been stitched into the culture. She knew that life was more hectic for those who lived in this city than for a tourist, but a certain amount of effort seemed to have been made to keep Zen in the culture. She had watched workers of all types take their time to do their jobs well, whether it was the girl polishing glasses at the bar or the old man washing the flagstones outside McDonald's. She knew she could learn from them all.

After her class, Bianca walked the short distance home and placed her arrangement in the *tokonoma* alcove where it belonged. She stepped back to admire it. She was proud of her amateur attempt and hoped she could find time to take a few more lessons while she was in the city.

Wrapping a scarf around her neck, Bianca stepped into the bustling Kyoto streets, her eyes scanning the unfamiliar landscape with excitement. She had assured Ian that she could make her way around the city on her own. All she needed was her trusty dictionary and map. Ian was in class, and she did not want him to interrupt his studies on her account.

She enjoyed how the city was an eclectic mix of old and new, with ancient temples and modern buildings coexisting in perfect harmony. The intersection of these two was not always beautiful, but it was always interesting. As she clutched her travel guide and map, she felt an overwhelming sense of adventure, ready to explore the city on her own. She decided to start small. A coffee and dessert.

She was on a mission. She reached into her pocket and pulled out the paper with the information she needed. According to her map, she needed to head south. She stopped for a moment at the window of an *udon* shop to watch as the cooks manipulated the dough into the soft, pillowy noodles

Ian loved so much. Even though she wasn't hungry, her mouth watered. She would need to sit down for a bowl soon, even if she always found those thick, long noodles the biggest chopstick challenge. For this reason, *udon* in soup was her preference, with a little crispy tempura—maybe shrimp or a nest of vegetables. She avoided the curry version completely. If the *udon* got unruly, she could run the risk of sending curry sauce flying across the room.

She walked by two cafes until she found the one she was looking for. The Bench & Mug Café. Back home in Batavia, Kay had explained that her cousin Kaori had started the original spot in Kyoto. With Kaori's recipes and interior design, Kay had started her own Bench & Mug Café. She had tried to keep it as close to the original as possible.

Bianca looked up at the second-story window. Colorful glass bottles and plants sat in the window. She followed the sign and walked up the narrow, winding stairs to the second floor.

"*Irasshaimase*," she heard as she entered.

When Bianca glanced toward the voice, she found a smiling young woman with her chestnut hair pulled back. She motioned to Bianca to pick her seat. Bianca looked around the tiny space and noticed there were only a couple of seats left, but the place remained hushed just the same. She hesitated, so her host guided her to the loveseat by the window. Bianca was thrilled. It was the best seat in the house.

"I am Bianca St. Denis from Batavia-on-Hudson in New York. Your cousin—"

"Oh, yes! Kay told me you would be in town. It is so nice to meet you. I am Kaori."

Bianca was charmed by Kaori's exuberance and her heavily accented English.

"Let me bring you a menu."

"There's no need for that. I would like a cup of your blend of the day and a slice of clementine cake."

"You must know the menu from home."

"Yes, your cousin has done a wonderful job with your recipes and ambiance. Everyone at home loves the Bench & Mug, and they especially love Kay."

"That makes me very happy. I hope to come and visit someday soon. I must go back to the kitchen, but we will talk again. I will bring your order."

Bianca was immediately at home in this space. She loved the simple décor, and the aroma of baked goods piqued her senses. Baking books and jars of coffee beans lined the shelves. A climbing plant wound its way around the ceiling while succulents lined the windowsills. She admired the rich glow of the wooden counter that sat only four. It faced Kaori's kitchen and coffee station.

Bianca took out her book and placed it on the table. The green glass of the bottles lining the window made an interesting play of light on the wood. It had just started to rain, and the trailing drops on the window added to the calming effect.

Kaori quietly placed Bianca's cake and steaming coffee on the table with a tiny bowl of three sugar cubes. Bianca thanked her and immediately speared the corner of her clementine cake, forgetting to say *itadakimasu*.

The dense, rich cake had just the right amount of give. A mouthful proved to be exactly what she had expected. It tasted just like Kay's at home. Made from almond flour, it was smooth and rich. The cake was bursting with a tart citrus flavor, which she followed with a sip of mellow coffee. A perfect mid-afternoon pick-me-up.

The patrons whispered, and soft music played in the background. Everyone was quietly conversing, reading, writing, or doing homework. There was a young couple at the far end of the counter. He was Western; she was Japanese, a common pairing Bianca was finding. They looked very in love or very interested in falling in love. They were playful with each other, and Bianca enjoyed watching them.

A small table for one had a tall young man hunched over a book. He looked like a Westerner to Bianca based on his height, his long wavy hair, and his clothes, but she couldn't be sure since his face was turned away. For Ian's sake, she was glad to know that the expat community was growing in Kyoto.

There were two elderly gentlemen at the only other table, each with his own newspaper. One was smoking, but Bianca noticed that their seats were tucked in the farthest corner near an open window.

She read as she sipped her coffee and nibbled her cake, trying to make it last. When she was done, she put her book away and took out her notebook. She recorded her impressions of this café and the others she had visited. The coffee culture was an unforeseen pleasure Bianca had discovered when she arrived for the first time. She had expected and was intrigued by the tea ceremony but had no idea the degree to which the Japanese had perfected the making of a perfect cup of coffee. Bianca also appreciated the way she could claim a seat in any of these establishments and linger for hours without any push to vacate her seat. She pictured herself and Ian here on the loveseat, reading and whispering for hours as they watched the sunset and the rivulets of rain on the window. She would need to bring him here soon.

Dusk had arrived. She finally cleaned her plate of the last of the crumbs and checked the time. She needed to get her dispatch to the *Kyoto Quarterly* before meeting Ian. Gathering her things, she said a few parting words to Kaori with promises to return with Ian.

"*Gochisousamadeshita,*" she thanked her host as she slipped quietly out the door and down the stairs.

Once on the sidewalk, she checked her map. Then she folded it up again and turned left. *Hidari,* she said to herself. Another left. *Hidari.* She made the next right. *Migi.* Then she stopped in her tracks. She was in an alley she didn't recognize.

She tried to review her map, but there wasn't enough light to read the small print. She retraced her steps, but as she turned the corner onto the main street, she bumped into the tall young man who had been reading at the café. He was as surprised as she was. He quickly turned without a word and left her wobbling there.

"*Sumimasen*" escaped her lips automatically. She had apologized even though she was sure it wasn't entirely her fault.

She righted herself, made the last turn to the café and checked her map again. One careful look and she realized she should have gone *migi, migi, hidari.* Just the mirror opposite of what she had done previously. Perhaps she should stick to English directions before she got herself lost.

Chapter Twenty-Four

Kyoto, Japan

Ian handed Jiro the business card.

"Where did you get this?"

"I found it. What do you make of it?"

"It depends on where you got it."

Ian hesitated. "I found it in the garden this morning."

Jiro turned the card over and over in his hand. "Kawabata doesn't give these cards to just anyone. I find it hard to believe that someone would lose it. It's valuable."

"Why would he give it to someone in the first place?"

Ian picked up some dirty glasses at the end of the bar and brought them over to Jiro by the sink. Together, they worked. Jiro washing, Ian drying and putting away.

"Kawabata isn't quite *yakuza*, but he fancies himself one. And he lives by their code. He's just a rich guy acting out against his father, and he takes this underworld stuff pretty seriously. Rumor has it that he even cut off the tip of his pinky as a show of loyalty after messing up a job for the local boss."

"How do you know all this stuff, Jiro? I mean, you don't…"

"No. Of course not. But I know things. I've got business connections, and they have connections. You know how it is."

Ian had no idea how it was. These were not people Ian had any knowledge of. Nor did he want any.

"But getting back to the card," Jiro continued. "If someone does right by Kawabata, this is how he reciprocates. He knows he has pull, and he knows that people who do business with him also do business with even shadier people. If they find themselves in trouble, they can use the card as a pass." Jiro dried his hands when he finished with the glasses. "The only person I can think of is—"

"J.C.," Ian said before Jiro got the words out.

"Yep." Jiro stacked the freshly cleaned glasses behind the bar. "I know J.C. can be irresponsible, but I don't see him losing this card."

"It must be J.C. It looks like his initials are scribbled on here." Ian pointed to the chicken scratch on the front of the card.

"Well, I guess it makes sense. Let's face it: Riku came looking for him last night. They obviously have some unfinished business." Jiro handed Ian a handful of lemons and limes and motioned to the fridge behind him. "J.C. and Kawabata don't make such strange bedfellows. Jay owes more debts than I care to count. He owes me five thousand dollars, and I doubt I will ever see it."

"I had no idea he owed you that much."

"Well, I wasn't so smart. I wanted to believe him when he said he had the money at home and it was coming soon. That was over a year ago, and nothing."

Jiro shook his head and kept cleaning the counter, but Ian could see his jaw clenching.

"He even stayed here for six months rent-free. A room I could have rented to someone else. He said it would only be a few weeks, and it turned into months."

Ian knew this story and didn't want to fuel the fire, so he said nothing. He rinsed a cloth and started washing down the tables while Jiro stacked chairs.

"Then I gave him a job! I actually paid him! I felt bad for him being away from home and hitting all that bad luck. It never occurred to me that he makes his own bad luck. Instead of paying me back with the money I was paying him, he went home to the States. I figured it wasn't so bad because he had money at home. I figured he would square it all with me when he got back."

Jiro started jamming the chairs into each other. It startled Ian—Jiro was the gentlest person he knew.

"But he never did, of course." Jiro swung around to Ian. "Remind me why we're talking about J.C.? This is my least favorite topic."

"I'm sorry. We were talking about Kawabata's business card."

"Yeah, yeah. So, no surprise that Jay is fraternizing with that type of guy. He'd better be careful and not cross him. Kawabata won't be as forgiving as I was.

"Or as forgiving as Daniel."

"Or you."

"Yeah, well, I don't want to talk about it either. Let's change the subject."

Jiro hopped around the bar to the mini fridge and took out a beer and a soda. He grabbed a stool by the bar and opened the beer. He pushed the other drink to Ian. They tapped their bottles together and took a cold sip, both happy to change the discussion, but both still thinking about J.C.—knowing that he was a problem that didn't go away.

Ian had a lot on his mind but didn't voice any of it. So far, he knew three people who had motive to harm J.C.—Daniel, Jiro, and possibly the most dangerous of the lot, Kawabata. Ian knew one thing: something serious had to happen to separate J.C. from his hat.

He sipped his drink, but his nerves were on edge. His gut told him that something was amiss. He hadn't believed his mother last night when she said that she had seen a struggle. There had been no proof. And maybe he hadn't wanted to believe it either.

But now he had to admit that something had happened last night. He just didn't know what.

Jiro finished his beer and started to peel the label. "Yeah, J.C. better be careful. Nobody likes him, but if he pulls on Kawabata some of the things he pulled on the rest of us...I don't even want to think about the consequences. All I know is that people who cross Kawabata often find themselves on the wrong side of a knife."

Ian decided he would keep his unofficial investigation to himself. There was no reason to worry his mom. She was here on vacation. A long-overdue one.

He considered talking to the police again before Bianca got home from her class, but he had no intention of giving them information that would make his friends look bad. So far, all he had was a lost cap, a friend who was a talented *tanto* knife instructor and who happened to have a grudge against J.C. for sleeping with his wife, and another friend who lent J.C. a great deal of money with no chance of ever seeing it again.

Not to mention his own issues with Jay.

And then there was a business card from a shady character who was known for settling scores with a knife.

Chapter Twenty-Five

Mike stood on the stage wishing he had worn his uniform and especially his sheriff's hat. He hadn't registered how much the uniform had become a part of his identity. It was his armor.

He normally wouldn't be nervous addressing the community, but he usually did it in his capacity as sheriff. Mike should have listened to Shelley's advice. He knew his uniform garnered respect, and it curtailed some of the ribbing.

He turned to his opponents. Vera had worn her uniform, crisper than usual. And her hat. Vera avoided eye contact and looked over his head when she nodded acknowledgment. Mike recognized that this event would be even more awkward for her than it was for him.

Off to her right, he spotted Edward Angleton. Eddie looked the part. He was dressed in casual but neat clothes. And he had a cowboy hat on.

When Mike realized that he was the only one without a hat, he knew he was sunk. His hat was the most recognizable part of the uniform. It could be seen from afar. In a crowd, he could easily be spotted. And although he was tall (many men were tall), the hat gave him the extra few inches he needed to assure some advantage in a situation. He loved his hat. He had even named it. He had never told anyone that. Not even Maggie.

Mike jumped up on the stage. If he were truthful with himself, he had to admit that he had chosen to jump as opposed to walking up the stairs as a show of vitality. He didn't want to seem like the oldest person on the stage—which he was. Vera was about thirty-five, and Angleton was only a couple of years older.

He strode over to Eddie and shook hands with as firm a grip as he could muster. It had its desired effect; Mike could see it on Eddie's face. He smirked to himself. Childish, he knew, but what the hell. He was here now, and he was going to fight for his job. Whatever it took.

He paused before approaching Vera. He smiled and put out his hand. He was gentle with her, and he could see that she appreciated it. She gave him an apologetic smile. His grandmother had always told him to take the high road. Be the better man. And he would.

He took his place behind the podium, and as he did, the audience clapped. Many with enthusiasm. Others out of duty, he was sure. Several stood. Kurt, Eugene, and Ernie clapped the loudest. Bert put two fingers in his mouth and whistled. Mike's heartbeat settled in, and with no effort at all, his carefully outlined notes came back to him.

Ben introduced him and, as the incumbent, asked Mike to open the remarks. He smiled at the crowd and started: "Good evening, everyone. It's good to see you all here. Thanks for coming. I'm here tonight to tell you why I should remain the sheriff of Onanda County. My capable opponents are here to tell you why they should be your next sheriff. It is my honest opinion that either one of them would work hard and do the job justice. I think I have been a good sheriff, and I think you know that I have given it my heart and soul. I have worked to be a member of your community, and I thank you for welcoming me. But I'm not one for speeches. I think my actions and my intentions over the years speak for themselves. So, I will leave the rest of the debate to Vera Weber and Edward Angleton. They need the time to talk to you. I don't.

"I have an unfair advantage. You know me; you know my track record. You know whether I have done right by you. You know if I have handled big and small problems well. If you think I have done so, we must give plenty of credit to Vera here, because without her, I certainly couldn't have done it alone. When it comes right down to it, there is no need for me to try to convince you. Either I've been good at my job, and you'd like to see me continue, or you want one of these worthy people to take it over. I leave it up to you. Thank you, and good night."

The audience watched in stunned silence as he walked off the stage and made his way down the aisle. The applause started when he reached the back of the hall and didn't stop until he turned the corner off Main Street.

When he arrived at the sheriff's office parking lot, he climbed into his truck, took his sheriff's hat off the dashboard, and clapped it on his head where it belonged.

Chapter Twenty-Six

Kyoto, Japan

Ian hooked his arm through his mother's as they walked down the boulevard. Bianca was so deep in thought she hardly noticed the bright yellow ginkgo trees lining the street. Takeru had called just before they left the house. Despite his best efforts, he had not been able to track down J.C. He said he would stay on top of it, and he had agreed that until J.C. surfaced, Bianca's story could not be dismissed.

Ian tugged Bianca to a stop before the Ebisu Café sign. They had arrived. On Bianca's last trip to Kyoto, when Ian had first started school, the Ebisu Café had been their regular hangout. Bianca would arrive about noon and have a toast and coffee as she waited for Ian to drop in between classes.

Ebisu, the god of good fortune, fishing, commerce, and prosperity, reigned over this café. Bianca was familiar with Ebisu's jolly and rotund image on the sign, and on the matching cups and napkins. This past summer, when a tiny wooden sculpture was retrieved off the dead body of an antique dealer visiting Batavia, Bianca had recognized that it was an Ebisu *netsuke*—a small carved figurine used to decorate a man's kimono belt. Putting the pieces together at the evacuation center during the flood had been difficult, but between her efforts and Mike's, they had determined it was a priceless antique. Mike arranged to have her return it to its rightful owner in Japan. And here she was. It had all started here.

She snapped a photo of the sign to include with her next dispatch home.

Upon entering, they were transported to the 1970s. The café walls were lined with richly polished wood panels. The bar gleamed. Forest green and burnt orange ceramic tiles covered the tabletops and the wall behind the bar. Amber leather chairs invited them to sit and linger.

She saw several men reading newspapers. Two women in the corner chatted quietly, three tables overflowed with students, their books open, their heads down. No one rushed them. They appeared to be settled in for the long haul. She looked forward to spending time here. The ambiance was perfect, the dated music soft and a tad upbeat.

They claimed their favorite seat near the window so they could have a view of the patrons. Outside, the streets bustled with tourists. Kyoto was the cultural capital of the country, and she wasn't surprised to see that many of the tourists were Japanese. Nonetheless, there were a fair number of Westerners. She even felt like she recognized one or two as they stood at the bus stop outside their window. As large a city as Kyoto was, even Bianca felt its intimacy.

"The usual?" Ian asked his mother.

"Of course."

"*Sumimasen.*" Ian called the waitress over and ordered two Vienna coffees.

"*Hai.* Extra cream. Coming right up Ian-chan," the waitress said with a light accent.

"Obviously, you still come here regularly."

"Almost every day. It's still my favorite place."

They both remained quiet for a bit, enjoying the atmosphere and music. They watched the barista, an older gentleman, pour their coffee. He was meticulous, as usual. Then he added two dollops of cream to the top of each.

Once the coffee was delivered, the girl returned to her spot behind the bar to her open books.

"She's the owner's daughter. Rina is in my economics class. We have an exam coming up."

The music switched to an instrumental piece reminiscent of the Beatles.

"I like that sound," Bianca mused almost to herself.

"I do too." Ian nodded in agreement.

"I'm glad you're back to playing. Are you still composing? And the band. Whatever happened with that?"

"I've started dabbling in composing again. It's been hard with my studies. But I started out playing at a few small solo gigs here and there, and I tried out a couple of my new originals and got some good feedback, so I think I might keep at it." Ian fiddled with the matchbook on the table. The smiling Ebisu on the cover matched the image on the sign and the cups holding their coffee. "It was hard. After J.C. and Irvin and that whole thing."

"Tell me more about that episode. Everybody here seems to know about it, but you never told me."

"I didn't tell you, not to worry you."

"Is there something to worry about?"

"No, not really. But the whole incident really took its toll on me at the time, and you were dealing with so much yourself, so—"

"Ian, never feel like you can't tell me something. You know I can always listen. Besides, it might have been a good distraction for me." She smiled to take the edge off her words. "So, tell me now."

He sipped at his coffee and gave her his cool side-eye. "You know that dad is…well, dad. And as much as I wanted to come to Japan because of my love affair with this country, a lot of it had to do with getting a chance to assert my own, I don't know what…identity, I guess. Dad is so much Malcolm Grant that it's hard to find my father in there." He stopped for a moment, but Bianca didn't interject. He needed time to gather his thoughts.

"And, you know how everything has to be his way? It got worse once the fame really kicked in. No one can have a better way or a better idea, because look how successful he was doing it his way. I guess I needed some distance."

More side-eye. He was checking to see how she was reacting, but over the years she had mastered the non-reactive face. Parenting is full of situations where parents can't show their true emotions, such as fear and anger. Especially fear. She wanted him to open up and not feel judged.

"I figured you needed some space. That's to be expected. We all need space sometimes." Bianca's mind wandered to Mike and Maggie in a trial separation. Which brought her thoughts to her first marriage with Ian's dad, Malcolm. They, too, separated first and divorced later. Space can grow on you.

Ian interrupted her thoughts. "You don't feel bad that I moved so far away?"

"Have you moved? Or—"

"Am I coming back after school? I don't know yet…"

Bianca exerted more facial control as she absorbed this information.

"Look, you seem very happy here. You will decide your next step as it all unfolds. You can't come back to the States for me. You have to live your own life. I will never guilt you into returning. But you better be prepared for me to visit more often."

They laughed two nervous laughs. He covered her hand, the one tearing at the napkin.

They both turned at the sound of patter on the windowpane. The ever-present rain had started again. The sky, a dove gray, was a perfect backdrop to the quiet afternoon scene in the café.

"So, tell me about your music."

"Okay, so, along with a little space, what I've found here is a new sound. A new vibe. And I discovered that I could compose and play again. That was very liberating for me. Not having Dad's music prodding me. My own voice. My own sound."

"That's great news. But?"

"The band I told you about with J.C. and Irvin backfired. The Three Dogs were doing well. We were getting gigs. Everyone knew us around town. My original pieces were everyone's favorites, but I misjudged. I thought these guys were for real. I missed the signs of what kind of people they really are. I'm such an idiot."

"Ian, you can't fault yourself for seeing the good side of people. That's a positive trait. Granted, sometimes it means we can be taken advantage of, but who would want to live being suspicious of everyone? Tell me what happened."

"They took my music. They just took it from me."

"How can they do such a thing?"

"Well, they did it. They recorded my original songs without me. The CDs are selling well, and they never even included my name on the credits for writing the songs."

Bianca's face was no longer passive. This, she hadn't expected. She had been nervous when he first left for Japan. She worried if he would find friends. Just like kindergarten. But once he told her he was thriving, she believed him. But his friends had hurt him. How had that happened on her watch?

"Mom, it's okay. I'm starting to get over it."

"That's good, but is there anything you can do?"

"I asked a friend who is studying law, and he doesn't think I have much to stand on because there is no proof that the music is mine. I never asserted any rights. And J.C. and Irvin have been telling everyone that the music is theirs. No one has any reason not to believe them. Although, lately…"

"Lately, what?"

"Irvin has had some trouble with the law. No one's seen him for months. J.C. hasn't been performing either, and he's been scarce too, except for his brief appearance at the party."

"My best advice is to move past this."

"I'm trying, but it's hard."

"If that's the case, then can't you approach them? Reason with them?"

"At first, I thought I could. But I had gotten so angry I didn't trust myself in a room with them. I didn't know what I might do. So, I avoided it. Another stupid thing."

"It's not stupid to avoid confrontation when you're so angry. That was smart. Now you're calmer. Maybe knowing exactly what you want them to do and asking them to do it would work."

"Well…"

"Well, what? Is there more?"

"Late in our partnership, just before the breakup of the group, Jay and I had an altercation."

"How serious of an altercation? Was anyone hurt?"

"We weren't seriously hurt, but we didn't come out of it unscathed. And…well…he filed a police report."

"He filed a report? Why?"

"He claimed I assaulted him. And he was just defending himself."

"Is that true?"

"I have to confess, it is. You may have heard what he did to Daniel. J.C. had an affair with Daniel's ex-wife. She was still married to Daniel at the time. J.C. was talking about it one day, boasting. I couldn't take it any longer, and I lashed out at him. It turned real ugly, real fast. I got some beautiful bruises, I must say. But…" A smile escaped. "But Jay got the worst of it."

"You never told me any of this. What came of it?"

"Nothing, really. I was called down to the precinct and questioned. Takeru helped me out and got the charges dropped. But the report is on file. That's another reason I'm concerned about my visa. I'm afraid if they consider me a bad element, they won't give me a new visa. That's why I've been avoiding renewing. And, of course, now it's expired.

"Nothing good comes from dealing with J.C. I think he had already hatched his plan to steal my music and had coaxed me into a fight so he could file a police report. It would make his claim stronger by making me look bad. Making it sound as if I was angry about the police report and was retaliating by claiming they stole my music. I think it was sort of insurance for him. His plan worked. Because of the police record, I'm nervous to make legal trouble for myself."

Bianca couldn't help thinking that it also made Ian an ideal suspect if anything had happened to J.C.

Chapter Twenty-Seven

Kyoto, Japan

Ian offered Bianca his arm. She was always so proud to show him off as her son and now she realized, as he introduced her, that he was showing *her* off. This was his turf, he knew everyone, and he was proud to call her his mother.

"I'd like you to meet my mother, Bianca St. Denis. She's an author."

"I haven't published anything yet," Bianca interjected for the third time.

"That's just a matter of time. Don't listen to her. She has an agent and one great book written and another in the works."

Everyone bowed and was patient with her Japanese. They spoke to her in English of various abilities. It reminded her just how much more effort she needed to put into her Japanese language studies.

Bianca and Ian entered the main hall of the building—an art gallery in the north of town. It was known for its support of emerging artists, much of the sponsorship coming from the Nakayama family.

A fusion of modern and traditional design, the room wasn't grandiose, but it could second as a small ballroom. It was not quite sunset, and Bianca could still enjoy the light streaming through the atrium skylight. It was a room of understated luxury with hand-painted silk upholstery, large stylized woodblock prints on three of the walls, and soft lighting housed in floating paper art sculptures. Bianca admired the entire effect, but most of all, she was delighted by the vertical garden on one wall, with water trickling softly down the face.

There was quiet *koto* music playing in the background. According to the program, there would be a special performance after dinner.

Bianca surveyed the crowd, looking for Kenzo. He had made plans to meet them at the gala with his guest. She was curious to see who it would be. Could he have a long-lost sweetheart here, she wondered?

A distinguished gentleman in a perfectly tailored dark suit approached her.

"Mrs. St. Denis, it is my pleasure to finally meet you. I am Nakayama Masuji, your host. Thank you for recovering our family heirloom."

Bianca responded with a shallow bow and accepted the business card he had produced. She could not read the complicated *kanji* symbols, but she placed it in her clutch, and with two hands and a bow, she presented her own card, which read, *Bianca St. Denis, Author*. Ian, at her side, also pulled out a card and presented it to Nakayama-san.

"*Dōzo yoroshiku onegaishimasu.*" Ian introduced himself. Bianca noticed that his bow was deeper than Mr. Nakayama's. She would need to learn all the protocols.

A beautiful woman approached their small group. She wore a kimono of blush-colored silk with a maple leaf design. Along the left hem and the right sleeve of her kimono, some of the leaves were embroidered in ivory threads. She reached Mr. Nakayama and stood quietly at his side. She had the kind of beauty that Bianca noticed was common in Japan. Youthful at almost every age with clear skin, shiny hair, and delicate features. No wrinkles or the soft middles that Western women often get as they age.

Mrs. Nakayama didn't seem to speak English. She bowed and spoke to Bianca in Japanese only. Ian translated words that were similar to the sentiments expressed by her husband.

Kenzo appeared and introduced himself to the Nakayamas. He stepped aside, and a beautiful young lady about Ian's age stepped forward.

"Let me introduce my granddaughter, Aki Hashimoto."

Everyone bowed, but Ian bowed and blushed.

"Do you two know each other?" Kenzo asked.

"Yes, I met Aki at the record shop below the *Kyoto Quarterly*. Lovely New and Used Records."

"Natsumi and I have hosted him for a few guitar events. Ian is very...*jōzu*. I'm sorry. My English. *Jōzu*—"

Kenzo interrupted. "Talented."

"Yes, Ian is very talented at guitar."

Bianca wasn't sure what she was witnessing, but she could see that both Ian and Aki were stammering and blushing. This had suddenly turned very interesting.

Kenzo and Nakayama-san continued talking. Bianca noticed that they talked rather comfortably. Not unfamiliar, not stiff or business-like.

"If you will excuse us, we will need to continue mingling. Please help yourselves to hors d'oeuvres and champagne. We will proceed to dinner shortly."

The Nakayamas bowed and moved to the next circle of guests. Bianca could hear Nakayama-san introduce himself again, this time in French.

Ian bent to reach her ear. He whispered that the group next to them included the cultural ambassador and his wife, as well as the head of the Bank of Kyoto and his wife. Hovering outside that circle was another group: an actress, her husband, and the Kyoto City Hospital director, waiting to greet the Nakayamas.

Kenzo turned and explained that his family and Mr. Nakayama's family had been neighbors for generations. Although the men did not really know each other, they knew of each other and knew the history of each family. Mr. Nakayama had been adopted by his in-laws since they had no male children to take over the business and family name. This was a common and accepted practice, especially in prominent families.

Bianca surreptitiously kept an eye on Ian and Aki. They were deep in conversation. Bianca marveled at what a small world it was. Kenzo's granddaughter and Ian were friends. Or maybe more.

Kenzo inquired about her stay, and Bianca elaborated to allow her son more time to talk. Aki had her back to them, and when Ian caught Bianca's eye, he made an almost imperceptible wink of thanks. Kenzo led Bianca to their table as the dinner announcement was made. Ian did the same, offering his arm to Aki this time.

The dinner was a display of Japanese perfection. Every dish was presented with exquisite care. Special touches made each dish unique to the season and the event. Bianca knew that these dishes would never be reproduced in exactly this way again. Each dish was only two or three bites. The idea was to indulge in a series of flavors and textures that would ultimately satisfy, without being overfilling.

The first course started with a cup of a rich miso soup of sea urchin with thin tendrils of soft custardy tofu that melted in her mouth. Next came a tiny salad with thin slices of persimmon, followed by a plate of two slices of sashimi.

"What kind of fish is the sashimi?" Bianca asked Kenzo to her right.

"Seabream. This is the season for it."

"Oh, that's very clever of the chef. The fish Ebisu carries is a seabream, isn't it?"

"Now it is you who is very clever."

Every dish was garnished with autumn leaves of red maple or yellow ginkgo, either real or formed from ingredients such as chestnuts or tofu.

Next came the grilled course with one succulent slice of beef, then a vegetable plate comprised of three ginkgo nuts, a small mound of pickled mustard greens, and several sweet potato chips in the shape of maple leaves. A simple bowl of mushroom rice rounded out the main course.

The meal ended with *wagashi*, three traditional sweets made into the shapes of a chestnut, a maple leaf, and a miniature persimmon.

After dinner, the ceremony of reuniting the collection began. Nakayama-san moved to the front of the room.

"We are grateful today to add Bianca St. Denis to our family. She has made a long-held dream come true by returning the Kawakami Shinji Ebisu to us. The entire collection is now complete. It will be on exhibit here for this week and then will be on loan to the Kyoto Netsuke Museum for an undetermined amount of time.

"This set was commissioned by our ancestor Nakayama Hosei in 1757 to commemorate the imminent birth of his first child. The artist created one piece a month for seven months. The last one was delivered one week after the child's birth. The final piece, the Ebisu, represented the prosperity the family would see with the arrival of a son. This collection stayed in the family until it was lost during the war in 1945. Since that time, we have been recreating the collection. The only piece that remained at large was the Ebisu. We are forever grateful to Bianca St. Denis."

Once again, Bianca found herself the center of applause. She looked sheepishly at her audience. The room was full of Kyoto's most influential citizens, and they were applauding her. Some were dressed in the trendiest fashions, some in rich traditional kimono.

The group quieted down as the host removed a paper from his chest pocket. "In addition, I have a fax to read that arrived this morning from the Cultural Office."

As Nakayama-san read in Japanese, Bianca understood nothing, but the applause she understood.

Kenzo leaned over. Between claps, he said, "The collection has gained the status of national treasure."

Bianca felt a flush of pride that she had helped bring this unique item back home where it belonged.

When the applause subsided, Nakayama-san continued, "We are pleased to present the complete collection this evening." He nodded, and two men in tuxedos removed the drape covering the small display on the table next to him. The room again erupted in applause as Nakayama-san invited the guests to come forward to view the collection. Everyone disbursed to form a line toward the front of the room where the entire collection was on display. As the line slowly moved, it reminded Bianca of mourners lined up to view a body at a wake—very somber and slow. But when she arrived at the table, she saw a stunning display of craftsmanship. She realized the viewers were quiet out of respect and awe for the intricately carved statuettes.

All the *netsukes* could easily fit in her tiny silk purse. So much fuss over something so small. But they were exquisite, she had to admit. Had the seven gods of good fortune been reunited because of who they were, she wondered. What were the chances that a collection of seven little wooden pieces could survive for more than two hundred years? They had already made it through war and possibly fire. Then lost or stolen. One even found its way to the United States just to be lost once again. It turned up in the tiny hamlet of Batavia and was almost washed away in the fury of the flooding river. Ebisu was indeed a god of good fortune.

Bianca was invited to join the Nakayamas in a few photographs with the collection. Once the photographers were done and the guests returned to their tables for more coffee, Ian excused himself. "Wait just a second, Mom. I think I see someone I know." He approached a woman.

"Mariko?"

A young woman in a bob turned around at the call of her name.

"Ian-chan? So good to see you!" She embraced him, and Bianca stood by, wondering just who this version of Ian was.

"Come here and meet my mother, Bianca. Mom, this is Mariko. A dear friend."

As Bianca came in for a hug, Mariko bowed. They struggled around this until they ended in a hug and then a bow. A young man appeared at Mariko's side with her coffee.

"Jonathan, I'd like you to meet Ian Grant and his mother, Mrs. Grant."

Both Bianca and Ian started to correct her, but Ian's voice was louder. "Actually, my mom is Bianca St. Denis. She uses my stepfather's name." Mariko seemed so uncomfortable at her faux pas that Bianca felt guilty for correcting her.

"I was Bianca Grant for a long time. Please don't worry. I am fine with either name."

"Let me apologize. Mrs. St. Denis, this is my husband, Jonathan Curtis."

Bianca wanted to correct her again but wouldn't. Bianca never went by Mrs. Not in her first marriage and not in her second. But she did take their names. Mostly because Grant and St. Denis were easier to spell and pronounce than her Italian maiden name, d'Alessandro. She settled for using her first name, which she preferred anyway. "Please call me Bianca. Nice to meet you both."

Jonathan and Ian shook hands and exchanged cards. Ian scrutinized Jonathan's card. Jonathan towered over his wife and was obviously half-Japanese. "Curtis? Jonathan Curtis? Any relation to Jay Curtis. J.C.?"

"No, we're not related. I'm from Los Angeles. My father is Harrison Curtis, and my mother, Chizuko, is from Kyoto. I've heard of J.C., although I've never met him. Is he a friend of yours?"

Mariko looked up from her coffee. "Isn't that an odd coincidence? I asked him that too the first time I met him. I assumed they were cousins."

Ian looked relieved by Mariko's interjection. Ian and Jonathan continued talking as Bianca and Mariko chatted about Kyoto sights. Bianca tried to eavesdrop but was not very successful.

"Time to get back to our table. Mariko, it was good to see you. I'd like to finish catching up."

"Please come visit soon, while your mother is still here."

Ian escorted Bianca back to their table. She was disturbed that J.C.'s name came up again, as it never failed to sour the mood in the room. Bianca concluded that Mariko's husband was a lucky man that he didn't know J.C.

Chapter Twenty-Eight

Batavia-on-Hudson, N.Y.

As Mike entered Stella's he could hear the change in pitch, all the voices taken down a notch. Everyone pretended it was normal, that nothing had changed just because the sheriff had walked in. But they all knew what had happened. They had been talking about the debate. And for anyone who had missed it, the *Gazette* had a minute-by-minute write-up.

The villagers were still stunned that he had walked out and left Vera and Edward to duke it out. Mike had said what he needed to say, and he had looked strong while doing it. Then, he just skipped out.

Some probably wished he had stuck around to take his licks, and the op-ed had covered that very neatly in the paper, too. What was he afraid of? Was he worried that his opponents would call him out? Did Vera have secrets she could share about him as sheriff? The newspaper had been merciless.

Eugene cleared a space at the counter. Mike removed his jacket, took his seat, and avoided looking at the paper. He had hoped for a few minutes of relaxation as he listened to the jazz playing overhead. The music could be heard more clearly today over the hushed voices. He listened to Paul Desmond and Jim Hall playing some bossa nova.

Eugene brought a cup and saucer. "Mike, quite a show last night. I have to admit you surprised me." Eugene poured the coffee and leaned a little closer. "Honestly, I laughed all night about it."

"Maybe we should change the subject? I presume the debate's all that anyone's been talking about." Mike pretended he wasn't curious about how Eddie and Vera did, but he finally succumbed. "Actually, I changed my mind. Tell me…did Vera hold up okay?" Mike wanted to keep his job, but if he had to lose, he hoped it would be to Vera and not that blowhard Angleton.

"Yeah. She was great. A little nervous at first, but as she warmed up, she was fine. Not as polished as Angleton, but that might have worked in her favor." Eugene straightened up just in time to hear the chime above the door. "Speak of the devil."

Vera walked in. The voices of the neighbors hushed a little more. Mike had to admit he was glad that he wasn't the only one they were gossiping about. But he didn't want her to feel the awkwardness more than necessary. He picked his jacket up off the stool next to him and motioned for her to take a seat.

Eugene left them to their business. Mike looked up, hoping to fix Eugene with a stare to keep him from walking away, but Eugene pretended not to notice.

Vera was a tall woman of Dutch stock. Strong and attractive, but all business. As usual, she wore her blonde hair in a tight bun. Not a crease on her uniform. Always in order, that was his deputy.

Vera approached with dignity despite her obvious discomfort. She hesitated a moment. "Listen, Mike, I know I should have said something sooner, but I honestly didn't know how to go about it." She looked at the seat but didn't sit.

Mike motioned to the seat again. "Vera, why don't you sit and grab a coffee with me? I understand why you're running, and I don't hold it against you."

"That's hard to believe. I would hold it against you if the tables were turned."

"Okay. I admit I was a bit stunned when I read it in the *Gazette*, but I got over it pretty quickly. I think I was more hurt that you didn't tell me yourself, but the more I thought about it, the more I realized just how hard that would be."

"Yeah, I guess I'm a coward. Not a great way to start a run for the job that requires the most courage in this county." She looked away, but she eased herself into the seat next to him.

"You're not a coward. You're running, and that takes guts. I don't like running, and I'm the incumbent."

"Well, if it makes me look any better in your eyes, I thought about it long and hard before I entered the race. If it hadn't been for Ben, I probably wouldn't have—"

"Big Ben? Oh boy, are you saying Ben recruited you?"

Vera looked down at her lap, confirming his guess.

This wasn't good. The village president had lost faith in him? Ben was recruiting a new sheriff? That news hurt more than Mike thought it would. He had come to terms with the fact that the village was testing the waters, checking to see if they needed new blood. But for it to come from Ben, his friend, was tough.

"Look, don't blame Ben. I think he knew that since Angleton was running, it would be better if you ran against one of our own. If you know what I mean."

Mike did know what she meant. It was a smart move, he had to admit. But as much as he understood all of this intellectually, and as much as he was trying to be "the bigger man" where Vera was concerned, he was unsure now what more to say. He wished he were alone again or still chatting with Eugene over coffee. Not facing his failings so openly.

The silence between them became awkward. Mike heard the vinyl scratching on the player as the music came to a close. Then Eugene sifting through the albums to pick the next record. Slipping it out of the sleeve. Was it really so quiet that he could hear all that? And then he realized that everyone had not just lowered their voices but had silenced themselves to eavesdrop on their conversation. He and Vera were the hottest news, and here they all were—with front row seats. They weren't going to miss the debate a second time.

"Okay, everyone, listen up." Eugene had come around the counter with the *Gazette* in his hands. "For those of you who missed it, we have another dispatch from Japan."

This time, Eugene didn't have to repeat himself or whistle to get everyone to listen. They were all quiet, and Mike was relieved for the change of attention.

Konbanwa Batavians—Good evening,

This trip has been quite a revelation. Last time I was here, Ian was new to the area and had very few connections. Now he has a world. The day after I arrived, he and his friends threw me a welcome party. I got to meet the large contingent of expats he calls family. We had music and drinks and octopus balls. Yes, you heard me, little fried balls stuffed with pieces of octopus.

Bert made a noise that edged on disgusting.

Eugene held up his hand to continue. *Stop making those noises, Bert—they were delicious.*

Everyone laughed when Bert started to take offense, but then he snorted a laugh, too.

The evening was lovely, but I was still jet-lagged and fell asleep standing at the bar listening to my son play his guitar with his friends. I've been going to bed early, but the jet lag is getting the best of me. I swear I've got brain fog, and I'm even questioning my memory these days. So, remember, if you come halfway across the planet, you will not be in your best shape.

Eugene went on reading. She described her *ikebana* class and then her language misadventures. These brought a giggle out of the neighbors.

Mike watched them all traveling vicariously through Bianca. But throughout the entire reading, he heard something in Bianca's words that sounded off. What was wrong? He wasn't sure, but something seemed not quite right. Maybe he was reading something into it. She had said she was jet-lagged. He should take her at her word.

"Oh, now here is the good part..." Eugene cleared his throat before continuing.

Last night, Ian was my escort at the netsuke *ceremony for the Nakayama family. I was fêted and introduced to many of Kyoto's most illustrious citizens. It was a bit much, honestly. But the best part was seeing the Ebisu reunited with the collection. It was remarkable to see the attention this tiny statuette garnered.*

And to top it all off, the night ended with a letter from the Ministry of Culture explaining that the netsuke *collection would be entered into the national registry of cultural treasures!*

The neighbors applauded and nodded and elbowed each other, as if they had all had a hand in this memorable event. Mike marveled at how quickly Bianca went from outsider to one of their own. He would love for her to hear this applause. But most of all, he hoped she was fine. He could hear all the right words. How interesting it all was. But underneath, he heard something else. Something he hoped he was wrong about.

Chapter Twenty-Nine

Kyoto, Japan

Bianca was pleased with herself. She had opted to meet Ian at Mariko's rather than making him backtrack to pick her up. She had spent the day shopping along Shijo Boulevard, and she felt confident that she could get herself up to the north of town and into the hills where Mariko's house was located.

She double-checked the map, then the bus schedule. On the display at the bus kiosk, Bianca watched the little animated image of the bus approaching her stop. Eventually, she saw the real thing turn the corner and stop at the kiosk in front of an elderly gentleman ready to board.

There was no pushing despite the bus being fairly crowded. A young woman gave up her seat for the older man. He nodded in thanks and sat down, placing his cane to the side. Bianca walked to the back and found a free spot on the bench seat along the rear of the bus. She stared out the window at the sights. All the shoppers along the streets were impeccably dressed and stylish.

She spotted a mother with her child, probably just coming from picking him up at school. He seemed about six years old and wore a pristine navy uniform with a yellow cap. He carried a miniature square bookbag on his little back.

Bianca checked her watch. They should be approaching her stop soon. Unfortunately, the man in front of her was taller than the usual Kyotoite, and his wild hair added another few inches to his height. She couldn't see the information board.

Excusing herself with one *sumimasen* after another, Bianca politely inched her way to the front. She checked the board against her map. Her stop should be coming up.

She stood for the remainder of the bus ride, glued to the window so as not to miss her stop. Ian had told her that she would recognize it from the persimmon tree on the corner.

When the bright orange fruits came into view, the bus pulled over. Bianca paid, stepped off the bus, and took a moment to admire the lovely tree, whose fruit dangled like Christmas ornaments. *Hidari* or *migi*, she wondered? She turned left, *hidari*, and rounded the corner. Then she stopped. She looked around at all the houses. Ian had said that the short walk would take her past a wooded area, including a small bamboo grove. Bianca realized she was going in the wrong direction. *Migi*, definitely *migi*. She made an about-face and turned back around the corner, crashing into the tall young man with the wild hair from the bus. The man dipped his head in apology, turning on his heels.

She bent to gather her map and bus schedule. By the time she stood up, he was gone.

Bianca and Ian crossed paths a block after the bus dropped her off. They walked the last piece up a steep hill together. It was peaceful in a way the city couldn't compare. They passed a few small homes, the owners sweeping up. Then, they found themselves before a locked gate. The house was barely visible, hidden behind a robust hydrangea bush.

On the right was a bamboo grove and stone steps off to the left that wove farther up the hillside. Ian noticed her gazing at the path.

"It leads to a shrine. It's a serious climb, but once you get to the top, it's a treat. There's a shaded bench and a view if you peek through the trees.

"I've spent a lot of time alone there since I arrived. I wander the streets at night. It's so quiet and safe. I can think. On the weekends, I roam around the outskirts to the various hiking paths and shrines. And in the evenings,

I try a different place to eat every few days. I just wander into the places I know I can afford and try something new on the menu.

"I felt that if I wanted to make this place my home, I needed to get to know it. My wanderings eventually paid off. There are very few areas I'm unfamiliar with.

"I even try a new *onsen* occasionally. I have my favorites, but they are all different. We really need to get you to the hot springs. Trust me. You'll love it."

Bianca nodded and mumbled an agreement. She trusted him. She knew he was right. That once she tried the hot springs, she would love them. Who doesn't love a hot bath or jacuzzi? But that was in the privacy of her own home. She still needed to get up the nerve to try bathing in a public place, in a foreign language, with foreign rules, and then be naked with a room full of women. Not just any women, but thin, petite women who never seem to age. Bianca had yet to see an overweight Japanese woman. She didn't consider herself overweight, but in her forties, she wasn't as lithe as she used to be.

"Would you like to climb up to the shrine after our visit to Mariko?"

"I'd like that."

Ian rang the bell and the gate unlocked remotely. They stepped inside the garden and closed the latch behind them.

Upon entering the house, Mariko offered them slippers. Ian and Bianca left their own shoes in the entryway and followed her into the living room. The décor was tasteful and spare except for several baby toys strewn about.

They could hear the baby making quiet cooing sounds in the other room. Mariko put up her finger as if to shush them. "Maybe if we keep our voices low, he will go back to sleep," she whispered.

In hushed voices, Bianca and Mariko talked about her trip. Before long, the baby's cooing turned to cries. Mariko went into the next room and came out carrying a beautiful boy with a tear-stained face. He leaned into his mother's shoulder, rubbed his eyes, and slowly stopped crying. When he finally took his hand away from his face, Ian gasped.

"I know what you're thinking. Kentaro looks just like him? Doesn't he?"

"Yeah, he really does. I had no idea…"

"Don't be angry. Irvin was not good to me, that's true, but he didn't know about the baby. I tried to reach him to tell him." She fussed with the baby and brought him his pacifier before she continued. "I confess maybe I didn't try hard enough."

"Then he doesn't know?" Ian looked relieved. "I'm glad to hear that he didn't just abandon Kentaro."

"He knows now. I recently heard from him and I finally told him about his son, and I also told him about Jonathan. He's coming back from the States to meet Kentaro. In fact, he'll be here this week. I can't say I'm not nervous. But I've decided it's the right thing to do. I can't keep a child away from his father."

The baby's mood had lightened as he sat happily on the *tatami* mat with his toys. The three of them took a few quiet moments to watch the boy. How he played. How he smiled. How he seemed to be oblivious to them. He was enjoying his own little world.

"How did Irvin react to the news that he had a child, that he was a father?"

"It's hard to tell. We did it all in writing. I think even Irvin can rise to the occasion and do the right thing. Sometimes."

As Ian and Mariko spoke, Bianca continued to enjoy the boy's antics. She found it soothing to watch his awkward playfulness and wondered if someday her grandchildren would also be half-Japanese.

Kentaro's ball rolled outside his reach, and in that split second, he broke out in a wail. Ian jumped up and rolled it back to him. In no time, Kentaro was giggling and batting it back to Ian. They continued this game, but Bianca could see the concern on Ian's face. This pleasant visit had somehow turned uncomfortable.

At the top of the steps, Bianca and Ian arrived at a clearing where a small wooden shrine stood. They took a seat side by side on the one bench. Other than the soft rustle as the leaves swayed in the breeze, it was silent. Bianca enjoyed the vista of the tree canopy and the rooftops. The branches limited the view, but Bianca thought it was intentional since the leaves framed the city in the way a photographer might frame a photo.

Although Bianca appreciated the meditative nature of the place, she felt the tension rising off of Ian. The climb seemed to have helped relieve some of the stress, but not all of it. She knew all of this boiled down to his music and his identity. When Irvin had left town, Ian could ignore the problem, but now that Irvin was coming back, Ian would have to make a choice—to try to claim back his music or to cut his losses and move on. He would have to decide, or the decision would be made for him.

A shuffling sound in the copse of trees nearby startled Bianca. She turned toward the trees.

"Did you hear that?"

"Hear what?"

Bianca was used to this problem. Her hearing was acute, and she often heard things others did not. At night in a creaky old farmhouse, it was particularly nerve-racking. She didn't want to be nervous for nothing, but she also didn't want to ignore something that might be of concern.

There was the sound again, this time it seemed to come from the other side.

"Oh, that? I'm sure it's just a squirrel or something." He smiled, then added, "I suppose it could be a wild boar."

If it hadn't been for his sideways glance, she might have taken him seriously. Ian loved to pull her leg.

"It's not a boar. Maybe a squirrel." She said it mostly to calm her own nerves. She turned to the stone steps leading down the hill from the shrine. A shadow passed over the last step in view as the shuffling occurred once again.

Despite the warmth of the setting sun, Bianca felt a chill in the air. Twice, she had been knocked into by a stranger. If she didn't know better, she'd say it might even have been the same man—a tall Westerner with lots of hair and a red backpack. She was sure it was only a coincidence, and she knew Japan was virtually crime-free, so she shouldn't worry. Or so she tried to convince herself.

And yet, the encounters were unsettling. She was jumpy. The noises from the glen were disconcerting. Was she being followed? What was preferable, she wondered: a stalker or a boar?

Chapter Thirty

Mike sat in the dark in his favorite armchair. The end of another tough day. Work had been uneventful, but it had been tough in a way that exhausted him just the same. He felt "on" lately, as if he were always posing for a photo. The way he had been at his wedding. Smiling for the camera, for the guests, for his parents, for Maggie. By the end of that day, his face actually hurt. That was how he felt today. An artificial smile plastered on his face. All day.

He had always been a law enforcement officer. He had never needed to defend his job before. Never needed to campaign for his position. This was not what he had bargained for. He was losing his will to go on with this game.

He held his beer in both hands. The coolness of the glass helped relax him, but he did not drink. He daydreamed. He picked up the remote but didn't turn on the television.

How had this year taken such a turn? He was separated from Maggie, and he was developing feelings for a woman he hadn't even known a few months ago. He was fighting for his job and wrestling with the discovery that his former partner was crooked and was probably murdered. He didn't even know where to focus his attention.

If he fought for Maggie, he'd probably lose the election. If he focused on the election, he'd probably lose Maggie forever. Or was Maggie lost already?

He hated to think about it, but it might just be the case. If not, how could he possibly feel so drawn to Bianca? If his love for Maggie had stood the test of time, no one should be able to distract him. This was troubled ground. He needed to avoid thinking of Bianca when he thought of Maggie. He needed to keep his head straight.

Then there was Sal. What should he be doing? How could he crack this nut? He had to pursue it. But how?

And what about the election? His work? His mind raced, and his thoughts whirled around each other. He got up and paced the living room.

How he wished he still had Maurice. He missed that damn fat cat. He should have offered to care for Shelby while Bianca was gone. It would have done him some good to have a pet. He needed to fill the space. But he knew the town would have gossiped about it; they talked so much already about the two of them.

He took a swig of his beer and was surprised to find it warm. He had wandered into the study. It was really Maggie's office since he never worked from home. But it didn't look the same. She had taken all the personal identifiers with her. The plant, the letter opener Mike had given her, her blotter with the doodles in the corner. It could be anyone's desk now.

He put his sweaty bottle down on the wooden surface and took a seat at the desk, then he wiped his hands on his pants and picked up the phone. He flipped through his wallet until he found what he was looking for. With the card in his hand, he dialed. "Charlie? Yeah, it's me. Can I come up to see you tomorrow? I have some more questions about Sal. Fine. 5:30. I'll be there. And Charlie? Thanks. I really appreciate it."

He hung up and grabbed his beer bottle, leaving the wet ring behind.

Chapter Thirty-One

Kyoto, Japan

Bianca was glad that Kenzo had joined her on this trip. He was a connection to her home so far away. She was surprised to notice that, despite her doubts about being considered a member of the village of Batavia, now that she was far away, she called it home.

But Kenzo, despite being in his home country, seemed out of sorts. Something was not right. She couldn't put her finger on it, but she knew he was here on a mission; perhaps it was a serious one. There must be a reason he hadn't returned to Japan in all these years. She considered that maybe language and culture weren't all one needs to call a place home. Maybe Batavia was now home for Kenzo, too.

Bianca had witnessed it with Ian. How he had found a place here in a new culture with a new language. It suited him. She thought about how, as they had walked into the house on her arrival, she had heard him say, *tadaima,* I'm home. That one word in Japanese meant everything. He had called it home without a second thought.

She had her eyes on Kenzo and was startled when he jumped from his chair and walked over to Jiro. They bent their heads over the paper, pointing and chattering in incomprehensible Japanese. Ian walked into the room and joined the conversation, though Kenzo and Jiro needed to slow down to accommodate him.

Bianca saw something odd in Ian's reaction. If there was anything Bianca knew, it was her son's face. She had seen every emotion unfold across his face over the years and she knew she was watching something momentous now. She hesitated to ask the question that would solidify her concerns. The longer she waited, the longer she could hold on to this peaceful moment.

When she could stand it no longer, she asked, "What? What's wrong?"

All three looked up at her and hesitated. Then Ian stammered a few words but said nothing coherent. Kenzo brought the paper over to her and pointed. "I think they have found J.C. Here it says that they recovered his body from the river last night."

Bianca looked at the newspaper in his hand. Her eyes moved to where he pointed despite knowing that she couldn't read it. The characters danced before her eyes. She could speak a few pleasantries in Japanese, but the writing was beyond her. J.C.'s name would be written in *katakana*, the Japanese writing used for foreign words. She recognized the *katakana* by the more angular design compared to the flowing lines of *hiragana*, but that was the extent of her ability to read the newspaper.

Kenzo pointed more emphatically at the letters. "Curtis, that was his last name, correct?" After Bianca didn't answer, he turned to the others. Both Ian and Jiro nodded. Bianca realized she wasn't the only one in shock.

Bianca was momentarily relieved to find out that she had indeed seen something the other night.

Then it sank in. She had seen something. She had witnessed a murder.

Chapter Thirty-Two

Kyoto, Japan

Bianca placed the phone back on the cradle without dialing. She couldn't just run to Mike whenever she had a problem. Could she? She was seven thousand miles away from Batavia-on-Hudson. He had his own work to do and his own problems. But Ian's life was upside down, and she was at a loss to help him. Mike was her lifeline. Someone who could show her how to navigate this problem.

She picked up the phone again and started to dial.

"Bianca, are you there?" A voice came from the other room.

She slammed the phone back down with a crash. She turned toward Kenzo's voice. Her heart thumped. She felt like a child with her hand caught in the cookie jar.

"Bianca, I was thinking. Perhaps we should call Sheriff Mike at home? He might have some help he can provide us."

Bianca couldn't believe her ears. Kenzo was always surprisingly astute. Did he know she was contemplating calling Mike? Or was this a genuine coincidence?

"I think you're right, Kenzo. Let's call him."

"If you don't mind, I will leave that to you and your sleuthing skills. You have proven that when you and the sheriff put your two clever brains together, you can solve any problem. Even murder." He took a mandarin out of the basket on the table. "I'm on my way to the train station. I want to go to Arashiyama, my hometown. I have an old friend there who is a retired police officer. Maybe he can give us some advice."

Bianca was relieved to know there was progress being made.

She had to make the call now, or she would miss him. 7:00 a.m. Japan time was 5:00 p.m. New York time the day before. The clock on the wall was showing 6:45.

After Kenzo left, she pulled Mike's card out of her wallet, but she dialed from memory. Her thumb rubbed the raised sheriff's emblem in the center of the card.

The phone rang eight times. Ten times. She was surprised that not even Shelley had picked up yet. She flipped the card to see his script on the back. He had given her his home phone number months ago. In the middle of a previous investigation, she had called that number just once and hung up when Maggie answered.

Her heart raced as she listened to the ring. But it rang and rang, and her heartbeat slowed to match her disappointment. She removed the phone from her ear and then heard, "Onanda County Sheriff's office."

"Shelley, is that you? It's—"

"Bianca. I'm so happy to hear your voice. How is it going in the land of the rising sun?" Shelley's enthusiasm reached across the miles and made Bianca homesick. It was the first time she had ever felt that way for Batavia. It was a new sensation, and despite her problems, she liked it.

Mike froze at hearing Bianca's name. He was stunned by the coincidence. He had spent the day contemplating calling Bianca, then talking himself out of it. How could it be? Had she heard him across the world? Did she know he needed her? Needed her advice, that is.

Or did she have a problem?

He rushed into the main lobby and motioned to Shelley to pass the call back to his office. Now that he thought about the possibilities, he started to worry. Anything could have happened.

"Bianca, is everything alright?"

Mike was met with silence. An unnerving silence.

"Bianca?"

"Can you hear me now?"

"Yes. Are you okay?"

"Yes, yes. I am, but…"

"But what? Your son? Kenzo? What's wrong? I can hear it in your voice."

"Mike, I'm fine. We're all fine. I'm sorry to worry you. But there was an incident here, and I didn't know who else to call."

Bianca told Mike everything about the night of the party. How she had been exhausted. How she had heard a struggle and seen a glint of steel. And how there was no body.

But now there was.

"I witnessed a murder. Mike, you're the only person I know I can talk to about this. Now that I'm on the phone, I have no idea what I thought you could do for me…"

"That's what sheriffs are for. Calm down and explain it again, but with a little more detail. What exactly did you see and hear? And who is this guy? And why was he at the party at all?"

Bianca went through the details methodically. She told him everything she knew about J.C.—his name, his age, where he was from, his background, the bad blood between him and the community. As she talked, Mike could hear her calming down. Her cadence had slowed; she was choosing her words more deliberately. He took careful notes just in case there was some way he could help.

The more he listened, though, the more he realized this was a real murder investigation that she found herself in, and from the details, it sounded to Mike that Ian might be considered a suspect. He kept that concern to himself for now. What started as a joyful trip to visit her son and receive some recognition had turned into a nightmare.

Shelley knocked and walked in. She motioned that he had a phone call.

Mike looked up at the clock. Mike's heart sank. He needed to take the waiting call. He had no choice. He had to hang up on Bianca.

"Okay. Listen, Bianca, I have to go. Let me think about this and let me see if I can help in some way. In the meantime, keep me posted. Call me anytime. You have my home number. Use it."

He hung up and tried to regroup before he took his next call. What could he do for her other than listen, he wondered. She was seven thousand miles away. This murder was definitely out of his jurisdiction, but he was determined to try and help Bianca.

Chapter Thirty-Three

Batavia-on-Hudson, N.Y.

Eugene sat down at the counter with his afternoon espresso and scanned the old diner. It was a rare moment of silence. Stella's was the town hub in Batavia-on-Hudson, and he was grateful for that. It ensured that he always had good company and a good laugh and that loneliness could never get a stronghold. He had his family, and it was at Stella's. But still, a little quiet during the day was good.

At times like these, he would change the album to Stella's favorite, Ella Fitzgerald's "Blue Moon," and make himself a fresh coffee. These days, he was just as likely to make himself an espresso. The rich aroma tempted him now, and he took his first sip.

He welcomed the moment to rest his feet. Working behind the counter at the grill was exhausting, especially for his bad knee, but he loved it back there. Not like his Stella, who thought of the diner as one ongoing party. The more the merrier, as far as Stella was concerned. They had made the diner work because she had handled the front, and he worked the grill. But now that she was gone, he had learned to take his place out front. He learned that it wasn't just Stella that his neighbors had loved, but him, too.

Slowly, he had come out of his shell. He gradually ventured out from behind the counter to sit with his buddies from the old school days. Bert Henderson, Ernie McCrae, Big Ben Sawyer, and Claire Koop all loved Eugene, and he soon realized that the rest of Batavia-on-Hudson was open to him as well. To this day, he was surprised that he continued evolving, that life wasn't stagnant, that he could grow, even without Stella. At first, he refused to move on without her, but it was nine years since she died, and he understood she wouldn't want his life wasted. He had had a close call a few months back. He had been given a second chance. And he was taking it.

He opened the paper and flipped to "The Last Page." Olivia Last, the editor of the *Gazette*, wrote a weekly column of musings. This week, her column was entitled *Autumn Embers*.

In a few weeks, we will have the annual Autumn Harvest Bonfire.

I long to be in a circle of friends in the heart of the town. I want reassurance that all is well. The last few months have been hard on this village. The storm has changed what it looks like. Some people have moved on; others are suffering and trying to heal. Hopefully, they will rejoin us soon.

I thought I knew who I was—a cancer survivor, a journalist, a friend of the village, a single woman. Now, I am a soon-to-be mother and editor-in-chief of the Gazette. *The changes keep coming. I plan to continue growing and evolving. I expect my chosen family to grow and evolve as well.*

I have recently learned that some of my neighbors are not who I thought they were. But I don't see them as flawed. I see them as new versions of the people I knew. More complex. More vulnerable.

We all have a past; we all have made mistakes. Every one of us.

Let's not define ourselves by our failures, but by how we bounce back. By how we reimagine who we are, and everyone else, as well. We need to make room for these changes. We are not who we were yesterday or last year, or twenty years ago.

We are who we are now, at this moment in time. Embrace it. We have worked hard to get here. We are fluid, and tomorrow we will be someone new once again. Thank goodness for that.

Thankfully, autumn is a new beginning of sorts. A time of second chances. The leaves are dropping to make way for new, stronger growth in the spring. We can't live in the past—that is where resentment, anger, and regret reside. And we can't live in the future—that is where fear, envy, and anxiety reside. I know it is cliché to say so, but let's remember to live in the present. There is only always now.

This year, bring your blanket and your marshmallows, but mostly, bring yourself—your whole self—to the harvest bonfire. Bask in the warmth with your friends—your chosen family. Hold them close; they are valuable. Without my chosen family, I would be unmoored, like the vengeful ghosts of this Halloween season.

My favorite part of the bonfire is when the flames diminish, and all that remains are the embers. The glow of soft embracing heat, rather than the dynamic flickering of violent flames. I love to watch the small sparks that pop and drop in a delicate arc. Red and yellow, like falling leaves.

Let the autumn embers warm you and illuminate you.

Eugene marveled at how Olivia had captured the mood in the community. He knew that the villagers were at a crossroads after the upheaval of the recent months, grasping at second chances and holding on for dear life. But until he read Olivia's column, Eugene hadn't completely thought it through. Olivia had an uncanny way of encapsulating what others couldn't and presenting it quietly to the villagers so that they might take the time to reflect on her words and incorporate them into their lives. She was a preacher, a therapist, a friend.

Chapter Thirty-Four

Kyoto, Japan

Bianca sat in the corner and made herself as small as possible. Two police officers had arrived to take statements. She worried now that calling them the other day when there was no body had made her, Ian, and Jiro the primary suspects. The officers were polite, but cautious. Or maybe she was being paranoid.

Jiro's cousin Takeru arrived as the other officers were introducing themselves to Jiro and asking for a place to sit and talk to everyone. Jiro turned and translated for Bianca.

"Takeru, I'm so glad you're here." Bianca was relieved to see a friendly face among the officers.

"I decided it would help if I were here since I know a little background. As weak as my English is, it must be much better than Kaito and Haru here." He smiled at Bianca then he bowed to his colleagues and spoke to them at length in Japanese.

Takeru turned away from the other officers and approached Jiro. "Okay, the first thing we need is a list of people who attended the party. Jiro, can you do that for me?" He took out his notepad, turned to a fresh page, and handed it to Jiro with his pen. Jiro took it and sat back down to jot down the names in a script that Bianca could not decipher.

Takeru started with Bianca. "Mrs. St. Denis, can you tell us again what you saw and heard that night?" Bianca dreaded revisiting that memory, but she knew that her information was vital. As far as she knew, she was the only witness—even if she witnessed very little. She recounted how she had been suffering from jet lag, left the party early, and how in the garden she had heard what sounded like a struggle. Then, the flash of metal. Then a thump.

"Could the flash of metal have been a knife?"

"Yes, that's what I think I saw. I mentioned it in my statement the other day."

Bianca thought it was interesting that today the police asked if it could have been a knife, whereas the other day Takeru had tried to suggest that it could have been something else. But of course, now they had a body. She shivered, realizing that Takeru asked her because the body must have had stab wounds.

Takeru turned to his cousin. "Jiro, have you finished with the list?"

"*Chotto matte.*" He held up a finger, asking Takeru to wait. He showed the list to Ian. "Did I miss anyone?"

Ian reviewed the list. "What about Akane?"

"*Sou, desu ne…* Yes, she came for a few minutes at the beginning. You're right." Jiro added her name and handed the notepad to Takeru.

"Don't Andrew and Akane live near here? Can we ask them to join us?"

"Yes, they live next door. I'll go get them." As Ian started to turn, he caught Bianca's expression and hesitated. Jiro jumped in. "You stay here with your mom. I'll go get them."

Bianca exhaled in relief. "Thank you, Jiro."

One of the other officers walked over to Takeru and half-whispered in Japanese. Takeru nodded and turned to Ian.

"Ian, now that I know who attended the party, can you tell me where everyone was when your mom returned and told you what she had seen?"

"Well, we were all here, I think. Except Akane and Andrew. Andrew left early because he works an early shift, and his wife was only here for the very beginning."

"Can you tell me why she left early?"

Ian looked around, flushed. He was twirling his watchband around in circles on his wrist.

"You're not thinking that Akane had anything to do with this?"

"Ian, I am not making any judgments. We just need to know where everyone was at the time of the struggle."

Ian nodded with resignation. His friends were under suspicion. He knew that was the case no matter what Takeru said.

"She came early to meet my mom but left pretty quickly to get home to her child. Her mother was babysitting, but she didn't want to stay long because her mom sits with the baby all day while she's at work. She was just being thoughtful. There's nothing to it."

Takeru nodded as he jotted the information in his notes. "And Andrew, what time did he leave?"

Ian hesitated, then looked at Bianca. "I think a little bit before my mom left. What time was that, Mom?"

"I think it was about 10:30."

Ian thought for a moment. "That's right. I remember looking at my watch. I was trying to convince him to stay."

"Are you saying he couldn't be convinced? Was it strange that he would leave a party so early?"

"Takeru, come on. You know Andrew. He didn't do this."

"I'm sorry, Ian. I need to ask these questions. It's nothing personal. I know Andrew, but I don't know him that well."

"Well, I do, and he has nothing to hide."

At that moment, Jiro returned with Andrew and Akane. "Of course I don't have anything to hide. What's going on?"

Takeru gave Andrew a brief nod and then a deeper bow to his wife and introduced himself. "I am investigating what Mrs. St. Denis believes she witnessed on the night of the party. Could you tell me about your evening?"

After Akane reiterated that she returned home early to care for her son, Takeru continued questioning her. "And Andrew. What time did he get home?"

"He came home pretty late, I think."

Takeru turned to Ian. "I thought you said he went home early."

"He did. I'm pretty confident it was about 10:30. Isn't that right, Andrew?"

"Yes. I think you're the one who told me it was 10:30 just before I left." He turned to Akane. "Don't you remember me coming home?"

"I'm not sure because I fell asleep early."

"So, you didn't hear him come into bed?"

She blushed and hesitated. "I fell asleep in the baby's room. After I read Toki a bedtime story, I was so tired that I dozed off in there." She continued blushing. Bianca remembered how many nights three-year-old Ian had fallen asleep in her bed. She also remembered how it had added further strain to her marriage with Ian's dad.

Takeru turned to Andrew. "Did you and J.C. have any issues?"

"Listen, I'm not going to lie and say I like the guy. Uhm…liked. But I would never do anything to him. Everyone had an issue with Jay. If you think that finding a motive will find you a killer, you're mistaken. We all had a motive. What you need to know is who had the opportunity."

"Andrew, where were you around 10:30 that night?"

"I was in bed, like I said."

"With no one who can vouch for you?"

"Well, no, I suppose not. But that's where I was." Andrew's face was reddening, and Bianca saw that he had come to the uncomfortable realization that he had just revealed how he had both motive and opportunity.

An announcement came over the officers' walkie-talkies. One of the two officers took the call, then walked over to Takeru and whispered in Japanese. Takeru nodded, and the officer left the house.

Jiro's cousin turned to Bianca. "*Sumimasen.* I'm sorry for the interruption. Now, Mrs. St. Denis, tell me again. What kind of sounds did you hear? And how could you hear them above the music?"

"I was surprised by how peaceful the garden was. The music was very well contained inside. The garden was quiet, and I heard grunts and thrashing. Like an animal attacking his prey. In fact, at first, I thought it was animals, perhaps cats. But the sounds were indistinct."

"No words? No voices?"

"No, nothing like that. That's why I wasn't sure what I had heard. Once

I zeroed in on where it was coming from, I saw what appeared to be an arm, maybe a torso. And I could see and hear the bushes shaking from the commotion."

"But I also heard something that night." Everyone turned to Akane. "Toki's bedroom faces this side of the garden. It was a nice evening, and I had the window open. When I tucked him in, I heard a rustling in the bushes. I didn't think anything of it. A cat, I thought, or a dog. Our neighbor Saito-san has a Shiba that wanders occasionally at night. And then there are the stray cats. They fight sometimes. But then…"

"Please continue." Takeru prompted her to go on.

"But then I heard a thump. I looked out and didn't see anything. So I went back to reading to Toki, and then I fell asleep."

"And if you were home, Andrew, presumably you heard it also?"

"I didn't hear anything. I was asleep in the bedroom on the other side of the house."

Takeru took some notes, then stepped closer to Ian. Bianca noticed Andrew and Akane intertwine their hands with a small movement that could easily have been missed. She could see that Andrew wasn't wearing his ring. She wondered what, if anything, that meant.

"Ian, you and Andrew play music together now, but isn't it true that the two of you used to be in a band with J.C. and that he ousted Andrew—"

"Well, yeah, but that's not the whole story." Andrew interrupted. "J.C. would replace me on the nights that I couldn't play. He didn't really oust me…he just started playing more and more often, and he sort of slipped into it."

"But you weren't happy about it?"

"Well, no, not really. But it was my fault. I let my guard down—" Andrew couldn't finish his thought before Takeru continued.

"And he took advantage. And you didn't like that, I heard."

"No, I didn't like that. But I wouldn't kill him for it either."

"But what about him flirting with your wife?"

"J.C. was a jerk. I know I shouldn't speak ill of the dead. But that's what was. And just because he flirted with my wife doesn't mean my wife flirted back."

When Bianca saw how Akane fiddled with her sweater and did not make eye contact with anyone, she wondered if there might be more to this story. But at that moment, Takeru turned to Ian, and Bianca's focus shifted too. "Can you tell me about your run-in with J.C.?"

Ian stuttered before his sentences started to make sense. If the situation wasn't so dire, Bianca would have found this endearing. As a little boy, Ian always had trouble getting off the runway with a story. He would be so excited to share his day that he couldn't organize his thoughts. Or when he was nervous or telling a lie. Bianca felt the color drain from her face as she listened.

"J.C. and Irvin were my bandmates. J.C. played keyboard, and Irvin played drums. I composed all of our original music, and I played guitar. They deserted me, took my music, recorded it as their own, and gave me no credit. It was a miserable thing to do." Ian's voice elevated with each sentence. "I admit it took me a long time to get over it." He stopped and looked at Takeru.

"It seems to me that you're not over it."

Chapter Thirty-Five

Batavia-on-Hudson, N.Y.

Mike looked up at the clock ticking above his office door. It was finally time to go. He grabbed his jacket off the peg and walked out to the lobby.

"Shelley, I'm heading out. You can reach Vera if you need anything."

"Half day?"

"Business. I'll be in Albany if you need me. But Shelley, only if you really need me. Got it?"

"Got it, boss."

"Oh, I forgot." He handed her a slip of paper with the name of J.C. Curtis and his last known address in the United States. "Do me a favor and call the Lincoln District Police Office in Chicago. I think that's the 20th District. And see if you can get any information on this guy. He goes by J.C. and Jay. I need anything they can give me on him. Tell them we have an incident here, and we are following any leads. Be vague."

"I've never heard of this guy."

"I know. It's for Bianca."

"In Japan?"

"Yes. There's an issue going on there with a couple of expats, and she asked me to find out anything I could. So be vague when you call."

"Is she okay?"

"Yes, she's fine. But this could involve Ian, so you can imagine that she's anxious to clear it up." He skipped over the part about the murder. Shelley wasn't a gossip by nature, but there was no need to test her.

Mike traveled the Thruway with anticipation and trepidation. He usually enjoyed the drive. Trees bursting with autumn colors lined the road, and traffic was non-existent. It was one of the joys of living so far outside New York City.

Despite the pleasant drive, his mind was not at rest. He thought and thought. What was he trying to find out from Charlie and his sidekicks? They had called him in the other day hoping that Mike could shed some light on the situation. They had grilled him, but Mike had nothing of value to contribute. Mike had managed to close his eyes to all of Sal's exploits, it seems.

He was heading back to Charlie's office this time to gather some information of his own.

Once he arrived in the office, Charlie offered him a seat.

"Thanks for seeing me again."

"What brings you back so soon? Do you think you remembered something?"

Mike didn't like the tone of Charlie's voice. He wasn't sure, but he thought there was a hint of sarcasm or skepticism.

"Not really, but something has been bothering me. You never told me the purpose of dredging this up. What do you think I can tell you? What are you and Internal Affairs trying to accomplish? I mean, it was years ago and what could you all be interested in?"

"We are just trying to tie up loose ends. Trying to understand what happened."

Mike mulled on that a moment. He looked down at his hands, clasped together. Knuckles white. He unclasped them in the hopes of relieving the tension. It didn't work. He looked back up at his former boss. "Charlie, you're not even on the force anymore. What's up?"

Charlie didn't answer. He walked to the back of his office. He poured two coffees and brought them over to his desk. He placed the I Love NY cup in front of Mike.

Charlie took a sip out of his Best Grandpa cup. "Nothing's up. I just want some closure. Sal was important to me too, you know."

"That doesn't explain why Internal Affairs was here. I was too stunned the other day to question it. But I see now that this 'closure' doesn't make sense. There's got to be more you're not telling me." Mike stood up, ignoring the coffee, and paced around the office. "There is obviously something going on that ties to Sal's death. Or you wouldn't be interested. You wouldn't dredge up a corrupt cop. Especially a dead one. In fact, you'd keep it buried. What do you know?"

"We've told you what we know. Sal was taking money on the side to protect certain elements, and we think that relationship went south, and Sal was killed to keep him quiet."

"That's too simple." Mike was losing his patience. And he had very little these days. "Don't take me for a fool." His voice was losing its normal calm control. He decided he didn't mind. Maybe it was better not to show too much restraint. Charlie was no longer his boss. A little force might get him further than being nice.

Charlie didn't blink. He just kept silent.

"Look, cooperation and silence are what you want from me. So far, I've given you both. But I can't guarantee that I will keep silent if you're not straight with me."

"You're threatening me now? That's none too bright, Mike."

Charlie's assistant knocked and walked in, much the way Shelley believed that the knock was just a formality in Mike's office. "Your next appointment is here. What do you want me to tell him?"

"Show him in." Charlie stood up and buttoned his suit jacket. "Like I said, Mike. Thanks for coming down. If you think of anything helpful, let me know."

The door opened, and Charlie extended his hand to the newcomer. "Senator, thanks for stopping in. Let's get down to it."

He turned to Mike and the assistant. "Please close the door on your way out."

Chapter Thirty-Six

Kyoto, Japan

Bianca's heart jumped. Takeru had just cornered Ian. She couldn't stand by and watch this.

"I don't understand what you're saying to him. He *is* over it. He told me so himself just the other day. And even if he has some lingering issues, he would never kill anyone."

Bianca looked around at the faces in the group. Jiro almost looked embarrassed. Ian was stunned. Takeru just stared at her. He opened his mouth, but she stopped him. "Everyone knows he has a temper. Don't we all? I know he is excitable and flies off the handle. But…"

Takeru's eyebrows shot up. Ian's face dropped. "Mom. What are you doing? Are you trying to help? Because it's not working."

Bianca stopped mid-sentence and realized that her nervous gabbing had taken over, and she had said more than she should have. She had to fix this.

"Even if he has a temper—"

"Mom! Stop!"

"What I mean to say is that he was on stage playing his guitar in front of the entire party. He couldn't have done anything." Bianca had broken into a sweat. She promised herself she wouldn't say another word.

Takeru turned to his cousin with an expectant look on his face.

"*Sou desu ne.*" Jiro nodded his agreement to what Bianca had just said.

Takeru turned back to the rest of the group. "Okay. Ian, I may need to talk to you some more about this. Next on the list. Where was Daniel?"

In an effort to redeem herself, Bianca spoke up. "He was definitely inside at the party. I spoke to him just before I left." Takeru jotted down his notes and then looked around at the others for agreement. Jiro nodded. Andrew spoke up, "He took my place on my drum. So he was there. I'm sure."

Ian was not nodding. He was pensive, and Takeru noticed.

"Do you have something to add, Ian?" The detective poised his pen, ready to take more information down.

"Honestly, now that you mention it, Daniel was not on the stage when my mother came looking for me. I was playing solo. I can't remember now if he told me where he went, but he wasn't there…"

Bianca frowned and thought back to the moment she went into the party to retrieve Ian. She clearly remembered that Ian was on the stage alone. Where had Daniel gone?

Takeru took more notes, and Ian swallowed hard. "I am just telling you he wasn't in the room. That doesn't mean I think he did anything."

"I understand."

Bianca could see the stress behind Ian's eyes. He just ratted out his dear friend just as she had ratted out Ian. What was it about the presence of authority that flustered them so much, she wondered.

"I will need to speak to Daniel. Does anyone know his hours at the *Kyoto Quarterly*?"

"He's there most days until five or six. Even when he isn't busy getting out an issue, it's his favorite hangout," Ian explained.

The detective jotted that down and looked up again. "So, is there anyone we missed?"

Everyone shook their heads and looked around to verify they hadn't forgotten a guest.

"Wait. I forgot all about Kawabata." Ian turned to Jiro.

"Right. Another uninvited guest. I think I will lock the doors next time," Jiro said.

"Which Kawabata was that?" Takeru flipped to a new page in his notebook and then looked at his cousin for clarification.

"Kawabata Riku. You know him. He arrived out of nowhere and escorted Jay out after…"

"After what, Jiro?"

"After, well, after I had an altercation with him."

"Jiro! *Nandeya nen?* When were you going to tell me you had a fight with him? You are my cousin. It could look like I am showing you special treatment." He turned to Bianca and excused himself for the outburst. *"Sumimasen."*

"I'm sorry. I should have told you sooner. Nothing came of it," Jiro clarified.

"Still. It is the first thing everyone should have told me." Takeru slowly looked at each of them, one by one, before returning to Jiro with his questions. "What did you fight about? Was it physical? Did anyone get hurt? Were any threats made? You must tell me every detail."

Jiro explained how J.C. was intent on crashing the party and ruining Bianca's evening. How he had tried to get J.C. to leave, but it had turned into a shoving match. "Nothing really came of it. No threats, no hitting."

"And then Kawabata walked him out?"

"Yes."

"And why was Kawabata here? That is another important piece of information I needed to know immediately. He is not your ordinary guest."

"I told you, we didn't invite him. He just showed up. It seemed he was looking for J.C."

"I guess he found him."

Chapter Thirty-Seven

Kyoto, Japan

Ian watched Takeru and realized that the more they all talked about that evening, the more it was clouded in mystery. So much remained unexplained. Kawabata arrived unexpectedly looking for J.C., and Jiro went missing right after the fight. He couldn't recall seeing Jiro until the evening was almost over. Where could he have been?

And Daniel. He had thrown Daniel under the bus. Takeru wasn't even aware that Daniel had a real grudge against J.C. What really bothered Ian was that Daniel used to teach *tanto* knife fighting. He was a master. It was something Ian knew he couldn't keep from getting out. Too many people knew these tidbits about Daniel. This information would get out, but he was damned well not going to be the one to tell the police about Daniel's history with J.C. He knew there was no way Daniel could have killed him. But the more he thought about it, the more he realized there was so much about Daniel he didn't know. He had always been notoriously quiet about his life in England and his reasons for emigrating to Japan twenty years ago. Ian had also seen him lose his temper, especially when he had been drinking. And he had had several drinks that night.

Ian felt a flush reach the back of his neck. Daniel was a father figure to him. He had always been there for advice and companionship when he missed home and when he tried to convince himself he didn't miss home. Daniel understood it all firsthand.

"Ian, what is troubling you? Do you know something? If you do, I need you to tell me," Takeru said.

Ian looked up, not realizing that his face was so revealing of his internal turmoil. "No. Nothing. I have nothing to add."

Jiro interjected. "Takeru, you need to understand that everyone disliked J.C. for many reasons. He owed everyone money. He cheated everyone one way or another. He had mastered the art of screwing people. He didn't care. He just used people." It was obvious the conversation had upset Jiro.

Takeru looked closely at his cousin, shook his head, and then sat down.

"Okay, Jiro, now I need to know what J.C. did to you to make you so angry that you cannot talk about him without getting so visibly upset."

"I'm not upset. He just has that kind of effect on people."

"Jiro, sit down. We need to discuss this at length. You are certainly upset. Look at you. Your hands are shaking. I have known you my entire life, and I have never seen you get this angry. You are the calmest person I know. In fact, my mother always said I should learn from you. I know when you are upset."

Bianca watched as Jiro's cousin wrote furiously in his notebook. He had pulled his chair closer to Jiro and lapsed into Japanese. They went back and forth for a few moments. The remaining officer in attendance was finally able to take some notes now that the discussion had shifted to Japanese. Bianca couldn't follow the rapid conversation, but she remembered what Ian had told her about how J.C. owed Jiro several thousand dollars and had overstayed his welcome here at the guest house. How Jiro had given J.C. work, and how when he returned home to get money, he had never repaid Jiro. She could see why he was so upset.

Everyone had a motive against J.C. But who would actually kill him? And then Bianca remembered something. Something that broke her heart. "Oh."

Everyone turned to her. The sound had escaped her lips. "Uhm, it's nothing."

Takeru looked doubtful. "Bianca, I don't want any more secrets."

"It's just that…I'm sure it can be explained," she answered in a near whisper.

"What can be explained?" Takeru asked.

"It's not important."

"Let me decide what is important."

Takeru stared her down until she couldn't stand it any longer.

"It's just that I don't recall seeing Jiro that night after J.C. left…"

Everyone looked to Jiro for an explanation.

Jiro shifted on his feet. "I was here. Maybe I left for a few minutes. But…"

"Where were you? Jiro, it looks bad that you are keeping secrets." Takeru's voice rose slightly.

"I am not keeping secrets—"

"Yes, you are. You did not tell me you had a fight with J.C. You were not at the party when he was probably killed. Those are secrets. Explain."

"It was nothing. I went out for a smoke."

"Is that true, Bianca? Did Jiro come out to the garden for a smoke?"

"I…I didn't see him."

"No, I went out the front door. I don't smoke in the house or the garden."

"I thought you did not smoke at all," Takeru said with an impatient tone.

"I don't." Jiro looked flustered. "I mean, I don't usually. Just when I'm stressed."

"And why were you stressed? And why did you keep it a secret? And did anyone see you out there?"

As Jiro and Takeru went into another huddle of rapid Japanese, Bianca's anxiety ramped up. She could no longer follow the discussion, so she wandered into the kitchen to put up some tea. Everyone would appreciate it, and she needed a break from the frustration of not understanding.

Keeping one eye on the door where his mother had just disappeared, Ian reached above the refrigerator behind the bar. He removed J.C.'s hat. "Before I forget, I think I should give this to you. Remember, we found it here the next morning." Ian hesitated, then pulled out his wallet and removed the business card belonging to Kawabata. "And this also. I found them together under the bush over there."

Takeru took a close look at both sides of the card. His eyebrows rose, he frowned, and shook his head. "I will need to get this tested. I've only seen one other card like this before. Kawabata is on this side of the law, but just barely. This could be important. I'll see what we can find out."

He carefully passed the card to the other officer, who placed it in an evidence bag.

As Bianca reappeared with a tray of teacups, Takeru turned to the group before him. "I wish you would all remember that I am here to help you and to find J.C.'s killer. I want you to think about that evening and make sure you have told me everything. I want no more changes to your stories. I know you are all friends and that some of you consider each other like family. I know this is hard for you. You do not want to turn on a friend, but this is too important." He waited and looked at them each in turn. "So, does anyone have anything to add?"

They each looked at one another. Jiro, Bianca, Ian, Andrew, and Akane.

Takeru watched them shake their heads. He, in turn, shook his. He was not convinced they had told him everything.

Chapter Thirty-Eight

Kyoto, Japan

Bianca knew that Kenzo was hoping to distract her by inviting her out to Arashiyama, his hometown on the outskirts of the city of Kyoto. She had woken up extra early to catch the train and meet him there for a quiet walk in the bamboo forest. He had told her that the only way to experience it properly was to get there before the city woke up. She was happy to oblige.

She arrived more quickly than expected, another perk of early morning travel. When she got off the train, she consulted her map and turned right. *Migi.* She walked straight along the route for a bit, but she wasn't sure she was headed in the right direction. She saw no one to ask.

She kept on until she saw a woman sweeping the pavers in front of her ice cream shop.

"Ohayou gozaimasu," Bianca wished the woman good morning before launching into her question. *"Takoyaki wa doko desu ka?"*

The woman looked confused, so Bianca repeated herself. The woman was smiling and trying to help but spoke no English and did not seem to understand. Bianca repeated it one more time. The woman motioned for her to follow and escorted her past several shops just opening for the day. She stopped before a kiosk where an elderly man was setting up for the day. The woman motioned to the man behind the counter. *"Takoyaki."*

Now Bianca was confused, but she thanked her and let the woman return to her shop. In broken English, the gentleman told her he wouldn't be ready for several hours. And then it dawned on her. She had asked for *takoyaki*, the famous octopus balls, instead of *takebayashi*, the bamboo forest.

Too embarrassed to ask him her actual question, she blushed and thanked him, then walked on, hoping to find another shopkeeper to guide her.

When she finally found her way, Kenzo was waiting for her and held a cup of coffee in each hand. He gave one to Bianca and led her onto the path.

They sipped and walked, and Bianca knew he had been right. The serenity of the forest could not be appreciated if there were too many others around. Any talking, or even footsteps, would have detracted from the experience. The quiet allowed the natural sounds to be heard—the whispering of the leaves, the trunks clacking against each other as they swayed in the breeze.

She looked up to watch their delicate movements. She was under their spell.

Kenzo and Bianca took their time, but as the path began to fill up with visitors and tourists, they exited the tranquil forest and headed into town.

They walked along the main road, quiet in each other's company. Bianca slowed in front of the lovely shops. One after the other. She ducked into one to buy a happy family good luck charm for Olivia now that she was expecting a baby. When she exited the shop, Kenzo was waiting for her, this time with a soft serve ice-cream cone in each hand.

"*Matcha* or *kurogoma?*"

"Green tea, and what's the other?"

"Black sesame."

"Oh, I'll take sesame. That's a new one for me."

At first, the charcoal color wasn't appealing, but she was determined to try new things while she was here. She licked the dripping sides of the cone and discovered a sweet and savory creaminess that was unlike any other flavor of ice cream.

They reached the end of the street and turned the corner to find the wide river roaring under the bridge. The vista opened up to the mountains on the opposite bank with red and orange maples painting the side of their slopes. The contrast against the crisp blue and white of the sky and the cool green of the water made for a stunning view. He escorted her across the street to the bridge. He stopped her exactly halfway across, where they turned to admire the view. The rushing waters were loud and refreshing. Bianca closed her eyes and felt the breeze and the mist. She pictured herself alone on the bridge, diving into the coolness. She wanted to forget all the darkness that had been following her since the night of the party. She simply wanted to enjoy her time with Ian.

Her feet were in need of a rest, so Kenzo led her to his favorite childhood restaurant. They ordered rich bowls of ramen and then more coffee. They spent a couple of hours there as Kenzo shared his childhood memories of Arashiyama.

When they were well rested, they returned to the riverside.

"How has your trip been so far, Bianca?"

"It's been wonderful…" She tried to squelch the anxiety of what she had witnessed the other night.

"But you're still worried about what happened to J.C. and what you may have seen that night. I don't blame you. But remember, the police are doing their job."

She nodded and then changed the subject. "It's beautiful here in Arashiyama. How lucky you are that this is your home."

"Yes, indeed. It is a beautiful place. It holds important memories for me. Mostly good. But it's no longer my home. Batavia-on-Hudson is my home now."

Bianca had not expected this answer.

"You seem surprised."

He was right. Bianca had just assumed that he was a Japanese man living in Batavia. But that was naïve of her. She should have noticed that he had moved on. That his identity had evolved. "I should have realized."

"I know that I seem like an outsider to Batavia, even to you, but I have lived there many years. I am a private person by nature. I would not be any more social if I lived here. I think some people assume that because I keep to myself, and live in the hills, that I don't consider Batavia my home. But I learned a long time ago that home is where I am. My presence, in every sense of the word, decides that. I make my own home. You make yours."

"Lately, I've been thinking a great deal about what makes a place a home."

"I have had plenty of opportunities to live elsewhere, but I feel at home in Batavia. I've lived many happy years there. I would not move. I have chosen Batavia. That is what makes it such a perfect home for me. When we have choice, we have great freedom. When we exercise that choice, even more so. I still have family here, but I have chosen the villagers of Batavia as my new family."

"Chosen family. I've been thinking a lot about that since I arrived. What an interesting way of looking at it, isn't it? In a way, I've chosen Batavia as my family and my home, too."

"And it appears that Ian has a chosen family here. He seems well cared for. Do you agree?"

Bianca had hoped to avoid the logical conclusion to this discussion, but in fact, it was true. Ian had a warm family here, and she believed that he was putting down roots in a way that resembled making a home here. Once he finds the right girl, his fate would be sealed. She turned away from Kenzo to allow the breeze to dry a loose tear. This was all too new for her. She used to think that Ian was here, in school, for a temporary stay. That he would experience all the city had to offer and bring those adventures home with him to the States to start his adult life. But now she realized that he was already in his adult life. That Kyoto held so many possibilities for him. And…and he seemed in his element. At home. It was true.

"Now, it is my turn to apologize. I upset you. I did not mean to. I meant it as a positive observation. But naturally, you would be sad if Ian made Kyoto his permanent home."

"No need to apologize. You're right. I'm happy for him. He has a tribe here, and he fits so well in this environment. I think he has evolved for the better since he's been here. I think he's a different Ian. A better Ian. I suppose we all have many identities, don't we?"

"Yes. I believe that is true."

Between the dipping branches heavy with bright red leaves, she spied the fishermen pushing their boats down the river.

Kenzo and Bianca reached the stone steps that led up the mountain. They took the path and once again found themselves alone in nature. It reminded Bianca of the isolated footpaths through Batavia that she preferred for her walks. After a long stint up the steps, they stopped for a rest on a wooden bench before they headed back down the mountain and reemerged by the riverside.

The short autumn day had passed them by, and Bianca realized that dusk was falling. Everything became still except for the movement of the boats. As they had for centuries, the fishermen were now pushing off with glowing baskets of fire dangling from their bows to light their way and to attract the fish to the surface. They slipped into the night with their assistants, the cormorant birds.

The temperature had dropped quickly. She wrapped her scarf tighter and enjoyed the breeze off the river.

The darkness was creeping quickly, and before long, a sky of dark blue velvet showcased a full moon.

Chapter Thirty-Nine

Kyoto, Japan

Bianca sat at the tiny desk by the window and looked out over the canopy of the colorful garden beneath her. The rain was soft and made a quiet pitter-patter on the vibrant leaves. She looked across the garden toward Ian's room, a mirror image of hers, but the maple and its glorious leaves obscured her vision.

"Richard, you would love this view. I wish you could see it." She wiped off a little bit of dust that had accumulated on the frame of his photo.

A gentle breeze wafted in the window and refreshed her. She was almost done with her dispatch and then planned on delivering it to the *Kyoto Quarterly* office. She was behind in her dispatches.

She worked hard to create a memorable transcript of her unique experiences while also keeping silent on the murder. Although she suspected, the Batavians would be equally interested in the investigation.

She wrote about the bamboo grove. And how the trunks swayed so gracefully. And how, despite the mere whisper of the branches, she had been able to hear them and enjoy them in the tranquility of the early morning. The few other people she had encountered in the forest had been respectful and quiet so that everyone could enjoy the serenity. She explained how she had stopped in her tracks at the base of the tall bamboo stalks and looked straight up until she was dizzy. How the very tops of the bamboo narrowed to thin tips and leaves, and how the swaying motion became larger and more exaggerated all the way at the top.

Then, she wrote about how the Kyotoites had created a community by the Kamo River. How lively a spot it was with picnics and gatherings. Bicyclists, pedestrians, lovers walking hand in hand, impromptu lunch breaks, and musicians along the banks at all hours. She found it peaceful but also bustling and welcoming. She wrote about how home is wherever you find yourself, and family is whoever you love and spend time with. She was learning a lot about home and family.

Once she was happy with the finished product, she folded it up, slipped it in an envelope and into her backpack. With one strap over her shoulder, she headed down the stairs to find Ian before his classes.

At the bottom of the stairs, she stopped to enjoy the garden. It was at the center of the traditional *machiya* house. The maple extended past the roof line. The rain had intensified the moss green and autumn colors as well as the stones and revealed earth. It was a dream for her to have a garden in the middle of her living space. She could get used to this. No wonder Ian was happy here.

She was ready to start her day. She missed the aroma of coffee in the morning but headed to the kitchen to join Ian for tea. When she got there, Ian's bookbag was there, but no Ian. Jiro appeared and stopped in his tracks.

"Jiro, what's wrong?"

"I wanted to go with him, but Ian asked me to wait for you."

"Go where? Where's Ian? What's wrong?"

"They have brought him down for questioning."

"Who? What?"

"The police want to talk more with him. But don't worry, Takeru will be there."

"He should have let you go with him. I don't want him there alone. You should be there to help him. I don't want any language misunderstandings."

"I wanted to go, but he wouldn't let me. He made me promise to stay here with you. Are you ready? I have the car out front, and I already put a sign in the window that we will be away from the office."

Once they arrived at the police station, Bianca was relieved to see Ian signing some papers. He looked almost ready to leave. Jiro saw Takeru and waved him over.

They started talking in Japanese. Jiro was agitated and seemed to be arguing with his cousin.

"Jiro, Takeru, please tell me what is going on. I can't follow along." Bianca was out of breath from worry. She needed to understand. Needed to have this world translated for her. "Why did you bring him here?" Bianca quickly inserted.

"We followed a lead. J.C. filed a complaint against Ian a while ago."

"Yes. I remember. But what does that have to do with anything?" Jiro asked.

"We needed to look into it. Ask him more questions. J.C. filed a report. He claimed that Ian stalked him. When he caught him alone, Ian beat him up for no reason. He claimed that Ian seriously hurt him."

"But I know Ian didn't do that. He wouldn't do that." Bianca was exasperated.

"J.C. claimed that he did. He also claimed that Ian took some studio equipment and some music that was J.C.'s."

"But he didn't. You can't charge him with that. That equipment and music was Ian's. He was just taking his own stuff back." Jiro was fuming.

"We didn't charge him at that time because J.C. had no proof. But we felt we needed to ask Ian some more pointed questions about that evening."

"So, you're letting him go." Bianca held her breath for the answer.

"Yes, he can go home, but he is still considered a person of interest."

Bianca started to protest, but Takeru held up his hand. "All of the people from the party are still under suspicion. It is routine, but it is serious. Until we know what happened, we must consider everyone a suspect."

Bianca had always been proud of the fact that she never cried. She had mastered the art of keeping her hurts bottled up. It had taken her almost two years to have a proper cry over Richard's death. But this was more than she could handle. This was her child, and the tears came unbidden.

Chapter Forty

Batavia-on-Hudson, N.Y.

Mike signaled to Eugene for another cup of coffee. He really needed a stiff drink, but he couldn't very well go to McLoughlin's at this time of the day. If he did, he could probably write off whatever remaining chances he had to win this election.

The high school civics club had published the results of their election polls, and it wasn't looking good for Mike. They were in a close three-way race, but Angleton had a small lead. Mike, at least, was second, with Vera picking up the rear. How had it come down to this? Basically, this election was a referendum on his tenure as sheriff.

Eugene poured him a second cup and brought along some pie to distract him.

"Thanks, Gene, but no thanks. I have no appetite."

"Are you sure? I could grill you a sandwich if you prefer. On the house."

"Yeah, maybe you're right. I should eat something. But I'll pay."

"Whatever you say, Sheriff." Eugene turned to the grill. Mike didn't place an order. He knew that Eugene would bring him exactly what he liked. A BLT with extra mayo on sourdough bread baked by the Bench and Mug Café and Bakery.

Mike's mouth watered when he saw the sandwich. He was hungry and enjoyed the feeling. It had been a while since he had an appetite. He took a big bite, then wiped the extra mayo off the corner of his mouth before anyone caught him with a mayo mustache.

"Mike, don't be discouraged. What do high schoolers know about taking polls?"

"They ask questions, people answer. How hard could it be? It's obvious the villagers have lost faith in me. Heck, Big Ben even recruited Vera." He took a half-hearted bite. "Honestly, Gene, I don't know what my plan is if I lose. Do I go back to New York? I don't know how I feel about hanging around here."

Eugene waited before answering. Mike assumed that Eugene's pause meant that he was right, that he was going to lose.

"I say you're jumping the gun. This is your home. Win or lose. And I don't think you're going to lose."

"Well, you have more faith than I do." Mike finished his sandwich and stood up. He reached in his pocket and came up empty. "Damn, I forgot my wallet at home."

"Like I said. On the house."

"Thanks." Mike started for the door, but then turned back. "For everything, I mean, Eugene. It means a lot to me."

Mike walked in the door to his house.

"Maggie?"

"Mike? What are you doing here?"

"Are you really asking me why I'm in my own home?"

"I'm sorry. It was just a reaction. I thought you'd be at the office."

"So, you're telling me you snuck in thinking I wasn't going to be here?" Mike threw his keys onto the side table and headed for the kitchen and the refrigerator. He bent over to find two beers in an otherwise empty fridge. He came up holding both beers, a little sorry there wouldn't be a cold one waiting for him when he returned tonight.

"Now you drink on the job?"

"I'm not on the job. I'm at lunch. So, you haven't told me why you're here." He didn't sit because he didn't want her to sit. It was bad enough to see her there unexpectedly.

She claimed the beer he offered her. "Do you mind if I sit?"

"No, of course not." So much for that.

"I came to pick up some things." She pointed to the files on the table. "I wasn't sneaking around. I was going to leave you a note. I just thought it would be easier if we didn't run into each other."

Mike sat. He hated being mad at her. She really wasn't deceitful. He knew better than that. They had just drifted apart. They hadn't nurtured this marriage, and it grew wild and unwieldy. Now, they were paying the price with a separation. It was most likely the beginning of the end.

"Did you find what you were looking for?"

"Yes." She fiddled with the bottle label. "Mike, it's good to see you."

"You too, Maggie. You look good."

"You do, too." She paused. "Actually, you don't. You look tired. What's going on? Is it the election? I saw the signs on my way into town. I'm sorry about Vera."

"Yeah, well, me too." He took another sip of his beer. He snuck a peek at her, sitting there peeling the label. The Maggie he remembered. So pretty, so sure of herself, but still a little vulnerable.

Before he knew it, he started confiding in her. The most natural thing in the world. She had been that person for so many years. He told her about Vera, about the jerk Eddie Angleton, about Sal, and about his strange conversation with Charlie and Internal Affairs. He told her everything. And she listened and nodded at all the right places.

She moved her seat a little closer when he started to get emotional about Sal. She placed her hand on his knee and watched his foot tap as it always did when he got into uncomfortable territory.

She looked up to find him staring at her. She kissed him. Briefly. He wasn't surprised at all. He kissed her back. Slower, longer.

Then his radio squeaked to life. "Mike, it's Shelley." He ignored it and kissed Maggie again, but his dispatcher was persistent.

Maggie pulled away. "You should get it, Mike. It's probably important."

"Maybe it would be good for them to see what it would be like if I wasn't always at their beck and call." But he picked it up anyway.

He squeezed the button. "Hey, Shelley, what's up?" He released the button, impatient.

"Mike, I've got a call here from Bianca. She's frantic. When can you get back to the office? She says she needs you." Mike looked up at the mention of Bianca's name, but Maggie had already turned away, her files in hand, and headed for the door.

He squeezed the button. "I'll be there in a minute. Tell her to hold on." He released the button and punched the wall.

Chapter Forty-One

Batavia-on-Hudson, N.Y.

Mike made it back to the office in a matter of minutes.

"Shelley, what line is Bianca on?" He looked down, and neither line was blinking. "Where is she?"

"Well, she's in Kyoto. You know that."

"Shelley, seriously."

"I told her to hang up and call back in ten minutes. Relax. She should be calling any time now."

"I thought you said she was frantic."

"She was, and I didn't see how she would benefit from waiting on the line."

The phone rang, and Mike jumped to grab it before Shelley had a chance. She raised her eyebrows at him and let him have the call.

"Bianca, I'm sorry I missed you earlier. What's wrong?"

"Mike, I think—"

"What do you think?"

But he couldn't get her to say anything. She was obviously broken up. He felt a clenching in his chest. He felt needed—something he hadn't felt in a long time.

"They suspect Ian."

"I don't understand. Wait a minute, are you talking about that body they found?" Mike's stomach went from a clench to a flip. He had wondered if Ian might be a suspect, but he had dropped the ball. After talking to Bianca the last time, he had gone up to Albany to see Charlie. Then, the election polls were released. Now Maggie had appeared. He had not given Bianca's son any more thought, and now Ian was in the crosshairs. No wonder she was frantic.

"Mike, what do I do? I don't even speak the language."

"Okay. Hold on. Ian does speak the language, and he has friends and connections. Let's be calm about this. First of all, remember that everyone is usually a suspect until they are not. The officers would be remiss if they didn't consider everyone."

"I suppose…"

"This is what I want you to do. I want you to find out if there is an expat community center. A place where everyone congregates for events."

"Yes. In fact, I'm staying at that place. Why?"

"Do they have a bulletin board? Go find it."

"Here it is, it's in the lounge. What am I looking for?"

"I would put money on it that there is an English-speaking lawyer on that board. Keep looking."

Bianca made her way through cards on every topic: language classes, rooms and apartments for rent, cleaning services, airport shuttles, immigration advisors. "I don't see one."

Mike could hear her voice climbing an octave. He crossed his fingers that he hadn't given her false hope.

"Here! Here it is. Katherine Matthews. Attorney at law. But she specializes in immigration law. That's no good. Oh, Mike."

"Look, she may make a point of saying she specializes in immigration because that's what is most often needed. She can help you. And at the very least, she can find you someone who can help. Now tell me why Ian is a suspect."

"Because they used to be partners. In a band, I mean. And J.C. stole his music. Ian's music."

"Wait, you're telling me that they suspect him over some music?"

"It's more than that. J.C. and the other bandmate took the music and recorded it without Ian. They never gave him any credit, and they've cut him off from any proceeds. And apparently, it's doing very well. Ian never told me about any of this. He didn't want to worry me. They—"

"Okay, relax. Catch your breath—"

"There's more. A while back, J.C. filed a complaint with the police about Ian. Said Ian stalked him and beat him up and then stole some stuff."

"What did he steal?"

"He didn't. He was taking back his own equipment and music. And they did have a fight, but Ian didn't attack him. It was a fight. That's all."

"Okay. That's not so bad. No charges, right?"

"Right."

"Okay, good."

"Mike, this guy was a menace. J.C. slept with his friend's wife. He owes everyone money. He…" Mike could hear Bianca's breathing slowing down. She was catching her breath.

"It sounds to me that there are a lot of suspects. This J.C. did a lot of damage. I bet that they just have to rule out Ian. It does sound like J.C. and this other guy really did a number on Ian, but that doesn't mean that Ian hurt him."

"Of course not. Ian would never hurt anyone. And I'm not just saying that because he's my son. Well, maybe I am, but he's the kindest kid you've ever met."

"I believe you, and I'm sure the police will believe him too. Besides, didn't you tell me that Ian was on stage when this guy was killed?"

"When I thought I saw something, yes. But the police haven't agreed that the murder took place when I saw whatever I saw. And there's no proof I saw anything. And sometimes, when they ask me questions, I feel like they are trying to trip me up. Like they suspect I'm hiding something or lying. I think they are not sure what to make of me because when I first reported this, there was no body. And…and…"

"And what?"

"His visa. Ian's student visa is in danger."

"Why? They have nothing to charge him. Why would they revoke his visa?"

"He let it lapse. He was having such a bad time over losing his music, and he was busy with his studies. Well, he let it lapse. Stupid, I know. But there you have it. Now, with these new issues over his head—the police report, being a suspect in J.C.'s murder—there's a question about whether they will let him renew. If he gets deported, he won't graduate. It's just a mess. If they investigate his right to stay in the country, they may decide he isn't the kind of person they want here, and he will be deported. He mustn't be sent away. This is where his home is. As much as I miss him, I am coming to the realization that this just might be his new home."

To distract her, Mike called Shelley over. "Hold on, Bianca. Shelley? Where is that information you got me from that precinct in Chicago?"

Shelley brought him her notepad. He picked it up and read to Bianca from Shelley's notes. "This Curtis fellow at the address you gave me—because believe it or not, his name and various versions of it are not uncommon—it says here that he was a troublemaker all through high school. Had a few run-ins with the law. Nothing too major. But he was suspected in a breaking and entering case. A house break-in. A neighbor was sure he was the culprit. Cash, a few pieces of jewelry, and a handgun all went missing, but they couldn't pin it on him. He was brought in during a raid of a pub where they were serving underage kids. In college, he was brought in for stealing a car, but the charges were dropped. Turns out it was a friend of the family, and his father made the whole thing go away. Later on, right after college, he was suspected of passing some bad checks, but the case was dropped once he left town. I suspect that's when he left for Japan. He seems to leave a mess everywhere he goes. And it looks like he managed to get away with it repeatedly. So, not a nice person, but nothing to be murdered over either."

"Thanks, Mike. I appreciate you looking into that for me."

"Thank Shelley. She did all the footwork."

"Thank her for me, will you?"

He could hear the fatigue in her voice. He promised he would thank Shelley.

"Mike, I forgot to ask, how did the debate go?"

"The debate went well, at least that's what I'm told. I didn't stay long."

"What do you mean, you didn't stay long?"

"I didn't have my hat."

"Now, what does that mean?"

Mike told her about deciding against wearing his hat and how both his opponents had theirs. "Do you believe Eddie wore a cowboy hat?"

"Since when? I never saw him wear one before."

"Well, he wore one this time. And the audience loved it. And I felt naked without—"

"Without…?"

"Oh, nothing, you'll just laugh."

"I will not."

"I know you will, and I can't even blame you."

"Give a girl a chance, would you? Try me."

"I consider my hat special. That's all. So special…that I've named it. I feel better when I have it. I should have known better than to leave it behind. Bianca, are you there? I told you you'd laugh."

"I'm not laughing. I think it's natural. I always name my cars. So, what is it?"

"What's what?"

"What's your hat's name?"

"Nope. I've said more than I should." Despite Bianca's protests, Mike did not relent.

"Okay, I'll respect it for now. No hat, so you left?"

"It was more than that. I decided to take the bull by the horns and let them fight it out. I felt a bit powerful leaving the room. I think I made the right choice. Nothing good could come of being up there and getting grilled by everyone. They know me well enough. It's the others who have never been sheriffs before who need to defend themselves. I left them to it. It was a good moment, I must say."

When they finally hung up, he felt that he had been some help. But something nagged at him. Ian was a suspect because he had been close to the victim. Mike knew from experience that looking at the spouse, as well as any other person close to the victim, was always the first course of action.

Playing together in a band, having his work stolen, and J.C. profiting off it was definitely a motive, even if Mike didn't think Bianca's son could have murdered J.C. But wasn't he biased? He didn't know Ian at all. To be honest, if he were investigating this case, he would be looking at Ian, too.

Then it hit him.

How could he have missed it?

He was Sal's partner. Everyone knew how close they had been. Could Internal Affairs be looking at him? As a corrupt cop? As a murderer? Could they think that he was too close to Sal to not know what he had been involved in? What if they thought Mike had felt threatened by Sal somehow? Do they think he could have taken Sal's life to keep him quiet?

Mike realized he had just figured out the missing piece. Charlie wasn't asking him for input. He was interrogating him.

Chapter Forty-Two

Kyoto, Japan

Bianca helped Ian shake open the blanket and place it on the grass. They fought the cool breeze coming off the river until they finally managed to get all four corners down. They laughed at how silly they must have looked to everyone else. The Japanese people around them were relaxed but so reserved in comparison. By the time they sat down, the two of them were straining to keep from being those loud Americans.

Bianca realized that Kenzo was right. They all needed to distract themselves from the investigation and enjoy the time they had together. She thought it would have been harder to do, but now that they found themselves enjoying the view and the sound of the river, it was easy to slip into the comfortable companionship she and Ian had always shared. She watched the heron perched silently nearby, waiting for lunch to swim by. Big black birds circled gracefully above them. It was a perfect day for a picnic.

A gentleman on a blanket off to the side got their attention, pointed to the sky, and warned them to keep close tabs on their food. Bianca and Ian looked up again at the sky and assured him that they had it all under control.

"The *tombi*, black kites, are those hawk-like birds gliding above us. They are known for swooping down to the picnic blankets for a free snack. But don't worry. I've heard about it, but I've never actually seen them do it. Sounds like an urban myth to me."

Ian opened the bento box and offered her a tuna *onigiri*, her favorite, and he had salmon. Bianca poured them some hot tea from the thermos Jiro had filled for them.

The bank of the Kamo River was a beautiful stretch of nature in a busy city. Bianca looked around to see many picnickers out and about. Some with dogs. Mostly Shiba Inus. Others were skipping across the turtle-shaped pavers set just for the purpose of walking to the other side. Young children yelped as they jumped, exaggerating the close call. It was a lovely scene and a perfect way to get some perspective on the problems of the last few days.

They chatted and ate their way through a cold omelet and some rice. Eventually, they fell silent. But the kind of silence that was loud and imposing with unsaid words. Here they sat avoiding the topic most on their minds.

"Okay. I give up. I know we came here to distract ourselves, but let's face it, we both want to discuss the investigation," Ian finally said.

"I'm glad you said that. So, here is what I found out from Mike. It's not very helpful, but it paints a picture—"

"Mike? From Batavia?"

Bianca flushed, realizing that she had reached out to Mike without consulting Ian. "I'm sorry. I didn't know what else to do."

"No. You're right. We need all the help we can get." Bianca noticed that Ian snuck a glance at her. She couldn't tell what he was thinking, but she suspected he was being protective.

"What Mike and Shelley found out substantiates what you have been saying about J.C.'s character." Bianca recounted everything she could remember from her phone call. She had taken some halfhearted notes, but they were back at the guest house.

"That's all fine and good. But we know J.C.'s character. Everyone did. It doesn't explain why he's dead, though. Actually, it explains it but doesn't lead us any closer to who did this." Ian's agitation was plain to see. Bianca wished she could make his anger and pain go away. But she was no longer that person. He was a grown man, and she couldn't protect him anymore from others or from his own anger. She just hoped he could keep his cool and handle this in a level-headed way.

"Ian, I know you're angry. But let's try to stay cool-headed about this." She refilled his cup and handed it back to him. "You're right; this information doesn't shed any light." She sipped her drink. "But what really worries me is that all of you have motives, and some of you had opportunity."

Ian sat there nodding. "I'm worried about my friends, Mom. Jiro and Daniel have done so much for me since I've been here. But neither of them was in the room when you heard the struggle. They could have been outside. I don't know. I don't think either of them could do it, but what can you really know about a person? Maybe there's more to their relationships with J.C.? And then…"

"And then what?"

"Nothing."

"What? What were you going to say? You have more info you didn't share with Takeru, don't you? You have to tell me. How can I help you if you don't tell me?"

"I know you're trying to help, but what can you do? I am so sorry you are dealing with this on your trip."

Bianca unwrapped two slices of cake. They nibbled and remained silent until she heard Ian grumble, "What the hell?"

She looked over at him and saw that his eyes were focused across the river. Two young men were greeting each other. One was a Westerner wearing a baseball cap, a backpack slung over one shoulder, and headphones draped around his neck. The other, a Japanese man wearing bright blue exercise gear, was kneeling down by his bike. It looked to Bianca like he was fixing the chain. He stood up to shake hands.

Bianca couldn't hear what they said, but Ian's face had changed. His jaw was clenched, and he no longer ate the cake he had been so eager to indulge in earlier.

"What is it? Do you know them?"

"I wish I didn't. Hiroshi is okay. But the other…"

"Is he an American? Part of your expat group?"

The Westerner waved to the cyclist and moved on. Ian watched him until he was out of sight.

"Who is he?"

"That's Irvin Concannon."

"Irvin, Mariko's ex? Your old bandmate?"

"The one and only. I wish he had stayed away. Everyone was better off—especially Mariko."

"Maybe it's a good thing that he's back. Maybe now you can try to talk some reason into him and get your music back or at least have him credit you."

"Nothing good would come of a confrontation between the two of us, Mom."

"Well, he's moved on. Let's forget him. We've got enough to worry about."

She unwrapped the final treat, her favorite *matcha* cookies. She put two on a napkin for Ian and two for herself. She reached back in the bag for the thermos, and in the blink of an eye and a flash of wings, one of the birds swooped down and claimed both her cookies.

She was so stunned she yelped, and her cup flew out of her hand, landing clear across the grass on the neighbor's blanket. He turned at the commotion and picked up her cup, then brought it over with a polite bow.

"*Arigatou gozaimasu,*" Bianca tried her best to thank him. He smiled and pointed up at the sky. They laughed as he walked back to his blanket.

"How clever are those kites? They must have been waiting for just the right moment. Talk about opportunists."

"So, I guess it's true what they say about them. Now I've actually seen it with my own eyes. I'm just glad they didn't take my cake." Ian handed her one of his cookies. This time, she huddled over it as she ate, keeping one eye on the sky and one eye on her cookie.

Ian picked up the blanket to shake off the remaining crumbs. They looked around to make sure they left no trash behind and started their walk along the river toward home. They walked in silence, enjoying the change in light as the day came to an end. The temperature had dropped, and Ian offered his mother his scarf, then wound it around her neck for her.

He saw the beauty around him, but it wasn't as distinct and moving as usual. He had too much on his mind. He saw no reason to verbalize his thoughts. He didn't need to worry his mother any more than he had already.

At all costs, he didn't want her to know that Daniel taught knife fighting. He didn't want her to know that Jiro had been sneaking off to make private phone calls. And most of all, he didn't want her to know too much about Kawabata's card in J.C.'s hat. Kawabata was a dangerous man and if Bianca understood this, she would never feel comfortable with Ian staying in this country. Assuming he could stay. If he remained a suspect, he worried they wouldn't renew his visa. He was already on shaky ground with it since he had needed to file an extension. But he had let it lapse. Not too smart.

All this uncertainty made him tired. Tired in a way he had never really experienced before. He felt old. He had never understood the term weary. He understood it now.

Chapter Forty-Three

The cool morning air welcomed Bianca as she set out to deliver her latest dispatch. She found the stroll through town comforting, as she relished the small gardens and miniature shrines tucked in every corner. She took a shortcut Ian had shown her through the grounds of a temple, then came back out on the main street, and turned to approach the *Kyoto Quarterly*. She decided to put her dispatch in the mailbox slot and skip going upstairs to see Daniel. She wasn't in the mood to face any of Ian's friends. At this point, she wasn't even sure who his friends were anymore.

She turned to leave when the window before her caught her eye. Lovely New and Used Records was painted on the window. Some soft jazz caught her ear. It was muffled, but she could make out Bill Evans on the piano. She decided to take a look around. She could browse the vinyl and find a gift for Eugene while she listened to some soothing music.

She walked in to greetings from the staff. A pretty girl behind the counter offered the usual *"Irasshaimase"* with a smile.

Bianca moved through the store to get her bearings. They had a large classical selection, more than she expected. She admired the retro posters and album cover art on the walls. The door opened, and in came another lovely young lady. Bianca began to understand the store's name a little better.

The girl hung up her jacket and bag. The Bill Evans album had ended, and she replaced it with a classical piece Bianca couldn't name but found intriguing. She walked over to the counter where the album cover was displayed and saw that it was Janáček's Sinfonietta. It was an upbeat horn piece she had never heard before.

When the salesgirl turned around, Bianca realized that she knew her. It was Aki, Kenzo's granddaughter. The girl who made Ian blush at the *netsuke* ceremony.

They both smiled as they figured out how they knew each other.

"Mrs. St. Denis, so nice to see you again."

"Aki, yes, you too."

The other girl made her way over.

"Natsumi, this is Ian-kun's mother. I told you I met her—"

"Very pleased to meet you! Ian talks of you… Ah, *nandakke*, always. Yes, that is the word—always. No wonder he is so handsome. His looks are like yours."

"Mrs. St. Denis, this is my sister, Natsumi."

"Please excuse my English. I was not a good student of language. Aki is much better. Aki is much better in all school…all…*gakko no kyoka*…"

"Subjects, school subjects," Aki said, finishing her sentence for her.

"See. She is much better."

"You are both better in English than I am in Japanese. You must forgive me. I do want to learn Japanese properly someday."

"You must learn. Ian will be here, and you must speak to his wife and children."

Bianca was surprised by the comment, and she knew she could not hide it on her face. Before she had a chance to recover, Aki came to her rescue. "Natsumi! What are you saying?"

"Ian-kun, he wants to stay here. He told me. He likes it here." She said this last piece with a coy expression, and Bianca once again found herself wondering who her son had become here in Kyoto. She looked from one sister to the other. Both were pretty. Aki was somewhat demure but with a sparkly exterior. Natsumi was pretty, too, but in a louder way. Everything about Natsumi was loud. Bianca would never have pegged them as sisters.

She was sure Ian had blushed when talking to Aki at dinner the other night, but here, now, it seemed as if Natsumi was staking her claim. Bianca needed to see what she could wheedle out of Ian. She didn't like to be that kind of mother, but if her son was serious about one of these girls, she figured she had a right to know.

The horns got louder and more insistent. "Aki loves this music. I like pop and jazz. What about you, Mrs. Grant?" Natsumi replaced the vinyl with a modern, punchy Japanese song Bianca had heard often since she arrived.

"Her name is Mrs. St. Denis, Natsumi."

Bianca was touched that Aki remembered her correct last name. Here in town, it seemed that Ian knew everyone, and everyone assumed his last name and hers were the same.

"I wonder," Bianca mused aloud.

"You wonder? Is there some music you would like me to find for you?"

"Oh, it's nothing. I was just thinking out loud." Having to correct her name so many times since she arrived had clicked something in her brain. When she could get to a phone out of earshot, she would call Mike back and ask him to look into Jonathan Curtis this time, Mariko's husband. She had asked Mike to check out J.C. but not Jonathan. Maybe this was all a case of mistaken identity. Maybe J.C. wasn't the intended victim. Perhaps it was Jonathan Curtis all along. And if that was the case, then Ian would no longer be a suspect. Ian hadn't even met Jonathan until the other night. She didn't want to get his hopes up, but she would look into this. She got so excited about her new lead she could barely concentrate on the conversation before her.

Aki was looking at her with concern. Natsumi was flipping through the CDs.

Bianca finally turned to answer Natsumi's question. "I like it all. Ian plays a mix of jazz and ballads. His father is also a musician and started with classical. It's all beautiful." She ended with a smile at Natsumi; then she quickly turned back to Aki. She felt a kinship to this girl. This one she could approve of easily.

It seemed that the more time she spent in Japan, the more she realized that she was losing Ian to this beautiful country with the lovely girls and the intriguing culture. His home and his family were evolving. She hoped she could somehow find a way to remain a part of it.

Chapter Forty-Four

Kyoto, Japan

The kettle rushed to a boil, then clicked off. Bianca poured her third cup of tea. Normally, she would work on her novel every day, but she found she wasn't getting enough writing done. She had thought she would arrive in this peaceful city and be so productive, but the distractions had been endless. More caffeine was the only solution she could come up with, so she allowed her tea to steep a little longer.

A knock and the slide of the front door caught her attention.

"Jiro? Ian? Bianca?"

"Daniel? In here."

She heard Daniel slip off his shoes. He came around the corner to the lounge carrying a beautifully wrapped package. "I thought I would check in and see how you were holding up."

He offered her the box. "Thank you. How nice. Jiro and Ian aren't here, but please sit and join me for some tea," she said, reaching for a cup. "Or would you prefer something a little stronger?"

"No, no. Tea is perfect. Too early to be drinking, isn't it? If I sound like I'm convincing myself, I am."

Bianca smiled and poured the tea for him and topped off her own. "Shall we see what's in the box?"

"I hope you like them."

She carefully unleashed the package from its cloth *tenugui* wrapping.

The fabric was decorated with a pattern of gold ginkgo leaves. Inside the unmarked box, she found chestnut pastries. She placed the box between them.

"These are perfect. Thank you. We Italians love chestnuts at this time of year. The smell of roasting chestnuts never fails to make me think of my grandparents. But I have never seen the assortment of chestnut pastries in Italy that I have seen here. What a treat!" Bianca bit into the soft center of the roasted chestnut topped with red bean paste so that it appeared to still have a shell. Like all food presentations in Japan, Bianca found, this one looked so special she hated to bite into it, but she was happy she did. The outer sweet bean paste made a lovely compliment to the smoky chestnut inside. When she sipped her tea, she found the pairing perfect.

They ate in silence for a moment. Bianca hoped he didn't want to talk about the investigation.

"Oh, I completely forgot. Olivia sent this to me when I showed an interest in the Batavia *Gazette*. I thought you might like it."

He removed a crumpled paper from his pocket. He smoothed it before passing it to her.

She was curious and then realized that it was Olivia's latest Last Page essay.

"Oh, how nice. Thank you. A piece of home. She writes these wonderful essays every week. I must admit that I look forward to them. Did you get a chance to read it?"

"I did. You're lucky to have a friend like her with such great insight."

"I know. I was very fortunate that as soon as I entered the community, Olivia took me under her wing. She's been through a great deal, and she seemed to come out stronger and better. I admire her and always tell her that I hope someday to be half the woman she is."

"Her essay captures what so many of us in the expat community feel—the need to make new families and homes in our new community. But she also reminded me about how we evolve as time passes. We tend to think we are who we are, but she writes about how we change. But most of all, I appreciate that she talks about accepting our community for its flaws.

These events of the last few days are reminders that we all have a lot of dirty laundry. And if the community is to remain healthy and vibrant, we need to be there for each other and adjust our thinking to accept each other. It sounds like Batavia-on-Hudson had a tough year, and yet you seem to all be on the mend, based on what she says here and what I can see from you. It gives me hope that my expat community here in Kyoto, my friends—more like my family—can mend too and move past all that we have been through."

He munched on a chestnut and was engrossed in his thoughts. Then he paused and looked at her. She knew her eyes were glassy, but she hadn't allowed the tears to overflow. She didn't like looking weak, but it seemed that he saw something else there. He reached across the table and put his warm hand over hers.

"From what I can see, you are more than half the woman Olivia is. You are remarkable and strong. Not many mothers would handle having their son live so far away. I think I broke my mother's heart when I moved here. But you are supporting him in every choice. A very strong woman. Remarkable indeed."

She broke eye contact for a moment and looked at her hand under his, but she didn't remove it. She realized how nice it was to share a moment of mutual vulnerability with someone who was as warm and engaging as Daniel. And as free as Daniel. There was no awkwardness, no guilt associated with her feelings toward him. She enjoyed his company, his sense of humor, the constant glint in his eye. She wondered if that glint was always there or if it was there when he looked at her. Suddenly, she realized that he had been very welcoming to her from the first moment. That maybe she had been enchanted as well from the beginning. This unencumbered attraction was new to her. With Mike, she felt guilty. Guilty because of Richard, because of Maggie. Especially with the neighbors looking on and judging. But here, thousands of miles away from home, she felt freer. And she was able to enjoy his attention.

She left her hand under Daniel's, looked up, and smiled at him.

Chapter Forty-Five

Batavia-on-Hudson, N.Y.

Mike walked slowly along Main Street with the *Gazette* tucked under his arm. He needed a breather from the office. He was glad he had chosen to walk rather than take the truck. The air was crisp, and the brittle leaves crunched under his feet. He stopped at the town square, where the benches were empty for a change. He took a seat and opened the paper.

He immediately regretted it. There on the front page were the most recent projections for the election. The three of them were neck and neck. There was no way he was going to win this race. He felt an emptiness creeping through his body, starting at his toes and working its way up. He was going to lose. And then what? He was erasing himself one piece at a time. He left the city nine years ago after Sal died to start again. It took years, and now Batavia felt like home. In the process of finding a new home, he had lost Maggie. And now he would lose his profession. He would need to leave Batavia. He could not see a way to stay in a community that didn't want him. He wouldn't know how to hold his head up.

Where would he go? Where would home be? With no family and no job. No identity. He was at a loss for how he had arrived here. If someone had asked him five years ago, he would have said that he'd be a sheriff in this small town until retirement, when he and Maggie would start traveling. Now, it had all changed. Beyond recognition.

He crumpled the newspaper and threw it in the nearby trash can. He walked across the street to Stella's. He hesitated before opening the door. He hated the stares lately, as if everyone was waiting for him to self-destruct. He just wanted a good cup of coffee and a decent chat with someone like Eugene without pitying looks or questioning stares. They judged him for his marriage failure and for the anxiety attacks that no one should know about. He had been so careful, but the word had made the rounds. And now they judged him for not being able to hold on to his job. He wondered what the villagers would think if they realized that he was being investigated for corruption.

He took a deep breath. When he pushed open the door, the bell above him chimed. It roused a small group in the corner, and a few more locals scattered about, but otherwise, the place was uncharacteristically quiet.

He grabbed his usual seat at the counter. Eugene approached, and his eyes revealed that he had picked up Mike's surreptitious glance at Bianca's empty seat. Mike knew Eugene was no fool. Everyone seemed to be aware that Mike and Bianca had an energy, but at least Eugene was decorous enough not to say so.

"What'll be, Mike? Some pie and coffee?"

"Sounds just right. Thanks, Gene."

After seeing the election projections, Mike had forgotten to check for Bianca's dispatch. Luckily, Eugene was on top of things. After dropping off Mike's slice of coconut cream pie and coffee, he moved around to the front of the counter to get everyone's attention.

"Here we go, everyone, Bianca's most recent missive."

The group settled down. They were getting used to Bianca's reports, and were better behaved when Eugene tried to get their attention. There were always a few stragglers, and Monica took her pencil from behind her ear and gently poked Claire with the eraser.

Dear Batavians,

I am learning the meaning of chosen family. Here I have watched Ian in his new circle, and I realize that he has not just a nice place to live, and some nice friends to spend time with. He has a home and a family here. And if my eyes don't deceive me, he also has a romance (or two) brewing.

The last few days have been wonderful and difficult. You may have heard by now that one of Ian's expat acquaintances was found dead. There is an investigation going on and I must say it has colored the entire visit. Please don't let this influence your feelings about Japan. This is highly unusual; Japan has very little crime. But, alas, it did happen.

In an effort to distract ourselves, Ian and I had a picnic on the shores of the river, and I had a quiet walk in the bamboo forest with Kenzo Ishikawa. Both were lovely ways to change our dispositions.

Mike listened as Eugene read Bianca's descriptions of the bamboo grove and the intense quiet and meditative benefits of walking there before the path got busy. The story of how the birds stole their desserts at the river got a hoot and howl from a few neighbors. Mike was glad to see that she was willing to talk about the death. It was preferable to keeping things bottled up as he knew she was prone to do. But he also noticed that she avoided her concerns about Ian as a suspect. And the fact that she had witnessed the struggle that most likely led to the murder. He knew she was still holding back.

"Onanda County Sheriff's Office. Is this an emergency?"

Bianca was taken off guard when she heard Mike's voice rather than Shelley's.

"Hello, is anyone there? Onanda County Sheriff. This is Mike Riley. Can I help you?"

"Mike, it's me, Bianca." She exhaled. Then inhaled. She wasn't sure anymore why she called.

"Are you alright? How's Ian?"

"We're both fine. At least in theory." Bianca stirred her tea before she continued. "Mike, can I ask you a favor?"

"Of course. I told you I would try to help any way I can."

"Can you do a little research on a guy named Jonathan Curtis from Los Angeles?"

"I thought you said he was in Chicago."

"This is a different guy. I know I'm grasping at straws, but I started wondering, what if this was just a case of mistaken identity?"

"You mean that the wrong guy was killed?"

"Yes. Maybe. I don't know. It's crazy, I know. But if Jonathan was the intended victim, then that means—"

"Ian wouldn't be a suspect anymore."

"Yes. That's what I'm hoping. Maybe Jonathan has some history at home, and he came here to leave it behind."

"And it followed him. Is that what you're thinking? It's certainly a possibility. I'll look into him, and I'll let you know what I come up with." Mike took down all the information. "But, Bianca, please don't go getting your hopes up."

"I know. I won't. I'm just thinking that maybe the similarities in the names could have led to some confusion. J.C., Jay, Jonathan. It can be confusing."

"I see your point, but like I said, don't get your hopes up. I would think that most perpetrators would know the person they intend to harm."

"You're right. I know it's a long shot, but please check him out for me."

The conversation was over, but neither said goodbye.

"Mike, have any polls given you an idea of how you're doing in the race?"

"We are running in a three-way tie right now. I think there is no way this will work out for me."

"You need to be optimistic. When all is said and done, the voters know how hard your job is. They don't want to lose you. I know Vera is well-liked, but you need to point out her lack of experience."

"I won't run a negative campaign. The voters will have to figure that out on their own. It's Vera. I can't do that to her."

"Believe me, you'd be doing her a favor if she wins and isn't up to the job. It doesn't need to be mean-spirited. You just have to find a way to lean into your own level of experience, and that will call attention to her inexperience. Of course, you'd have to actually get on the debate stage or write an op-ed..."

"I know I haven't been much for campaigning. You make a good point. Let me think about it."

"You do that. It's one thing to be defeated kicking and screaming. It's another to sit back and let it happen. Go fight for what's yours."

Bianca hung up and hoped she hadn't just advised him to go fight for Maggie.

Chapter Forty-Six

Kyoto, Japan

Bianca stepped to the front of the bus, threw her coins in the machine, gave a nod to acknowledge the driver's goodbye, and stepped off the quiet bus.

Ian called from behind her, "*Hidari.*" She nodded and turned right.

"Your other *hidari.*"

They both laughed as she turned to her left this time. For some reason, she couldn't seem to get those two straight. *Migi, hidari.* Right. Left. Simple. But apparently not.

"I'll eventually get it straight."

"That's what you said last time."

"I know, I know. This language isn't easy. You count differently whether the item is tall and long or round and flat? I don't stand a chance."

"Tell me about it." He pointed to the green traffic signal ahead of them. "What color is that?"

"I'm going. I'm going."

"No. I mean, really. What color is the light?"

"It's green, why?"

"Because even though it looks green to you, to me, I presume to everyone, it's a blue light here. *Ao.* So are green beans. *Aomame.* And then…"

"Okay. I get it. But you have to love a language that has the words *tokidoki, magomago,* and *nikoniko.*"

"Yes, you do. Then you'll love this word. *Kuchisabishi.* Which means lonely mouth. When you eat to entertain your mouth. Not because you're hungry, but because your mouth is bored."

"Oh, I love that one. My favorite though is *tsundoku.* I suffer from the wonderful affliction of *tsundoku,* the act of buying lots of books and not reading them, leading to a pile of unread books."

They wandered down the street, passing chestnut vendors, kimono shops, and cafés until they reached the corner and stopped for the light and the chirp. "Let's wait here for the light to turn blue before we try to cross," Ian said with a smirk. "Seriously though, no one really jaywalks here. I don't want to be that person."

It had started to drizzle, so Ian led her to the nearest building to stand under an awning while they waited. Someone opened the door behind them.

"*Sumimasen,*" said a Western voice.

Bianca stepped out of the way, and Ian turned to excuse himself.

Even Bianca recognized Irvin when she turned around. Ian was correct—Irvin and baby Kentaro looked like father and son. There was no denying it.

"Ian. What a surprise to bump into you."

"Well, yeah, considering you're the one who's been away—"

"Irvin, I'm Bianca. Ian's mother." She put out her hand for a shake. He took it and shook it quickly.

"I just got back into Kyoto, and I'm settling in here at the hotel." In his hand he held the key to his room, and with it, he pointed above him to the Joli Hotel Kyoto.

Bianca nodded, but Ian kept his eyes on the traffic light. Finally, the light turned, and he grabbed Bianca's hand and started to cross the street.

"Goodbye." Bianca had no idea how to act. She was livid at what Irvin had done to Ian, and yet her manners were so ingrained that she felt compelled to be polite. She was relieved to be across the street.

Once on the other side, Bianca turned to Ian, but he shook his head. "Let's not talk about him. He's done enough damage as it is. Look, we're here." He pointed to the tall gate before them.

Kitano Tenmangu was a large shrine with extensive grounds where a monthly flea market was held. She was so excited to be there that it went a long way in distracting her from meeting Irvin.

They wandered up one busy aisle and down the other. She knew that the term flea market was not a fair description. There were antiques and vintage items, along with old toys and food stalls. And art of all types. Bianca favored the kimono stalls where she could find gently used kimonos at affordable prices. They made wonderful gifts. She would never spend the money for a new one. She had nowhere to wear such a thing, but a short *haori* made a beautiful jacket. She had accumulated several already.

She admired the feel of the silk as it fell through her fingers like sand. And with so many patterns, it was hard to choose just one or two. This month, most booths showcased autumn patterns: brilliant maple leaves, golden ginkgo, chestnuts, orange persimmons. These warm colors were her favorites.

She searched the entire market, row after row, looking for an inexpensive replica of the Ebisu *netsuke* that she had returned to the Nakayama family. She was disappointed not to find one, but she had known her chances were slim.

She strolled down the last row with Ian, where she found one last antique and novelty stall. She carefully picked through the piles. And then there he was, with his round face and jolly smile, a small wooden Ebisu. He brought luck and prosperity to fishermen and merchants. She couldn't believe her own good fortune at locating him.

"*Ikura desuka?*" She asked with her fingers crossed. When the vendor said the price, she did a quick calculation and realized it was only fifteen dollars. She happily paid the vendor and grasped the Ebisu to her chest. This would be her special purchase of the day, which was quite a place of honor for she had purchased several unusual items. A pair of colorful earrings made of miniature *hanafuda* playing cards. An antique incense burner in the shape of a fisherman on his boat with his line cast. An inkstone and brushes for the art of *shodo*, Japanese calligraphy. She even unearthed an intricate antique *hanko*, a traditional seal carved out of soapstone. She had found one prize after another, but the Ebisu would be dear to her above all the others.

They passed through the shrine garden and into the courtyard, where they joined the queue at the temple proper. When it was their turn, they each threw a coin into the wooden receptacle. Ian motioned for Bianca to go ahead. She wrangled the thick rope to ring the bell. The gong reverberated as they bowed twice, clapped twice, and then bowed their heads one last time.

Chapter Forty-Seven

Kyoto, Japan

Bianca held her breath, waiting for Mike to continue.

"Okay, so this is what we found on Jonathan Curtis out of Los Angeles. Once again, we had to wade through the various people with the same name, but I'm pretty sure we have it narrowed down to the right person. It looks like you may have something here.

"First of all, the family of Jonathan Curtis had a business for several generations near Little Tokyo. A business on his mother's side of the family. The Kawabatas ran a noodle company. They had a shop and a small factory that employed quite a few people. It was very successful for several generations, but it recently went under. I'm thinking there could be something there. Maybe a disgruntled former employee."

"Hold on, I'm writing." Bianca took down notes to share with Ian, Takeru, the lawyer, anyone who would listen. "Okay, what else do you have?"

"Jonathan went to UCLA and studied journalism there. He worked on the University paper and was charged with plagiarism on an award-winning article he co-authored. I'm thinking this kind of problem can be a career buster. Maybe his co-author has it out for him. I'm just spit-balling here.

"And finally, probably the most damning thing I found, several years after he graduated, Jonathan made a name for himself with a three-part article that eventually was turned into a book. And this time, guess what the subject was? The *Yakuza*. I'm sure the crime syndicate wasn't happy with an exposé."

Bianca exhaled. This was meaty information. "There could be something here. Thank you, Mike. I owe you."

"Tell me what else I can do."

"I don't know. I feel like this can help. But there's so much that needs to be untangled here. The murder, maybe mistaken identity, Ian's visa, his music…"

"Bianca, the visa will work itself out." Mike said this to put her mind at ease, but he knew that legal entanglements would probably harm Ian's chances of getting his visa renewed. That might be fine with Bianca, but if Ian wanted to stay and make a life there, then this would blow it all for him. "And I think you're just as upset about Ian losing his music as you are about the entire investigation. You can't do much about the process the cops are going through. They have to go through their steps until they can eliminate Ian as a suspect. But maybe you should ask the lawyer about the music. You said the other bandmate is back in Kyoto. Maybe the lawyer can find a way to corner him on this issue. Send him an official letter. Maybe she could scare him into doing the right thing. I don't want to get your hopes up, but maybe you can get the ball rolling for Ian."

"Do you think so, Mike? Really? I would hate for him to lose his creative work. He tried so hard to move past his father's shadow, to create a sound all his own. I think it was the main impetus for him coming to school here in the first place. To have something all his own."

When Mike put down the phone, he looked up to find his deputy in his office. He blushed. He knew he did. He didn't even need to look in the mirror. He felt as if Vera had caught him flirting. But he hadn't been. He was just helping a friend. But that friend was Bianca, and both Mike and Vera knew that was a different thing. Everyone in town seemed to know it, even Maggie. Maybe he was the only one left who needed to come to terms with it.

He tried a half smile. He and Vera had been working well together, but it had been restricted to work. The easy way they used to banter around the office had stopped, mostly because Vera rarely stuck around long enough.

It was awkward. They both knew it.

She handed him a burgundy takeout cup from Rudy's Market across the street. He nodded and took it.

"Thanks."

Now that the cup was in his hand, he realized it was Trudy Bauer's famous German hot chocolate. "Trudy is serving her *heisse schokolade* already? I guess it is that time of year. Isn't it?" He reached into his pocket.

"What are you doing? Are you trying to pay me back? Oh boy, have I made a mess of things." She took a seat facing his desk. "Mike, I came here to tell you I've dropped out of the race."

Mike stopped the cup midway to his mouth and stared. "Why would you do that? I never asked you to do that."

"I know. But it's the right thing to do."

"No, it's not. You have every right to run."

"It's not that. I know I do. And honestly, you've lost some of your edge in the last year. And I thought it was my opportunity. If Eddie could run with no experience, so could I. I thought it could be done with no hard feelings. But I was wrong."

Mike started to interrupt, but she put up her hand.

"Let me finish. But I'm not dropping out for any of those reasons. I was up all night, and the way I figure it, I'm going to lose. I want to make the right choice this time. I want to step down with dignity. And if I do, there is no doubt you will win."

"I don't think it's a given. You were right when you said that I had lost my edge. Because of that, I think Angleton still has a very good shot at winning. There is no guarantee that your votes will come my way. I don't want you sacrificing your chances for me. I'm not worth it."

"You're wrong. You are worth it. And even without your edge, you're better equipped to run the harder cases, especially the murders. I'm hoping we don't need to face those again, but I learned that I'm not the best person for that job. You are." She took a final drink from her cup and threw it in the trash near Mike's desk. "Besides, all I will do is draw votes away from you, and then that jerk will be my boss. I have purely selfish reasons for doing this."

Before she reached the door, she turned back to him.

"Give me a few years, and I will really give you a run for your money."

183

Chapter Forty-Eight

Kyoto, Japan

Bianca sat down at a corner table of the empty lounge in the guest house. It faced the glassed-in garden, and Bianca found herself relaxing in spite of the recent turmoil. She was always surprised by how soothing this city could be. Despite all the concerns swirling in her mind, she was repeatedly blessed with serene moments. This was the true gift of Kyoto.

She sat there listening to the patter of raindrops on the glass. The darkness had crept up quietly. Soft lights in the garden gave her just enough visibility to appreciate the rivulets on the windows.

"Ian, are you sure I can't help you?"

"Nope, Mom, I've got it under control. You'll be helping soon enough."

With that, he came out and placed a pot, something along the lines of a dutch oven, in the center of the table. But this pot had the tail of an electric cord. He plugged it in, added some broth, put the cover back on, and ducked back into the kitchen.

He returned with a platter full of goodies. Thin sliced pork, various mushrooms, cabbage, fresh tofu and fried tofu slices, bean sprouts, and lotus root. Bianca was about to be introduced to a *nabe* dinner. They picked what they wanted for the first batch and added it to the pot. They sat there and watched it all come to a bubbling boil. They waited a few minutes for the ingredients to cook, then they served themselves and added more ingredients to the pot. On and on they went until there was nothing left.

"I can't believe we ate the whole thing."

Bianca laughed at Ian's words.

"What's so funny? It was a lot, even for me."

"I laughed because it's the old Alka Seltzer commercial. 'I can't believe I ate the whole thing.' But it's true. There was so much, I never thought we'd eat it all."

Bianca and Ian each used their chopsticks to pick up the last of the thin *enoki* mushrooms and bean sprouts from the bottom of their bowls.

Bianca hesitated but then decided to ask the question that was foremost on her mind.

"Ian, I've been thinking. Now that Irvin is back in town—"

"Mom, I know what you're going to say. I'm not going to seek him out and beg for my music back. I'm over it."

"But clearly, you're not over it. And you have every right not to be. What if you just go speak to the lawyer about it?"

Ian reached over and placed his hand over his mother's. "Mom, I appreciate you're trying to help, but I want to leave it alone. It's just too stressful, and I don't want to deal with it. I'd rather put my energy into something more positive."

There was nothing Bianca could say to that. These were lessons she had spent years teaching him. How to see the glass half full. How to move on from challenges. How to cut losses. She should be glad that he was so level-headed about it.

"Promise me we won't keep talking about this?" Then he removed his hand from hers and picked up the empty bowls and chopsticks. "Now for dessert."

Chapter Forty-Nine

Kyoto, Japan

Bianca stopped to watch as the breeze caused the branches to shudder overhead. Bright red maple leaves floated to the ground. So many fell in unison that it sounded like raindrops as they detached with a click and then reached the crisp leaves below with a quiet but perceptible landing.

When the wind settled, Bianca continued her walk along the Philosopher's Path. Ian was in class, and she had decided to take a stroll along the meandering path.

The walkway curved alongside a narrow canal. Bianca didn't know where to look first—up at the branches or underfoot where leaves had created a blanket of color. And then there was the canal where the leaves were carried away like children's paper boats.

Bianca found herself with a clear head and heart as she walked down this meditative path. She was able to keep her head free of thoughts for most of the walk, but eventually, her pristine mind was exactly what allowed her worries to resurface.

She had to face the fact that Ian was probably going to remain in Kyoto. In March, he would be graduating. That was just a few months away. He had said nothing about returning to the States, and she suspected that was because he intended to stay in Kyoto. He was so happy it was hard for her to suggest any good reason why he should leave.

And she had to be honest with herself. If Ian stayed, she would spend more time in Kyoto. What would keep her in New York? In Batavia?

Then again, Batavia had Mike. She tried not to think about him, but he was always right there. She wondered why Mike had even entered into the equation. He was a married man. Yes, he was separated, but he remained married nonetheless. Just because the two of them had hit it off and could solve a murder together didn't mean anything more than that. There were other men. Even here, she had found an interesting man. Not that she was looking.

Her time in Kyoto called her attention to the fact that she rarely lived in the moment. She read her Zen books, tried to be present, but she found it very hard to practice. But here, here in this magical city, she found peaceful, thoughtful moments even when she wasn't trying. She was more clearheaded here even while worrying about the murder, Ian's predicament with the police, his visa, his music. So many things to worry about, and yet, this city helped her keep it all in perspective. She wrote better; she thought better here. Walking the Philosopher's Path was just another metaphor for finding her way—living in the present and not grieving her past or daydreaming about the future.

She walked a little farther, but the path was getting crowded. She saw a couple walking hand-in-hand. A few young women chatting quietly together. Across the canal, a young father and his son collected leaves, the boy squealing every time he found one he particularly liked. A beautiful young woman in a rust-colored kimono leaned toward a branch and pulled it down toward her face while a young man took photos. Bianca walked and watched the others.

Bianca realized that she might enter the photographer's frame if she kept walking and stopped short so as not to ruin the shot. She was bumped from behind and almost lost her footing. She looked at the shallow canal below. It would not have been dangerous, but certainly unpleasant to fall into the water.

She had had enough. This time, she wanted to see who kept crashing into her.

She whipped around, ready for a fight. There, she found a teenage boy, blushing and bowing his apologies. She knew he had to be rather young, no more than seventeen. He still donned a school uniform, and he was hunched under the weight of his book bag.

He continued to apologize. All she understood were the words *hon* and *sumismasen*. Book and sorry. Then she noticed he held a book in his hand. She suspected he had been walking and reading, and when she stopped short, he had just kept walking.

She offered her apologies when she realized that it had been her fault. He walked around her and moved on.

The others on the path were watching. She had done the unthinkable. She had called attention to herself. In a city as densely populated as Kyoto, it was necessary to remain small and quiet so as not to disturb others. Being respectful of your neighbor was first and foremost. This was a city where you were discouraged to smoke outside because that was public space, space you shared. Buses and trains were silent. Cars moved along the busy thoroughfares with almost no sound and certainly no honking horns. But here she had gone and made a scene. Needless to say, the locals would think her another "ugly American."

Despite how the Philosopher's Path had worked its magic on her frame of mind, she must have been more on edge than she realized. These few unpleasant encounters were so unusual in a city that respected personal space that she had thought she was being stalked. It was ridiculous, and she knew that she had been keeping these confrontations from Ian because she thought they were real. She was relieved to let that worry go. She would tell Ian, and they would laugh about it. She had let her imagination run wild.

Chapter Fifty

Batavia-on-Hudson, N.Y.

An anonymous source states that Sheriff Michael S. Riley, a former NYPD detective currently running for re-election as sheriff of Onanda County, is being investigated for corruption along with his former partner, Sal Petruzzo, now deceased.

Olivia had warned Mike that the *Onanda Register*, the newspaper across the river, would be running an article. Even with the warning, it was a kick in the gut. Mike wasn't completely sure how this had leaked. He knew Edward Angleton was well-connected, and Mike would bet he was the anonymous source. Just because Mike wanted to run a clean campaign didn't mean Eddie would.

The Police Commissioner was quoted as saying, "The NYPD has zero tolerance for corruption of any kind, and the crimes this former officer is charged with represent a disgraceful violation of his oath of office and the public trust. Our NYPD investigators in the Internal Affairs Bureau, together with prosecutors in the District Attorney's Office, will work tirelessly to ensure that a measure of justice is achieved in this case."

Everyone knew that Jake at the *Onanda Register* liked to sensationalize his stories, but this was too much. The Police Commissioner had said nothing about this case yet. Mike would bet that the commissioner was indeed quoted, but from another case.

Mike couldn't read another word.

He threw the paper away, walked out of his office, got into his truck, and headed across the river to the *Onanda Register*.

Chapter Fifty-One

Kyoto, Japan

Bianca continued to pace, the phone pressed so hard to her ear that it hurt.

She heard Mike roll his office chair and plop down into it. "You need to be patient. Ian is in the same boat as quite a lot of people right now. Based on what you have told me, they are not zeroing in on him any more than the others. Unfortunately, you have to sit tight right now. I know that's not easy under the circumstances."

"I suppose you're right. I just wish I could make this go away. I know he's an adult, but I feel it's my job to keep bad things away from my son. I've only got one child. One job. If I can't do this, what good am I?"

"Listen, Bianca, Ian is the luckiest guy in the world to have you as a mom. You're doing everything you can. But you need to accept when things are out of your hands."

The front door slid open. Bianca heard Kenzo and Jiro talking as they removed their shoes. When they entered the lounge and found Bianca on the phone, they dropped their voices to whispers. Kenzo took a seat in the far corner of the lounge while Jiro went behind the bar to retrieve some drinks. He held a beer in one hand and a soda in the other and motioned to Bianca to choose. She pointed to the soda and continued with Mike.

"Mike, you're right. I feel powerless, but I have to be patient. I need to talk about something else. Tell me how the election is going. Any more news?"

"It's going. Nothing new to report. I'm not a shoo-in, that's for sure. But Vera dropped out of the race. Even so, I just don't see how I can pull this off." Mike refused to try and explain the leak and the newspaper article to Bianca. It was too much to make her understand the long history of this problem, and she had enough to think about.

"Vera dropped out. That's a big deal. I'm glad she did. She will have her chance eventually. But you need to stay optimistic. The villagers will lose confidence in you if you don't have confidence in yourself." Bianca took the lemon soda from Jiro.

"You can say that, but it's not easy. I just think my time may be up in law enforcement. I'm thinking of retiring early. Finding another direction. Maybe going back…to the city."

Bianca heard his words, but she felt sure he meant that he would go back to Maggie. She wanted him happy, but she didn't think Maggie would make him happy anymore. And if she had to be honest, it wouldn't make her happy either.

Bianca heard a knock on the front door and the sounds of someone entering. After the shuffle of removing shoes, Takeru entered the lounge.

"Oh no," she whispered under her breath.

"What, Bianca? What now?" The urgency in Mike's voice rattled her even more.

"I don't know. I'll call you back."

She hung up and turned to Takeru. "Is it Ian? Is he okay?"

"Ian is fine."

Jiro and Kenzo came over to stand by her. "Then what brings you here, Takeru?" Jiro asked.

"We've recovered another body."

Chapter Fifty-Two

Kyoto, Japan

Bianca felt guilty for feeling relieved, but her gut told her that any new developments could only help Ian. Any complications would make it less and less likely that Ian would be a primary suspect. But just the same, someone was dead.

"Who is it? Do you know?" Jiro asked.

"It is Kawabata Riku. How well do you know him?"

There was that name again. Kawabata. Mike said that Jonathan Curtis was half Japanese, and his mother's family were the Kawabatas.

"I didn't know Kawabata well, but we knew each other. He had a reputation," Jiro hedged. "What happened to him?"

"We don't have much to go on yet. A fisherman found him in Lake Biwa. Looks like a drowning."

"Was it *yakuza* related?" Jiro asked.

"Not necessarily. He could have committed suicide, had an accident."

"It's not exactly beach weather. I doubt he was swimming. And he doesn't seem like a fisherman to me. He's not the type to take his own life, either." Bianca and Kenzo stood by and let Jiro talk.

"I am more concerned about any connection between Kawabata and J.C. Curtis. Obviously, there was some manner of connection. What do you know other than the business card?"

"What business card?" Bianca looked from Jiro to Takeru.

"The card Ian found with the hat. Kawabata's card," Jiro explained.

"There was a business card, too? He never told me that."

"He didn't want you to worry. Kawabata is an unsavory kind of guy…and honestly, Kawabata's the reason Ian's been worried about your stalker."

Bianca saw the pieces coming together. This had to be something, but what? She needed to tell Takeru and Ian what Mike had said about Jonathan Curtis and the Kawabatas. If this guy they found today was connected to the mob, maybe Jonathan Curtis was as well. She would tell Ian first and let him decide how to proceed with the police.

"*Chotto matte.* Wait a minute. You have a stalker?" Takeru's English seemed to suffer when he was agitated.

"No, I don't think so anymore."

The front door slid open again. "*Tadaima,*" Ian called out.

Ian entered the lounge and frowned upon seeing Takeru. Once he saw Bianca, his face relaxed. "Good to see you Takeru, but why are you here? Is there an update?"

"Nothing yet on J.C., but we just retrieved Kawabata's body from Lake Biwa."

Ian's eyes opened wide. "So this means there must be a *yakuza* connection in J.C.'s death. This can't be a coincidence."

"Yes, it could be a coincidence. We do not know of any connections yet. Nothing except the business card."

Ian turned to his mother.

"They told me, Ian. I understand you didn't want to worry me, but…"

"I'm sorry. I just wanted you to enjoy your visit."

"Now I understand why you were so worried about my so-called stalker."

Takeru held up a hand. "Let us return to the stalker. Before Ian walked in, you said that you were stalked and then that you were no longer. Why the confusion?"

"Well, I thought she was being stalked. But not anymore."

"Why not anymore?"

Bianca interrupted Ian before he had a chance to respond. "What he means is that we don't think there ever was a stalker. That we were worried for nothing."

"Why did you think so in the first place?"

Bianca told him about the encounters, ending with the teenage boy who had bumped into her at the Philosopher's Path while he was reading and walking. "You see, they were all nothing. I was just giving my imagination too much room after what happened to J.C."

Takeru took some notes and then looked up at them. "It does indeed sound like nothing to worry about, but I want you to let me know if anything else occurs. Anything at all."

Bianca was taken aback by his firmness.

"Are you keeping anything from us? Should we be worried?" Ian asked.

"I think your encounters were just clumsy people, but we mustn't forget that someone may consider your mother a witness to a murder."

Chapter Fifty-Three

Kyoto, Japan

Bianca felt confident as she waited for the bus. She was getting a handle on the public transportation system. She wanted to get around without further distracting Ian from his studies. She needed him to graduate and decide his next move. He certainly wouldn't be coming home if he didn't graduate on time.

Her bus pulled up alongside the curb. She quickly embarked and found a free spot to stand near the front. There were no seats available. The only ones remaining were those reserved for the elderly, infirm, and pregnant.

The old woman sitting near her pointed to the empty seat next to her. *"Dozo."*

Bianca smiled and shook her head. She knew she shouldn't take one of the reserved seats, but the woman repeated herself. Bianca relented. She took the seat, balancing her packages on her lap.

Bianca's feet hurt after a day of walking in the city. Sitting on the bus would be a good reprieve before she made the climb up the last hill to Mariko's house, where she was meeting Ian again. Mariko had called them because she had some horrible encounter with Irvin. Bianca and Ian were hoping to take her mind off things or be a sounding board for her if she needed it.

Bianca watched the sunset through the window. The ride took longer than usual as the bus seemed to fill and empty at every stop. It was the end of the short autumn day, and many women were rushing home with groceries for dinner.

Bianca was worried that she was in a seat someone else needed. She decided to stand where she could see out the window and look for her persimmon tree, but darkness had fallen, and she wasn't sure where it was anymore.

She had lost her bearings.

Ian paced the block. Up and down. East and west. Nothing. He looked at his watch. She should have been here by now.

He was normally very protective of his mother. Lately, even more so. She didn't know her way around, and her Japanese was horrendous. In a city where he had always felt safe, he now had to worry about a murderer and a stalker.

Bianca stayed glued to the window, searching for the orange ornamental persimmons. Every time the bus stopped, she leaned closer toward the window. No persimmons.

After several stops, she began to worry. She seemed to be riding on this bus for more stops than usual. She stayed at the window and watched as streetlights illuminated their surroundings in little hazy circles of yellow. She looked closely only to realize she didn't recognize a thing. She couldn't be sure if it was the darkness or if she had overshot her stop. She had no idea where she was.

She looked around; the bus was almost empty—just a few young men in the back. Even the nice old lady had slipped out unnoticed.

Ian walked up the hill toward Mariko's place. Could Bianca have gotten here early and walked up there already? He doubted it. They had met at the bus stop last time with no incident. But last time, it had been daylight.

Two buses had passed since he had been waiting. One hadn't stopped. The other stopped only to drop off a young school child. No one else. Then it took off up the hill.

He turned back around. He didn't want to walk all the way to Mariko's place and lose sight of the buses.

Bianca was surprised when the bus pulled into a large, well-lit parking lot. It stopped to let off the last of the passengers. The driver turned off the engine.

She realized they had arrived at the university. But what now? She walked up to the bus driver. She pointed to the spot on the map where Mariko's house would be. He seemed to understand. She was relieved, but when he answered her, he spoke not a word of English.

"*Mou ichido, onegai shimasu.*" She hoped that if he repeated himself, she might pick up a word or two. But no such luck. She went back to her seat to retrieve her parcels.

She hoped she wouldn't have to walk from here. She had no idea how far she was from her destination. And it was dark. Very dark.

Ian stood at the corner and looked down the street again. According to the schedule, another bus should be arriving soon. He tried not to worry. He tried to think of something else. His mind wandered to J.C.'s murder. Something else…please. His visa… This wasn't working.

Bianca got up her courage and started down the aisle to the exit when a small group of students stepped onto the bus.

She took a deep breath. "Does anyone speak English?"

A young Western man shot up his hand. "I do!"

She hurried over to him before he had a chance to sit down and told him what she needed.

"I see where you're going, but I don't speak Japanese."

Bianca was back to square one.

The engine started up again. Now what?

The boy continued, "But I think this bus does one big circle. So, in a minute, we will head back down the hill, and you can find your stop on the way down. Just remember you need to get off on the opposite side of the street."

Bianca nodded and thanked him.

Halfway down the hill, the bus driver pulled over, turned to her, and motioned to the open door.

"*Arigatou gozaimasu,*" she happily said as she dropped her coins in the machine and climbed down. Across the street, she saw Ian standing beside her persimmon tree.

Ian saw a bus round the corner, coming from the other direction. It came to a stop across the street, and Ian heard the door open with a whoosh, followed by the unmistakable sound of his mother's voice saying *arigatou gozaimasu.* The bus continued down the hill. He watched in amazement as his mother waved to someone in the back of the bus.

No wonder she had missed the tree. In the dark, the orange fruit was barely noticeable. Only the branches hanging within the courtyard and lit by a small garden lamp had any visible orange orbs. She was so relieved to see her tree that she didn't notice that Ian was scowling.

He met her halfway across the street. She opened her arms for an embrace, but he gently took her by her shoulders to take a good look at her under the streetlamp. "Are you okay? What happened to you? I was worried sick."

"I'm sorry I was late. I missed the stop. It was the dumbest thing I've done so far. On the way up the hill, I was looking for the persimmon tree, like last time. But in the dark, I obviously couldn't see it and—" She took a closer look at Ian. His eyes glimmered, and she thought he was working to keep tears at bay. "Ian, what's wrong?"

"Mom, you were missing. You weren't where you said you'd be. I got scared. Are you sure you're fine?"

"Yes, why do you keep asking? I missed my stop, that's all."

"Well, with all that's been going on lately…." He took her parcels from her and motioned up the hill toward Mariko's house. "I, well, you know, I got worried. You said you were being followed. All of it, it's too much. I don't want you out of my sight from now on."

"Ian, you're worrying for nothing. I told you it was all in my imagination. I wasn't being stalked. There's no need to worry."

"I'm not so sure."

"I'm telling you, there's no stalker. Ian. Look at me. It was all in my head. That's why I told you. I thought it was funny that I had let my imagination go wild."

"Are you suggesting that if there really was a danger that you wouldn't tell me?"

"No. Yes. No. What I mean is, stop worrying for nothing." Bianca took back one of the packages from Ian, a stuffed animal for Mariko's baby. "Look. We're here. Let's change the subject. Mariko doesn't need to be concerned about this too. I'll take the toy. You take the pastries."

Chapter Fifty-Four

Kyoto, Japan

Mariko answered the door with baby Kentaro propped on her hip. She was gracious in welcoming them in but seemed less put together than last time. She placed Kentaro in his playpen, absentmindedly handed him a wooden car with big red wheels, and gestured for Bianca and Ian to take a seat.

Bianca took the pastry box from Ian and handed it to Mariko. "For you. My new favorite dessert. *Kuri wagashi. Wagashi,* right? Chestnut sweets."

Bianca turned toward the baby. "And this is for you." She reached over and placed the new stuffed octopus in the playpen for him. She squeezed each tentacle to reveal a different sound. One tentacle crackled, one squeaked, one made a sound like a cricket, and so on. He giggled with each new sound.

"It's so nice of you to come. Since my sister moved to Tokyo, I don't feel that I have anyone to talk to when things get difficult. It's not the same when I speak with her on the phone. The children are always needing her attention. It feels good to have you here."

"Tell us what happened. We bumped into Irvin yesterday," Bianca said to break the ice.

"He arrived unannounced. I knew he was planning on coming into town, but I thought he would have planned his visit with Kentaro, not just appear unannounced.

"But he showed up after I had put the baby to bed. Jonathan had just gotten home from the office." She moved to the playpen and brought the octopus closer to Kentaro. He had taken it by a leg and thrown it too far to reach, and he wasn't yet a good crawler. She continued playing with him, with her back to them for a moment. "And, of course, I wasn't happy that he arrived unexpectedly, but I invited him in. He was polite enough to me and to Jonathan. Then he asked to see the baby, and I told him to return the next day because Kentaro was sleeping. But he wouldn't listen to reason. He wanted me to wake up the baby. When Jonathan tried to intervene, Irvin raised his voice and started to antagonize him. You know how he can get." She took a moment to compose herself. Then she stood up and came back to the sofa.

"Yes, unfortunately, I do," Ian said.

"Before I knew it, they were pushing each other, and that quickly turned into wrestling and punching. No matter what I said, I couldn't get them to stop. Then, the baby woke up crying and wailing. We have a peaceful home here. Kentaro has never heard us raise our voices. He was very scared."

Bianca turned to the now cheerful baby. Despite the story, it made her smile to see him entangled in octopus arms. "Poor thing."

"They ended up wrestling on the floor. Eventually, I got Irvin to leave, but not before he got a few good punches in. Jonathan has to explain those marks today at work. I am sure it will not be easy." Mariko's cool composure started to weaken, and when Bianca moved to her side of the sofa to comfort her, she broke down in tears. "I think this is all my fault. I should never have told Irvin about the baby and Jonathan. Irvin is an angry person, and he has never figured out how to manage his temper. That's why we are no longer together. And now my poor baby will need to deal with Irvin's temper his whole life. I could have kept quiet, and no one would have known."

"But you would have known. You did the right thing. You are a good mother, and Kentaro should know who his biological father is. You knew that; that's why you told him." Bianca rubbed Mariko's shoulders and gave her a moment to cry.

"I know you are right. It was the right thing to do. But I keep wondering…" Her tears continued to roll down her cheeks.

Kentaro started to whimper. He finally broke out in a full-throated cry.

Ian picked him up and rocked him until he calmed down. It worked for a minute, and then he began to wail again.

Mariko looked up at the baby and extended her arms. Ian handed the baby over to her. As soon as Kentaro was reunited with his mother, he stopped crying. And as Bianca suspected, so did Mariko.

Chapter Fifty-Five

Kyoto, Japan

Bianca had been looking forward to this. She and Ian had just arrived at Jazz Spot Yamatoya. The sign outside made Bianca chuckle. Whiskey and Coffee. Something for everyone.

This was another retro find. It had been in the same location since 1970, and it felt like a step into the past. The wood-lined walls were painted in muted green, interspersed with rose and green floral wallpaper. It housed a gleaming red counter, an upscale music system, and a complete wall of vinyl.

An elegant woman in a kimono sipped her lemon squash at the counter. Bianca and Ian sat in the back, where they could watch everything unfold and enjoy the upbeat jazz number on the turntable.

An older gentleman sauntered in. He took off his cap, ordered a coffee, and bopped to the music. He sat directly in front of the owner, who gingerly prepared the pour-over coffee by the cup. They were obvious friends. They chatted sotto voce while the barista prepared the drink without asking what the customer wanted. Obviously, he knew.

The woman approached Bianca and Ian's table with a smile and two menus in the shape of pianos. One in Japanese and one in English. The menu stated that they welcomed music requests, but Bianca was so pleased to discover new music she wouldn't think of requesting anything. Bianca took out her notebook and jotted down the name of the album to share with Eugene when she returned home.

Ian ordered his usual Vienna coffee, but Bianca, a lover of all things citrus, ordered a lemon squash like the lady at the counter. They ordered toast to go with it. This was no ordinary toast. It was an inch and a half thick, grilled to perfection, and slathered with butter. Just delectable. No wonder Jazz Spot Yamatoya was one of her favorite spots.

They discussed Bianca's latest dispatch and Mike's election, but eventually, they returned to Mariko and her plight. Bianca had found it so distressing to see a mother broken up over doing the right thing for her son. Bianca knew the feeling. Ian had been a little older than Kentaro at the time of her divorce from his father. It had been a tough decision when she put Ian in the equation, but she came to the realization that Ian could not thrive when she and Malcolm were at odds. She knew that, in the long run, Ian would be better off if both his parents were happier. She had been right, but it had been an agonizing decision at the time.

Mariko had decided that Kentaro should know his biological father, but she lived with the guilt that her son would forever deal with this difficult man in his life. Perhaps suffer at his hands. Bianca considered that maybe Irvin would become a better man as a result of experiencing fatherhood.

Still, Mariko would second guess herself for years. Bianca knew this from experience.

Bianca had been absorbed in her thoughts and had missed Ian's comments.

The waitress brought over their drinks. Ian's rich coffee arrived in a delicate porcelain cup with a blue design, along with a tiny sapphire-colored bowl with sugar cubes. Her lemon squash came in a rose-tinted etched glass with several slices of lemon floating on top. A diminutive pitcher of emerald green glass contained some simple sugar so she could adjust the sweetness to her taste. Before she left them, the woman placed two miniature origami cranes by their beverages.

Bianca was delighted. *"Arigatou gozaimasu."*

The woman responded with a charming smile.

Bianca drizzled a little sugar in her glass and stirred.

"Then there's Daniel," Ian said.

"What about Daniel?" Bianca felt her face flush. And picked up her glass to shield her face from his.

"Well, like the rest of us, he's a suspect."

"But you don't believe he could possibly be involved with this, do you?"

"Mom, I don't know what to believe." He gently picked up a cube of sugar with the silver tongs and plopped it into his cup. He stirred and thought. "Just like you told me earlier this year. You know how Mike had to suspect his friends. It's hard, but it ends up that despite what we think, we are all more capable of violence than we realize." He stirred and thought some more. "Especially if we are provoked or we are protecting people."

"Which reminds me. You never told me about this fight you got into with J.C."

"I guess I wasn't proud of it. I didn't want to tell you that I had lost my cool to that extent."

"To what extent is that?" Bianca held her breath.

"I broke his arm. I hadn't planned to, but..."

Bianca was speechless.

"I'm sorry. I've shocked you."

"Well, yes, I think you have." She used her straw to macerate the lemon at the bottom of her glass. "You were right, I guess, that despite what we'd like to believe, we are all more capable of violence than we realize."

Bianca picked up Ian's train of thought. "I'm sure it's just a formality to suspect Daniel as it is to suspect you. We know you didn't do it. We know Daniel didn't do it."

"Well, there are some extenuating circumstances when it comes to Daniel."

"I know that J.C. slept with his wife. But that's no reason for murder."

"I've heard of lesser reasons to drive people to violence. But it's more than that..."

"What do you mean, more than that?"

"Nothing. It's nothing."

They watched as the woman placed a new album on the turntable. This time, it was Paul Desmond's *Bossa Antigua.* They smiled at each other. This was one of their favorite albums. Something they had played at home often.

Bianca didn't let Ian off the hook. "Tell me what you're hiding."

"I'm sure it's nothing, but when it comes out, it could be a problem for Daniel. He used to teach *tanto* knife fighting. He's a master."

Bianca sat back. Her face went from flushed to pale.

Ian shook his head. "I knew I shouldn't have said anything to you about this."

"No, it's fine. It's just so incriminating. Daniel is such a nice guy. I don't see how…"

"Mom, are you and Daniel? I mean, is he? I mean, do you like him?"

"Of course, I like him."

"That's not what I mean, and you know it."

"Daniel is just a nice guy, that's all. It's hard to find nice men my age who aren't married."

Ian's eyebrows shot up.

"I mean to talk to. To talk to. Relax."

Ian smirked, knowing how easy it was for him to tease his mother.

"It's one of the reasons Eugene and I are friends. We both lost our spouses. A married man can't really be friendly with a woman. People talk, jump to conclusions. Wives don't approve. Daniel is a man I find easy to talk to, that's all."

"That's all?"

"That's all."

Bianca took her straw, poked at the lemon, and hoped that Ian wasn't as good at sussing out a lie as she was. "I have to confess something."

Ian's eyebrows shot up again.

"No. I'm changing the subject."

"How convenient."

"Listen, I called Mike for some help. I hope you don't mind."

"No. Of course not. We can use all the help we can get. The two of you are pretty remarkable as a sleuthing team."

"The last time I called him, on a hunch, I asked him to investigate Jonathan Curtis."

"Mariko's Jonathan?"

"Yes. I know it's far-fetched, but…"

"No. I see your point. The names are almost the same. But what did you think could come of it?"

Bianca explained how finding out that the killer had someone else in the crosshairs meant that J.C.'s death was an accident, and that would mean Ian was no longer a suspect. Ian nodded, deep in thought.

"Actually, it would mean that all of you are off the hook."

"Wishful thinking. What did you find out?"

"Well. That's just it. Mike mentioned quite a few interesting things. I think they could be considered possible motives against Jonathan, but I've been trying to keep my hope in check."

Bianca went on to explain about his family's noodle business going under. "The Kawabatas were a major employer for a long time."

"Did you say Kawabata?"

"Yes. Jonathan's mother's family. That name just keeps popping up. According to Mike's research, his grandparents were from here, and he still has Kawabata cousins in the area."

Ian became pensive.

Bianca continued. "Maybe someone went postal?"

"You mean you think someone went ramen?"

Bianca laughed in spite of herself. "And then Jonathan was accused of plagiarism at UCLA. He was a student of journalism there—"

"That's a coincidence. UCLA is where Daniel studied journalism."

"I didn't realize there was a connection between Jonathan and Daniel."

They both sat around thinking of the consequences of Mike's information.

"Oh, I almost forgot. There was another issue. Jonathan wrote a *Yakuza* exposé. That certainly could get him into hot water with the wrong people." Bianca looked at him, hopeful.

Ian put his cup down. "First thing tomorrow, I'm going to give this information to Takeru and see if it leads anywhere. Maybe Jonathan was the intended victim. This could just be the break we need."

Chapter Fifty-Six

Batavia-on-Hudson, N.Y.

2:07 a.m.

Mike opened his eyes to the sounds of an infomercial and stretched to get the kink out of his neck. He had found himself sleeping on the sofa more and more often. The need to have the television lull him to sleep, to quiet his mind, was a new development. All those years at the NYPD, dealing with serious crimes, he surprisingly had little trouble sleeping. In fact, he would sleep deeply from the minute his head hit the pillow.

That had all changed now. Now, he had personal stakes.

This profession was his identity. How could he be Mike Riley without that side of him? He had no way to grasp, or even fathom an alternate identity.

The anxiety attacks, the community losing faith in him. He had a marriage on hold. And then there was Bianca. She was a distraction. He had to admit that she was a pleasant distraction, but still…

2:39 a.m.

Vera paced her small kitchen. She knew she had had a chance at the sheriff's office. Had she done the right thing by dropping out of the race? Or was she just another woman clearing the way for a man to take over. Was she a coward?

She knew that winning the election wasn't the same as being good at the job. On one hand, she felt she could be a great sheriff. And then other times, like last year when they dealt with a murder investigation, she realized she wasn't up for it.

But this county wasn't about murders, really. She couldn't remember a murder in her lifetime. Not until recently, anyway.

Her skills were perfect for the typical crimes around here. She knew everyone, she was respected, she could be intimidating when she needed to be, and supportive and warm when that was needed. She was an insider, and Mike's biggest problem was that he wasn't one.

Then, of course, there was Angleton. He was a local too, but he was a jackass. If anything, she was more concerned about keeping him out of office, than getting the seat for herself. But her bid had only complicated things. She had been in third place, and her friends were starting to cool toward her. Despite their rumblings over Mike not being a real local, the villagers were mostly behind him. It was clear to her—if she had persisted in running, Mike would lose to Eddie for sure. She hoped she had made the right choice.

Chapter Fifty-Seven

Kyoto, Japan

As the sun dipped below the horizon, casting a golden glow over the city, Bianca checked the address on the paper. "This looks like the right place."

"I think I can see the tea house on the far side of the garden," Kenzo said as he peered through the gate to the hidden courtyard.

Ian rang the bell on the pillar, and with a buzz, the gate unlocked. Once they entered the garden, they found themselves at a fork in their path. One led to the main house a few steps away, the other to the quaint teahouse. The delicate scent of incense wafted through the air, luring Bianca inside, but she wasn't sure if she should go directly to the teahouse or wait. She was eager to finally experience the revered tea ceremony.

A middle-aged woman in a burnt-orange kimono came out of the front door of the main house. She bowed to the group.

Kenzo led them in a bow and introduced himself to Mariko's mother. *"Tanaka-san, Hajimemashite, Ishikawa desu."*

"I am very happy to host you today. Please call me Kumiko. Mariko tells me you are good friends to her. Thank you."

They bowed in return and exchanged names.

"Please follow me." She turned with a soft rustle of her kimono.

When they arrived at the teahouse, Bianca removed her shoes. She stepped onto the *tatami* mat, feeling the firm yet soft texture beneath her feet.

The three guests were guided to a small room, the air filled with quiet anticipation. Kumiko took her place by the tea utensils and motioned with her hand for them to face her. Bianca watched the others and followed along. She knelt in *seiza*, with her legs tucked under her and sitting on her heels. She worried if she could sit long enough in this position, but her discomfort quickly faded when the ceremony began.

With graceful and deliberate movements, Kumiko meticulously cleaned each utensil. Bianca found herself mesmerized; her mind focused solely on the unfolding ritual.

Bianca had read that the rustling sound of the simmering tea kettle was referred to as *matsu kaze,* because it was reminiscent of the sound of the wind in the pines. It reminded her of the traditional play of the same name, *Matsukaze,* which she had seen performed on her first visit to Japan. The play told the story of two sisters, Matsukaze and Murasame, who were bound to the mortal world by their love for a nobleman. The sisters spent their days waiting for his return, their spirits wandering in the ethereal space between life and death. The play was a poignant exploration of love and loss, mistaken identity, and the human struggle to let go.

As Bianca recalled the play's tender scenes, her gaze followed the host's careful movements as she prepared the tea. Kumiko scooped the vibrant green *matcha* powder into a bowl, then whisked it with hot water using a bamboo whisk to aerate the tea. The swirling motion created a froth, intensifying the aroma in the small room.

The host offered a bowl to Kenzo first, who took it in both hands. He rotated his bowl two turns clockwise, then took a sip, his movements practiced and reverent. Next was Ian, who accepted his bowl and followed the same routine. Bianca was glad to have had the opportunity to observe the others before a beautiful deep orange bowl was passed to her. She rotated her bowl and took a sip. The tea tasted slightly bitter, unlike anything she had experienced before. She closed her eyes, savoring the moment, and with the warmth of the vessel seeping into her skin, she felt the connection to centuries of tradition.

When she finished her last sip, she handed the bowl back with both hands.

Bianca marveled at the diversity of the trio. Kenzo was deeply rooted in Japanese culture. Ian was a bridge between East and West, while Bianca was a newcomer. They all found common ground through the shared experience of the tea ceremony.

As they finished, the host cleaned the utensils once more, and they bowed in unison, a shared moment of gratitude. As they left the teahouse, the sun had nearly disappeared, the sky darkening to a deep indigo.

The three walked quietly through the back streets of Kyoto, streetlamps casting a warm glow on the cobblestones. Bianca felt that the experience of the tea ceremony, with its rich cultural tapestry, bound them together in a shared appreciation for the beauty and transience around them.

As the wind picked up, the maple leaves above them flickered and fell to the ground as if to prove her point.

Chapter Fifty-Eight

Kyoto, Japan

Bianca closed her book. She had been reading on the rooftop garden of Kyoto station for the last hour. Sky Garden and Happy Terrace it was called. She had walked part of the one hundred and seventy-one steps of the grand staircase and then took several escalators the rest of the way.

It had a breathtaking view of the city and was a perfect place to think, people watch, or read. She had done all three. Her mind was cleared, and she began to feel that everything would be fine. That it would all get sorted out. Somehow, no longer worrying about the stalker had released most of her tension.

A quick look at her watch told her it was time to get going if she wanted to arrive at the platform on time. She planned to take a detour through the Skyway Tunnel first.

Bianca took her messenger bag and switched it to the other side. A day's collection of souvenirs, along with the weight of her camera, her novel, and her notes, had made the bag heavier than usual.

She arrived at her platform early and found the area empty. She claimed a spot near where she thought the train would stop and took out her book again.

She was always early, but she preferred it that way. Just to be sure, she took a quick look around, but no one she was meeting had arrived yet. Ian was coming from an outing with his class, and Kenzo was coming from Arashiyama. Daniel would be arriving soon, he was returning from Tokyo. Then, they were off to the mountains of Kurama for the Fire Festival.

She opened her book to where she left off. She was quickly engrossed in Seicho Matsumoto's detective novel.

After a few chapters, a buzz filled the air. She looked up from her book to discover that the platform had filled with people.

She continued her reading, and before long, her creative juices were flowing. She rummaged in her bag to find her small notepad to jot down an idea for a story before she lost it. Her hands landed on everything but that darn notebook and pen. Her wallet, the bus schedule, then her map. She dug deeper with no luck.

She stuck her head in the bag, and no sooner had she spotted her notepad than she felt a shove so hard and debilitating it took her knees out from under her. She crashed to the floor, throwing her hands out in front of herself.

Petrified, she lay on the edge of the platform, one leg dangling. All she could see was a flash of red and black running away from her and then legs in dark denim running towards her. She called out, but her voice was weakened by fear.

She was hoisted to her feet, then steadied with an arm on each of her shoulders.

When she looked up, she found Daniel's worried face and a crowd that had gathered behind him. She put her head on his shoulder, and she cried. He embraced her and let her stay that way as long as she needed.

Kenzo approached them, concern etched on his face.

"Bianca, what is wrong?"

"I fell. I almost fell on the tracks," she hiccupped.

"Darlin', how did you fall?" Daniel asked. "Did you misstep? Lose your balance?"

The rush of a train passing the station almost drowned out his words. The wind tunnel it created chilled Bianca to the bone as she watched the train pass over her book. When the train had disappeared, all that was left were pages scattered everywhere and a broken spine.

"No. No. I didn't fall. I was pushed. I was definitely pushed." She pulled herself away from his arms and ran up and down the platform. "He was here. He was just here." The crowd made room for her, the faces concerned and curious. Everyone watched her frantic motions.

"Who? Who, Bianca?"

"I don't know, but someone hit me intentionally. One minute the platform was empty, the next minute it was crowded, and then out of nowhere someone pushed me. This was no mistake. Someone intentionally tried to push me onto the tracks."

Ian came rushing down the platform. "What's going on?"

Daniel walked over to Ian. "Bianca fell."

Kenzo interjected, "Luckily, Daniel was here and helped her up. She was dangling from the platform."

"Are you alright? What's going on with you, Mom? Were you dizzy?"

"No, Ian. I'm trying to tell them that someone pushed me."

"Pushed you? Who would do such a thing? Are you serious?"

"Of course I'm serious. Someone pushed me with the intention of sending me onto the tracks. If the platform had been empty, I have no idea how I would have gotten up on time, if at all. Luckily, Daniel came along to help me up."

"I had some help. Everyone on the platform was stunned at first but jumped right into action to help. I had just spotted you and was heading over."

"Is that—" Ian pointed to the book.

They all turned toward the tracks and watched the pages of the book pick up with the wind.

"Yes, that's my book. And I was almost finished, too."

"I'll buy you another one."

"I don't know. Maybe not. I might need a break from that book for a while."

Ian started pacing, fuming. Kenzo walked with him, attempting to calm him down.

Bianca wanted to go home. But she also wanted to go to the festival. Daniel looked down at her jeans. The fabric at one of her knees had ripped open. "Very stylish, Bianca. People pay a lot of money for that look."

"Very funny."

"Do you want to abort our mission? Maybe you'd rather relax. We could get some *udon* noodles at that old place near the guest house. That will soothe you, and we could all watch a movie."

Bianca thought about it and was tempted. "No, I'm going to this festival. I didn't come seven thousand miles to be scared into hiding." She wiped at her elbows and knees, trying to stifle tears. "Daniel, did you see anything?"

Ian walked over when he heard her question. "You must have seen something. We should report it."

"I saw you fumbling around in your bag. I was weaving my way toward you, but the platform was crowded. I was watching where I was going and trying not to bump into people. When I looked in your direction again, you were gone. Then I noticed you on the ground, and a few people had already rushed over to help you."

"What about who did this? Did you see anyone or anything?"

"At first, I thought I didn't see anything, but now that I think about it, I did see someone running away. I assumed—"

"Why didn't you stop him!"

"Ian, first of all, your mom was dangling, remember? Second of all, I didn't put two and two together. I assumed he was late for a train and had been on the wrong platform. I never imagined it was something like this."

"Of course. How could you know?" Bianca felt terrible that Ian was taking his frustrations out on Daniel. "Ian, give him a break."

"You're right. Of course, I'm sorry. So, what did he look like? Or was it a woman?"

"It was definitely a man. A tall one, but I didn't see his face, just the blur of his back. And I really didn't look. I saw what I thought was someone running for a train, and then I looked down and saw Bianca. I almost forgot I saw him. Bianca, did you get a look at him?"

"No, I was caught by surprise. Before I knew it, I was down on the ground. The only thing I saw were his legs running away. That's it."

Chapter Fifty-Nine

Kyoto, Japan

After speaking to security at Kyoto Station and filing a report, they arrived at Kurama Station later than they had planned. Late or not, Bianca was happy to be there. It was a one-day event, and she didn't know when she would get the chance to experience it again.

She had started to unwind about halfway through the second train ride. The first train had been packed, and the transfer station and last train even more so. But as they left the city behind and the countryside dominated the view, she had found herself decompressing. The vista of the autumn palette through the windows mesmerized her until finally she was nudged awake by Ian at their destination.

They had arrived at the Kurama station, and she felt a weight lift as she exited the train. Nestled in the mountains, the old wooden train station brought her back to a simpler time. The serene environment quieted her mind, and a canopy of maple leaves imbued everything with a crimson hue as the setting sun shone through their leaves.

Outside the station, Bianca was struck by the sight of an enormous red statue with a long nose. She wandered over to take a closer look and recognized the face from masks she had seen at souvenir shops.

"Mom, stand over there. I'll take your photo."

She posed while Kenzo explained to her that the statues were *tengu,* mountain Shinto spirits.

They started along the obvious path, falling into step with the crowds making their way up to the main street—the only street. "This festival has been celebrated since 940 when the city was hit by devastating earthquakes. The festival was started as a way to protect Kyoto from further disasters. And since the north is where it was believed demons came from, the emperor decided to enshrine a new deity in Kurama, the northern point of the city, as a form of protection. They held an imperial parade of torches to welcome and facilitate the passage of the deity. Our modern events are a recreation of those festivities. The entire festival is made up of many torches, two hundred or more. Carrying the heavy torches is a rite of passage for the youngsters. Originally, only boys participated, but, over the years, they allowed the girls as well."

"I'm glad they got more progressive about it."

"Not really. The population in these mountain towns has diminished over the years. I believe they allowed girls because they would not have had enough participants otherwise. These smaller villages have suffered a great loss of young people who leave for job opportunities in the cities and never return. It is hard to maintain the traditions without them."

"Not so progressive, then. But we'll take what we can get."

Bianca and her group needed no maps. They followed the other festival-goers until they reached the main street lined with traditional wooden houses and shops that had been there for centuries.

A small fire was burning before each home. In the windows, precious family heirlooms were displayed. She stopped briefly before a samurai uniform display. The police lined all the streets and repeatedly asked the spectators to move along, so she couldn't linger.

Once the official procession started, the young children, in full traditional garb, carried the small bamboo torches at the head of the procession, followed by the teenagers with larger torches. The real spectacle was the men. They carried massive torches that took great effort and several men to light and then hoist on their shoulders. Others carried the portable shrines. These were meant as tests of strength, Kenzo had explained.

The chants of *sairei-ya sairyo* repeated endlessly, wishing everyone a good festival. The repetition was calming, and she found herself chanting along with the rest. She and her group joined in the procession where they could find a spot, with the police ushering everyone along.

The largest torches released sparks and dropped small fires behind them. Bianca watched dreamy-eyed as the sparks rose like fireflies, higher and higher, like Icarus, until they eventually snuffed out. Only the smoke lingered.

The walkers before them stopped. Bianca couldn't see much, but she could still hear the chanting. Eventually, the police came through and loosened up the knot of spectators until Bianca was able to catch a glimpse. A circle of men and children chanted and danced a simple side-to-side sway. Bianca knew she had to keep walking, so she moved on to allow others a moment to watch.

Along the torch path, women distributed restorative cups of sake to the men carrying the biggest torches.

The Shinto priests wore red robes and carried paper lanterns. They led the procession to the front of the temple, where all the torches were thrown together to create a giant bonfire.

Bianca remembered that Kurama was known for its *onsen*—the natural spring mineral bath. She wondered about a village known for its water that was also the heart of a fire festival. She marveled at the wooden homes and shops, how vulnerable they all were to fire, and yet, here they were with torch after enormous torch parading down the narrow streets. She couldn't help but feel that one wrong move could lead to disaster.

It was particularly tense when the men were handing off the largest torches to each other. Bianca held her breath as she watched the sparks fall over their shoulders. Despite the weight of the torches and the awkward balancing act needed to accomplish it, they successfully passed their torches to the shoulders of the next man.

Jiro, the tallest in their group, wound a path through the crowd, grabbing Bianca's hand so she could easily follow and get a good view. The others followed close behind. As they got nearer to the bonfire, Bianca felt awed by the magnitude of the events, the heat from the fire. Participating in a traditional ritual that had changed very little in one thousand years helped Bianca keep her day in perspective.

The smoke gathered and gathered until Bianca could see nothing but shapes and dark colors running together. Bianca realized she was famished. Her earlier experience on the train platform had given her a rush of adrenalin that had left her tired and hungry. The ethereal atmosphere and the drummers' one-two beat put her in a trance. The smoke caught in her throat and stung her eyes. She swayed for a moment. Daniel put an arm around her shoulder to steady her.

"Hey, you alright?"

Bianca nodded but was grateful for the shoulder to lean on and did nothing to extricate herself. They stood there, side by side, as the embers floated upward.

Chapter Sixty

Kyoto, Japan

Once they were able to get a train, the men all made sure Bianca had a seat. They rode home in silence; the day had taken its toll on all of them. At each stop, passengers disembarked. Eventually, they all had seats. Kenzo to her right. Ian to her left, Daniel and Jiro across from them.

"Did you enjoy the festival, Bianca?" Kenzo asked.

"I have never experienced anything like it. It was almost disorienting. I felt transported a thousand years to another time, another place."

"You will have a similar experience when we go to Fushimi Inari. Another ritual with long roots. Fushimi Inari is the head shrine for tens of thousands of Inari shrines around the country and their fire festival is considered the most important of the Inari festivals. The belief is that the holy fire purges sins and grants wishes."

"I'm looking forward to it. I hope we have a chance to walk through the *torii* gates afterwards. I think the vermillion gates of Fushimi Inari are stunning, but I've never seen them at night. It must be quite a sight, thousands of them winding up the trail."

"Yes, it is. And don't forget the guardian *kitsune*."

"*Kitsune?*"

"The white foxes. They are the shrine's guardians against evil spirits."

"Yes, I remember now, the huge statues outside the shrine. I got a fox mask and a good luck charm last time. I hung it on my rearview mirror when I returned home. It's still there."

"Yes, they are good luck, but they can also be mischief makers, and sometimes they are downright malevolent. They are tricksters and shapeshifters who enjoy playing pranks on humans. Stories abound in Japanese folklore of *kitsune* using their magical powers to deceive people."

"The sly foxes, yes, Ian mentioned them to me." Bianca thought about how well mythology can capture the paradoxes of our personalities. How we were two people at once. Maybe even several people. How sometimes we weren't even sure which one was our real self. And how we tried these identities on for size over the years before we had a good sense of who we really were.

When the train came to a stop, the lack of movement woke Bianca. She rubbed her eyes and tried to gather her wits. It had been a long day. She stood with the others to get off the train, and no sooner had the cool bracing night air hit her than her hunger started to gnaw at her.

"*Oji-san udon,* anyone?" Daniel announced.

Everyone cheered and followed him. Bianca didn't know where they were going, but she recognized the word *udon*. She was happy to follow Daniel to those thick, delicious noodles that were so hard for her to balance on her chopstick.

They walked several blocks. Bianca didn't think she had it in her, but the slight flutter of a crisp breeze helped keep her awake, as did her empty stomach.

Daniel stopped at an empty lot between two traditional buildings. Bianca suspected that someone had taken down an old *machiya* house to build something new but hadn't started yet. Instead, there was a large tent with a rich, savory aroma emanating from it.

Daniel pulled aside the *noren* curtain to allow her to enter. To her surprise, there was a makeshift noodle shop set up under the tent. She spotted an older gentleman near the burner, busy preparing two bowls for a couple seated on one of the benches. He must be the *oji-san* Daniel was referring to. The shopkeeper had arranged a circle of benches around a small fire. The whole arrangement was cozy and welcoming. But most of all, it was delicious food at an ungodly hour.

Ian ordered for her, and she worked hard to stay awake. Bianca considered her day. It had been unusual, even for Kyoto. From souvenir shopping to her long walk through the rafters in Kyoto Station to the close call on the tracks and then up to the fire ceremony. Next week, they would go to another fire festival, and when she returned to Batavia, she would be in time for their annual bonfire. It was the autumn of fires, she realized.

She stared into the coals in front of her now. All that remained were the red and black embers. Glowing, pulsing, and radiating warmth. She felt in community here with strangers around the fire.

Before long, she had a large, warm bowl in her hands. After a whispered *itadakimasu*, she slurped the noodles the best way she knew how, and she decided that this simple soup with the slippery noodles was one of the most delicious treats in the world.

Chapter Sixty-One

Kyoto, Japan

Bianca changed into her pajamas. She was pleasantly surprised to have found her futon all set up and ready for her since she hadn't taken the time to put it away this morning. The bedding was a little messy, but it awaited her, and that was all she cared about. She slipped under the covers, inhaled the *tatami* scent, and checked the clock. It was 2:13 in the morning, and she was just getting to bed. Tomorrow would be a hard day. She wasn't used to not getting a full night's sleep.

She turned to Richard's photo. "I'm fine. I'm just fine. It's been a long day, but Ian is taking good care of me."

"Are you trying to do too much?" She was sure she heard him ask.

"I do have a lot on my plate. I'm writing a new book, I'm sending dispatches home to Batavia, and I'm trying to see all the Kyoto sights."

"And don't forget you are worrying about a murderer and a stalker. Bianca, maybe you shouldn't go around alone until you figure out what's going on." Bianca knew Richard would have been worried if he were still here.

"Maybe you're right, tonight *was* different. Very different. I almost landed on those tracks…"

Her eyes fluttered. She let them close.

3:37 a.m.

Bianca rolled over on her futon. She couldn't sleep. For all her fatigue, for all the desire to sleep, it simply eluded her. The moon illuminated her room, and under any other circumstance, she would consider it beautiful. Now, she found it irritating. She blamed her wakefulness on it. But she knew better. She knew there were other reasons she was awake.

She got up and walked over to the window, and slid it open. The moon filled the sky, like the mid-afternoon sun. Her gaze dropped from the sky to the garden beneath her window. The puddle in the stone fountain shimmered in the moonlight. The light, as it passed through the maple leaves, left a dappled pattern on the moss. It was captivating. Something she could not reproduce in Batavia for all its beauty. This particular beauty was for here. It changed her frame of mind. For a moment, it didn't seem so hopeless. She closed her eyes and tried to capture the image so she could take it home with her.

She slid the window back in place and returned to her futon. She got herself comfortable again and thought about the garden image. She attempted to will herself to peacefulness and sleep.

The beautiful afterimage remained with her for a moment but then was driven out by her worries. What had happened today on the platform? Was it her imagination again? Did someone just bump into her on the crowded platform? That would be a reasonable explanation, but she could feel his body crash into hers. So deliberate, she was sure of it.

The festival had helped keep her mind off the strange encounter. It was all so enchanting—the children, the Shinto priests, the flames, the sparks, and the danger.

4:02 a.m.

Ian rolled over and looked at the clock. It was almost morning, but not quite.

How had his problem with J.C. and Irvin taken a turn for the worse? He thought it was behind him. With Irvin gone, he had been able to move on a bit. Now he was back, and J.C. was dead.

Ian had begun to make so much progress, too. He had decided that he needed to focus on his studies, that the music problem was secondary. Now his visa was in danger, his whole future was in question. All because of one stupid mistake on his part.

In his rush to get away from his father's musical domination, he took up with the first musicians he encountered. Maybe if he had worked solo for a while and developed his music and his sound on his own, he wouldn't have felt the need. But the camaraderie, the collaboration, was a heady feeling. The more he thought about it, the more he realized that they weren't collaborating. They had been riding on his coattails the entire time.

He had felt more validated by working with others. It gave him more credibility. J.C. and Irvin had been in Kyoto longer, seemed to know the ins and outs of the music scene, and had been able to get them gigs. He had thought of it as equal work, but he realized now that the gigs wouldn't have meant anything without his music. It was his original work that had gotten them a name.

Ian considered what they had learned from Mike today. Jonathan Curtis, Mariko's husband, had a shady past, it seemed. And he was a Kawabata. That must mean something in this strange story. It couldn't just be a coincidence, could it? And Jonathan's article and book about the *Yakuza*. There had to be some connection here that he was missing. He needed to make sure Takeru knew all of this new information. Maybe if Jonathan had been the intended victim, Ian and his friends would no longer be suspects. It suddenly occurred to him that he needed to tell Takeru immediately in case Jonathan was in danger. Anyone who had meant to kill Jonathan earlier might try it again.

CHAPTER SIXTY-ONE

4:16 a.m.

Jiro knew he would not sleep. It had been an eventful day, but mostly, he needed to come to terms with his involvement with Kawabata. He knew he couldn't confide in Takeru. His cousin had a job to do, after all. And Takeru was always by the book. He wouldn't tolerate Jiro dealing with these unsavory characters. But he had had no choice. He needed the money, and only Kawabata could help him. If he hadn't done it, then he would have had to close the business. Maybe even move away. It wasn't just for him; it was for the others. For Ian and for the rest of his staff. Jiro worried about them all like a father might.

4:49 a.m.

Daniel stared at the ceiling. He had sworn off women for a while after the incident with J.C. and his ex-wife. And yet, here he was, thinking about Bianca. He knew it was ridiculous. She lived thousands of miles away. And yet, he couldn't put her out of his mind. It made him sad to think that she was leaving soon. He had been so lonely for so long and she had brightened up his days so effortlessly, to the point of easing his burdens and his bitterness. He no longer felt as vulnerable or as angry. He wished she had been in his life before. Before all of this.

5:28 a.m.

Bianca ran from one mossy boulder to another in the damp garden. She couldn't escape. Was he still there? She turned back for a quick glimpse. His long red nose, his enormous head on a tall man's body was still behind her, approaching.

She couldn't find her way out of the garden. She was trapped behind the glass. She carefully placed her hand on the panes, one after another, looking for an opening.

She knew she should move faster but couldn't. She had to be careful not to miss it, she knew the door had to be here. She knew it was close.

Slowly, slowly, she moved her hands over the glass.

One hand slipped through. Then the other. No more glass. Finally, an escape.

Carefully, she placed her leg through the portal.

She tried to speed up but couldn't. Looking over her shoulder again, she saw him. He was still there, just a few yards behind her, his white fox face grinning.

She turned back around to concentrate on her escape.

There, up ahead. The bamboo forest, empty and green and inviting. She ran with all her energy, though not covering much ground.

Just before she reached her destination, her speed picked up, and she sprang forward, teetering on the edge of a train platform. Her arms twirled in the air to keep her balance. She stepped back as a train rushed by, inches from her body.

She turned around. He was gone.

To her right, the forest appeared once again.

When she reached the path between the tall bamboo, she looked behind her and saw she was alone. She had lost him. Maybe he had fallen onto the tracks. Maybe she had slipped into the glen before he could find her.

She stopped and caught her breath. Her hands resting on her knees. Then she looked up and watched the cool green bamboo sway to the breeze. The sound of the leaves fluttering, the bamboo clacking against each other, deep and resonant. It mesmerized her. She stayed in that spot, watching and listening.

She lost track of time. She finally felt safe.

The wind picked up; the sounds got louder. She saw a movement at the base of a bamboo trunk. A little fox peeked his nose out. He saw her and came out, motioning for her to follow. She hesitated, stuck in place. Then another fox appeared. One after the other, fox after fox.

Finally, her feet were able to move. She tiptoed at first, careful not to make noise. Then she stopped and turned before moving any further. There he was. Following her again. Now, he was a tall man with no face. He was running toward her. She could not hear his steps, only the sound of the leaves and bamboo clanging. Louder and louder.

The wind picked up until it was a roar. She ran along the empty path, surrounded by the tall bamboo. She chased the foxes. One by one, they became warped and fluid, each one turning into a woman in a different colored kimono. They continued deeper into the woods, coaxing her to enter.

The faceless man behind her was closing the space between them. She ran, convinced that if she could turn the bend, she would lose him.

As she approached the curve, she slowed down, calmer now, knowing she would make it. She followed the path as it wound away from her.

Up ahead she faced the forest ablaze, flames licked the tops of the bamboo like torches. The women walked into the flames and shot up into the air like fireflies. Higher and higher until they were spent and then fell back down to earth in a beautiful arc of color. Sparks flew, and smoke engulfed the entire forest in a cloud.

She stood there, paralyzed.

She couldn't go forward, and she couldn't go back.

Chapter Sixty-Two

Mike woke to his alarm, groaned, and rolled over. This was the day he wished would never come. Election day.

The next time his head hit this pillow, he would know if he was still the sheriff of Onanda County. Whether he would remain in law enforcement or not. Maybe even if he remained in this town at all.

He made himself an instant coffee to start the day. It was pathetic, but he didn't see any reason to make anything better at home. It was merely to get him out the door. He'd grab a good coffee at the diner or the market on his way to vote.

On second thought, he dreaded showing his face in public today. He didn't know if the town was rooting for him or not. He changed his mind and rummaged in the cabinet. He pulled out the coffee grinder.

The brittle sound as the coffee beans started to break up made him sad. This had been Maggie's job. She always woke early and ground the beans for their morning coffee. Once the big beans were broken down, and the sound turned into a whir, he found it soothing and almost forgot to stop. He opened the cover and found the grinds were like powder. Finer than usual. But they smelled great.

He scooped four spoons into his machine and poured the water. He pressed the start button and got into the shower. By the time he was done, the coffee would have dripped, and he could avoid the diner. And if he hurried, he could get to the polls before there was a crowd.

After placing his vote, Mike headed to the office where he made another pot of coffee. It was still early, and he had the place to himself. A good time to make that phone call.

Mike hated this feeling. He had information that cleared someone's name, and yet he wished he had something incriminating. It was one of the paradoxes of law enforcement—the desire to see the world cleaned of the bad elements and yet unhappy when you find that someone is good and clean.

He sipped his third cup of coffee and watched the hands of the clock approach seven. It ticked so slowly, he thought he would throw his cup at it. As the minute hand reached twelve, he picked up the phone. He knew Bianca was waiting for this call.

After only one ring, she picked up.

"*Moshi, moshi,*" she said.

"Bianca, I'm glad you picked up and no one else. I wouldn't have a clue how to be understood."

"You would have been fine. Everyone here seems to speak some English. Certainly better than my Japanese."

"Well, I only know *konnichiwa* and *sayonara.*"

"At least they'd consider you polite."

Mike was surprised that Bianca was able to banter. "You sound better."

"Thank you. I'm just getting better at managing, I think." He heard her footsteps. He knew she paced when she talked on the phone.

"But?"

"But I had some horrible dreams last night. This morning, I was a mess. But I've had enough time to put it in perspective. It was only a dream, after all. Anything new there? How's the campaign going?"

"Well, I just came back from voting."

"I'm sorry. I forgot that today was the election. I keep losing track of the time difference—and with all that's been going on here. How do you think you'll do?"

"Well, I've got one vote for sure."

"Two, because I sent my absentee ballot in."

"Great. Two votes, just six thousand two hundred and forty-three to go."

"You'll get there. I have a good feeling."

"Thanks, Bianca. I needed that. There's nothing I can do now anyway. Just wait."

"Yeah, waiting is awful. But it's just one day. Do you have anything new for me on Jonathan Curtis?"

"Well, I do, but I don't think it will be helpful. In fact, I know it isn't. I did some more in-depth checking. I know it was a hope for you that maybe there was a mistake and that he might have been the target, and honestly, all that stuff I dug up seemed to support your idea…"

"But…"

"But…I think we're barking up the wrong tree."

"How can that be? He had so many potential ties here that could have gone sour."

"I think it was an illusion. It seems that the family business that failed wasn't as big a problem as we would have thought. The entire family was adored by the community in Little Tokyo. The Kawabatas helped everyone get new jobs. They even created a scholarship fund at UCLA for Japanese American students. They donated the equipment to the youth center, and family members teach free noodle-making classes to ensure the transmission of the culture. Jonathan's family remains well-loved in Little Tokyo.

"As far as UCLA is concerned and the charge of plagiarism. It turns out that Jonathan was clean. It was his co-author who did the plagiarizing. That other guy was expelled, and his name was removed from the article. The University issued a public apology, and they allowed Jonathan to rework the article, then they published it in the corrected form. In fact, it was Jonathan who discovered the problem and revealed it to the school. He jeopardized his own reputation in order to do the right thing. By the way, you said that one of the expats there went to the UCLA journalism program. Did anything come of that link?"

"No, it seems that Daniel had heard of Jonathan, but that's about it. They didn't really know each other."

"And last but not least—"

"The *Yakuza* exposé. What about that? That's pretty damning, don't you think?"

"Well, Jonathan got the inside scoop from an actual insider now on the outside. Jonathan showed both sides—the good and bad. So, it's not likely he will have enemies there. In fact, he had their blessing. So, this lead is a dead end. Your Jonathan Curtis is squeaky clean."

"Mike, where does that leave me? I'm back where I started."

"Bianca, it's never a bad thing to eliminate leads. It helps tighten the circle and bring the case into focus. Otherwise, the investigator is flailing."

"I suppose you're right, but you know what that means, don't you?"

"I know. It means Ian can't be eliminated as a suspect."

Chapter Sixty-Three

Kyoto, Japan

Mike was right, Bianca decided. This was what she was good at. She loved a problem to solve. Instead of focusing on the investigation, she would work on helping Ian get his music rights back. This was a manageable problem she could tackle.

She turned off the tea kettle, and before making her morning tea, she went back to the bulletin board in the lounge. She shuffled through all the advertisements until she found what she was looking for.

The business card for Katherine Matthews, Attorney at Law. *Walk-ins welcome. No appointment necessary.* She was confident that this woman could help.

She went upstairs for her jacket and scarf. She closed the windows in case of rain and did her best to rush down the treacherous stairs. As she reached for the door, the phone rang. She hesitated—she wanted to get to this woman early today. She decided a ringing phone held too many possibilities.

"*Moshi moshi.*"

"Bianca, two for two. I'm so glad you answered again."

Her heart jumped. The election results. She crossed the fingers on her free hand.

"Mike, it's you. Did you win?"

"Yes and no."

"What does that mean? Either you did, or you didn't."

"Well, I won by eleven votes."

"That's great! I knew you could do it." Bianca was so relieved to have one piece of good news amongst all the problems. She could feel tears pricking her eyes.

"It's not so simple. It's only eleven votes."

"I know it's not what you were hoping for, but—"

"No, it's not that. It's that the slim margin requires a recount. So, nothing is final, and with such a close count, anything can happen."

"Mike, this isn't a national election. They will do the recount and they will certify the vote in your favor. When all is said and done, even if there were one or two mistakes, you will win. You'll see."

"I don't know, Bianca. I'm not counting my chickens, as Lester would say."

"Remember when they had the recount for the village president? Big Ben won by six votes, and after the recount, he won by five. There just aren't enough votes to worry about."

"I'm still not going to rest all week until this is resolved. And for that matter I have to decide if I even want to stay in a place that is so unsure if they want me."

"Mike, now you *are* counting your chickens. Sit tight and see what happens in the recount. Then you can decide what to do. But remember, a win is a win. Don't be so quick to dismiss it. Besides…"

"Besides, what?"

Bianca did not want this conversation to go any further. This was the second time in so many days that she had almost told him she hoped he didn't leave. It wasn't her place to weigh in on his life decisions.

"Besides, I need to go to the lawyer's office. I'm taking your advice, and I'm going to see how she can help Ian get his music back. I want to get down to her office early before she gets involved in another case. I've got to go." Bianca gave him a few more encouraging words and then rushed off the phone.

Relieved about the election, she found tackling another problem easier now than it had been a few minutes before.

Bianca stepped out of the lawyer's office and into the glare of the setting sun, shocked by what she had heard. Katherine Matthews, Esquire, could not help Ian, at least not anytime soon. It was a long shot, she had said, and it would take months, if not longer. This was not what Bianca had hoped to hear. She meandered the streets, heading toward the guest house.

They were back at square one with the music problem. And Ian's visa was still in limbo as long as J.C.'s murder was unresolved. Bianca lost all her earlier optimism. No matter how bright the leaves, how fragrant the roasting chestnuts, Kyoto could not make her problems go away.

Chapter Sixty-Four

Kyoto, Japan

Bianca scribbled a note on the pad of paper she always kept on her desk. She tiptoed down the squeaky steps and placed the note on the counter near the teapot where Ian was bound to find it.

She grabbed an umbrella, her tote bag, the bus map, and her notebook. She had no idea if this would work, but she would try. She believed that the sheer will of a mother could overcome most things.

Once outside in the crisp morning, she felt confident that she was doing the right thing. She walked to the corner, and before she had time to review the bus schedule, the bus pulled up. She got on and chose a seat close to the front so she wouldn't miss her stop.

She settled in with her notebook and jotted down her observations as fodder for her next dispatch. The bus ride was silent as usual despite being half full.

First, the bus turned south. The long boulevard was awash in yellow ginkgo leaves. Then, they crossed the bridge over the Kamo River. She felt lucky to have landed a seat on the right side of the bus, where she had a full view of the river delta and the mountains beyond. She watched pedestrians and bicyclists along the banks making their way to work and to school. She wondered if they were aware of how lovely their surroundings were. Did they stop and realize that this stunning city was not what most people experienced every day?

Today, the trees were ablaze in crimson, amber, vermillion. She knew that come spring, the banks of the river would be lined with cherry trees bearing fragile pink blossoms. And in the summer, Kyoto would be bursting in full verdant splendor, lush and humid. But she was most tempted to return in the winter to see the delicate snowfall on the pines.

She turned her attention to the route and realized she had only one more stop before she got off the bus. She was anxious but optimistic. It was only a matter of reasoning with someone, and she was very good at that.

At her stop, she paid, thanked the driver, and stepped off to the left. *Hidari.* This time, she was sure it was to the left since she had seen her destination as the bus pulled up the block. She walked the half block back in the direction they had come and stopped before the modest Joli Hotel Kyoto.

She walked by the window twice to familiarize herself with the layout of the lobby. After she spotted the elevator, she walked in. She smiled at the clerk and said good morning; then she walked past the front desk as if she belonged there, heading straight to the elevator. She pressed the button to the fourth floor.

If her memory was correct, Irvin had a key ring with the number 402 in his hand when they had bumped into him outside the hotel the other day. She was counting on her memory now. She wanted to show up at his door. It would be harder for him to avoid her that way. If she called up, he might not choose to see her.

She knocked delicately in hopes he would assume it was housekeeping. She was surprised when the door swung open immediately, and Irvin appeared before her, all six feet of him, an unusual sight in Japan.

"Oh, hello. Don't I know you?"

Bianca looked up at him. She held out her hand, and he took it. "Yes, I am Bianca St. Denis, Ian's mother. We met the other day."

"Sure, sure. I remember you now." He stuck his head of unruly hair out into the hallway and looked both ways. "I was expecting someone with towels. I'm all out."

"I hope you don't mind me stopping by this way. I was hoping to talk to you for a minute."

"Come on in." Irvin turned back into his room. His unmade bed took over most of the room. He pointed to the comfortable armchair, then pulled out the desk chair for himself.

"Did Ian send you?"

"No, not at all. In fact, he doesn't even know I'm here." Bianca paused to get her thoughts together. "I wanted to ask if you would be willing to discuss his music. How we could make this all more equitable."

"Equitable?" Irvin looked out the window, then turned back to her. "And what do you mean, *his* music?"

"The music Ian wrote for The Three Dogs. From what I understand, you and J.C. recorded it without him. Without his permission. He did write the music and lyrics, didn't he? Why won't you consider at least giving him credit for his work? That's not much to ask." Bianca spoke deliberately, calmly, knowing she would get nowhere if she accused him.

"His work? His music? Where did you get that idea? That music was ours. The Three Dogs."

"But didn't he write it and compose it?"

Irvin stood up and walked over to the window. He unlocked the latch and slid the window open halfway.

Bianca welcomed the refreshing air in the small hotel room. She was beginning to regret having come here. Would she get anywhere? Could she get anywhere?

"Couldn't you just consider for a moment what it must be like to work as hard as Ian did on creating that music and to have it taken out from under him? I thought you were all friends."

"We might have been friends, but I have things I need to accomplish. I can't sit around waiting for them to make moves. They were too complacent. Ian is a good musician, but he doesn't have a business head. Same with Jonathan. They're both good musicians, but—"

"Jonathan?"

"Yeah, J.C., Jay, Jonathan. I never understood why he needed three names. Most of us do just fine with one."

"Jonathan? J.C.'s name is Jonathan?"

Chapter Sixty-Five

Kyoto, Japan

Ian left the police station and rushed home to find his mother. With these test results, they would need to start thinking differently about Jay's murder. Takeru had arranged to have the tests on the business card rushed. His supervisor understood that this was a family matter for Takeru and had imposed the necessary pressure to produce quick results.

On his bicycle, the trip to the station had gone by in a flash. It had been all downhill, but going back up north toward home was another story altogether. He was in shape and made good time, but when he got off his bike, he was winded.

He entered the guest house and could hear the noises in the kitchen. When he got there, he found only Jiro and Daniel, but no Bianca.

"My mother isn't still sleeping, is she?"

"No, I found this note for you when I came down this morning." Jiro handed him the note and offered him a cup of tea. "Where have you been?"

"I went down to the police station. Takeru said he would have the test results available early this morning, and I wanted to get a jump start." He took a sip of his tea and opened the note.

He read the first few words and wasn't happy.

> *Ian,*
> *Please don't be mad. I went to see Irvin ...*

Irvin returned to his seat across from Bianca. "Yeah, his name was Jonathan, what of it? He's another one who didn't understand the urgency. You have to strike while the iron is hot. We were hot, and they were too relaxed. Not enough hustle. Music is music. If no one hears it, it doesn't matter who wrote it. It won't go anywhere."

"But it was Ian's music. He created it."

"Let him sue me."

"But—"

"What you don't understand is that those two never had it in them to go places. Too many people let others decide their fate. They sit back waiting, as if the world would just deliver success to their doorstep. When we were a group, Jay and Ian were like that. They were always too willing to take a back seat. I act. If something is in my way, I remove it."

Ian slammed his fist on the counter and started reading the note from the beginning.

> *Ian,*
>
> *Please don't be mad. I went to see Irvin to try to reason with him about your music. Like you always say—I get results. I can't make any promises, but I will try. You never know. He's come back to care for his son. That means he has a heart. He sounds like a changed man. I'll be home soon. Hopefully, with some good news.*
>
> *xo Mom*

Ian's head got cloudy. His vision blurred a moment. He needed to process.

J.C.'s prints were not on the business card that Ian had found. Only his blood. What Ian had thought was mud from the garden had been a small blood stain. The only prints on the card belonged to Kawabata and Irvin. Kawabata was dead. J.C. was dead.

And his mother was with Irvin.

Bianca jumped as a loud knock resonated from the door. Irvin opened the door to find the chambermaid. The young woman handed him the towels, but before turning her away, Irvin engaged her with some questions. Bianca only understood a few words. It sounded to her like he had a problem with his heater.

Bianca was relieved to have the door open and to have another person nearby. She was beginning to feel uncomfortable in the small room with Irvin.

She called out. "Can you leave the door open, please? I think I need some air. I've got the beginnings of a headache coming on."

Although she did have a real headache, it was more than that. It was starting to dawn on her that she was dealing with an unstable man. Someone who could only see things his way. Who was unable to consider others in his calculations. A man who stopped at nothing to get what he wanted.

Ian turned to his friends.

"Jiro, call Takeru and tell him to meet us at the Joli Hotel Kyoto. Daniel, I need you to come with me."

"What's going on, mate?" Daniel chugged his tea and was up in a flash.

"Mom is with Irvin, and I think he killed J.C."

Bianca's eyes scanned the room and rested on the CD case on the desk. The image on the cover was a fox and the title of the album was *Shapeshifter*.

A chill shook her as she recognized the trickster fox.

The drive was short, but the traffic was thick and slowed things down. Ian could run faster than Daniel's car was able to move in the congestion.

Ian jumped out of the car and ran the last block to the hotel. Daniel double-parked and rushed after Ian.

"*Sumimasen.*" Ian's urgency didn't preclude the natural need to be polite in Japan. He addressed the clerk with a string of broken and stuttering Japanese. The clerk was unable or unwilling to understand.

Daniel jumped in. He argued with the clerk in Japanese, but the clerk refused to divulge the room number.

Ian, fed up with being polite, ran behind the desk to get what he needed himself. He fumbled around the desk while the flustered clerk picked up the phone.

"Fine. Call the police. We can use all the help we can get."

He found Irvin's room number and ran to the elevator.

Bianca stared at the fox on the CD cover. Her head was swirling now.

Irvin had said Jonathan. J.C.'s real name was Jonathan Curtis. Just like Mariko's husband.

Could she and Ian have been right in the beginning? Could the murder really have been mistaken identity after all? She was paralyzed in the armchair as the realizations started hitting her. She continued to search the room. Her gaze landed on the closet door. Half-open.

Inside, she could see a red backpack. Like the one she saw on the first man who bumped into her near the café and the stranger on the bus.

A red backpack, like the one she saw on the train platform.

Ian watched the number above the elevator. It was stuck on the fifth floor and wasn't budging.

He turned his back on the elevator and yanked on the door behind him. It led to the janitor's closet. Then he tried another, which was locked. The third door opened to the stairwell. He ran up the steps two at a time, leaving Daniel in his wake.

Irvin returned with the towels and put them away in the bathroom. "So, that's why you came here? To try to get me to give up my rights to the music? I think you'd better tell Ian—"

When Irvin left the bathroom, he discovered the armchair was empty. "Where'd you go?"

He turned to find her staring at the backpack. He walked over and closed the closet door. She looked up at him.

"It was you on the platform."

Ian ran down the hall following the numbers.

412, 410, 408, 406, 404.

The next door was open. 402. He ran in to find Irvin standing over his mother.

He pushed Irvin out of the way and grabbed Bianca's arm. "Mom, get out of there."

Irvin rushed Ian, and they both landed on the floor.

Bianca rushed past them but would not leave Ian alone with Irvin.

Daniel came running in, saw the altercation, and jumped on Irvin's back. He wrenched Irvin by the neck until they both rolled off Ian.

Irvin scrambled to his feet and was out the door before anyone could stop him. They chased after him and reached the corridor just in time to see Takeru tackle him. With a large grunt, Irvin was thrown to the ground.

Chapter Sixty-Six

Bianca and Ian walked out of the Fushimi Inari train station and wandered up a side street. They were in search of a specific café where they would meet the rest of their crew before heading to the Ohitakisai Fire Festival at the Fushimi Inari Taisha shrine.

"Ah, here it is. Just as I thought." He beamed. "I've only been here once a while ago. I wasn't sure if I could remember."

They ordered coffee and shared a bag of mini-castella cakes—a donut hole of soft sponge cake. This pastry was the type of thing the Japanese do beautifully. They make something delicious in its simplicity and perfection.

Before they finished the bag, Jiro and Takeru arrived with Kenzo and Daniel a few steps behind them.

They still had plenty of time to claim a spot at the festival. It wouldn't start until one o'clock, so they lingered at the pastry shop with their goodies.

"So, I know you have been over this many times with the police, but can you fill me in on what happened yesterday?" Kenzo had missed all the excitement when he had gone into Arahsiyama.

"Yes. Of course. We were so tired last night we were in bed before you returned." Bianca offered around the last castella in their bag. Everyone turned it down, so she popped it in her mouth. "I had hoped to talk some sense into Irvin about Ian's music. In hindsight, I should have minded my own business. I went to the lawyer first, but she wasn't sure she could help.

And even if she could, she said it would take quite a bit of time. With all the other things going on, I thought it would be nice if I could help Ian with this one thing. But, like I said, it didn't look promising. So, I decided that a conversation with Irvin was in order. I figured the worst that could happen would be a no from Irvin.

"But while I was there, he mentioned that the other band member was named Jonathan. And that got me thinking. Originally, when Ian and I had met Mariko's husband and discovered he had the same last name as J.C., we thought maybe there was a chance that her husband was the intended victim and this was all a mistake. We even asked Mike Riley at home to investigate Jonathan. At first, it seemed like a promising lead. He had all kinds of possible reasons why someone would seek revenge on him."

Ian picked up the story. "Then Mike called us back and explained that all the leads were dead ends. Mariko's Jonathan Curtis had an impeccable background. So, we stopped thinking along those lines. The problem is this really was a case of mistaken identity. We and Takeru had all been searching for motives and connections for the wrong person.

"Irvin had heard from Mariko that she had married Jonathan Curtis and that together they were raising his son. Irvin was furious. He assumed that her husband Jonathan was our J.C. They had been rivals for Mariko's attention years ago. At that time, Irvin had won. He just assumed that once he had left Japan that J.C. had jumped in to replace him. J.C. and Irvin had always had a tenuous relationship to begin with. Love, hate. Neither ever trusted the other."

"Then, Bianca, what you heard and partially saw in the garden really was a struggle between J.C. and Irvin?" Kenzo said.

"Yes. Irvin had come back into town and was following J.C. He was livid over what he thought J.C. had done and wanted revenge. When he saw J.C. leave our party, he confronted him. It quickly turned physical. And then deadly, apparently."

"But there was no body." Kenzo said.

"No, they struggled, and Irvin took out his knife. Then, when he realized that someone might have seen what happened, he 'walked' the fatally wounded J.C. out of the area and down by the river. In fact, Takeru said that no one remembers seeing anything odd. Just a couple of drunks near the river close to our house. That's not so uncommon as to raise eyebrows. So, they never followed up on that lead. In fact, that was probably Irvin with J.C. He eventually dropped his body in the river when he had the chance."

"And J.C.'s hat was lost when they struggled in the garden. But what about Kawabata's business card?" Kenzo asked.

Ian jumped in to answer. "Yes, I thought the card was J.C.'s. That it had fallen out of the lining of his hat where he usually put things like that, but the card belonged to Irvin. He lost it at the scene. When Takeru came back with the results on that card, that's when we realized that we had been misguided and following the wrong leads. Other than my fingerprints, there were only two sets of prints on the card, and they belonged to Kawabata and to Irvin. There were no prints belonging to J.C."

"But there was also a blood stain on the card," Daniel interjected.

"There was blood? I never noticed any blood," Kenzo said.

"Neither had I. I thought it was just dirty from falling in the garden. Maybe stepped on. But that dirt mark was blood, as Daniel said."

"And the blood was Jay's?" Kenzo asked.

"Exactly. Ian came home from the police station with this information to share with us and Bianca, but Bianca wasn't home. But she had left a note," Jiro said.

"And the note said that I had gone to Irvin's."

"So now Ian was frantic, because he's beginning to understand that Irvin was probably the murderer, and his mom was alone with Irvin. So, then we all headed out to the hotel where Irvin was staying," Daniel said.

Bianca interjected. "By that time, I had started to put the pieces together. Like I said, once Irvin referred to J.C. as Jonathan, I began to realize that maybe this was really mistaken identity as we had originally hoped." Bianca was lost in thought a moment. "Honestly, what really got me thinking was when I saw the CD cover for the album J.C. and Irvin had made with Ian's music. He had it there on this desk. It made me so mad to see it, and when I saw the cover, it gave me chills. It was called *Shapeshifter* and had a design of the fox. I remembered the little fox statues in Jiro's garden. How Ian had told me to beware of them because they are tricksters known for possessing humans to encourage them to make foolish choices and seek revenge. It made me so uncomfortable. Like an omen or a premonition.

"And then I saw the red backpack in Irvin's closet. The same one I had seen on the guy who had bumped into me a few days ago and the same one I saw on the guy running away from me at the platform. I *had* been stalked. It wasn't my imagination. I think Irvin had been watching me since the night in the garden. He must have been trying to figure out what, if anything, I did see and what I knew. At the train, he decided that he wasn't taking any more chances with me. He must have considered me a threat. And then, back at the hotel, I stupidly said something about the red backpack. I was so stunned. He was standing over me…

"I don't know what would have happened if Ian and Daniel hadn't arrived. Ian and Irvin wrestled, then Daniel managed to get Irvin off Ian. Irvin scrambled to his feet and ran out the door. Just when we thought we would lose him, he was tackled by Takeru."

"The Takeru Tackle. I like it!" Daniel had just coined another Danielism.

"I'm sure Takeru is well-trained in martial arts like all the officers in Japan. They really don't use their guns since there are no guns in the private sector. Irvin had no chance once Takeru arrived," Kenzo said. "So, all this happened because of mistaken identity. Irvin thought J.C. had wronged him. When all along it had nothing to do with him. It was Jonathan Curtis, a complete stranger, who had married Mariko and was raising his son. That is some story."

"None of you knew that J.C.'s name was Jonathan?" Kenzo asked.

Ian looked embarrassed but spoke up. "Honestly, no. Jiro and I hadn't known him all that long. He always went by J.C. and Jay. I never heard him use Jonathan. Remember, Irvin knew him for many years. I feel like an idiot that I didn't know, but I thought his name was Jay."

"But what about J.C.'s initials that Kawabata had scribbled on the card?" Kenzo asked.

"The initials were I.C., Irvin Concannon, not J.C. Since I jumped to the conclusion that the card belonged to J.C., I assumed the initials read J.C. Again, we were all simply following the wrong lead from start to finish."

They tucked in their chairs and wrapped themselves in their jackets and scarves. As they headed out the door, they all turned to the counter and said, "*Gochisousama deshita.*"

"Wait. I have one more question." Kenzo stopped them on the side of the road. "Kawabata? Where does his death play into this whole story?"

Takeru finally spoke up. "We don't know yet. It could be completely unrelated. But I don't think so, and neither does my supervisor. We are investigating whether Irvin had anything to do with Kawabata's murder. He may have realized that he lost the card. Maybe he was trying to reduce the chances of us making the connection. By eliminating Kawabata, we couldn't question him to connect him to Irvin. But Irvin will not talk on this subject. He has a lawyer who has made him keep quiet. All we know is what he told us before his lawyer arrived. We had put most of the pieces together by then. I know Irvin is not a good guy, but I don't think he intended to kill Jay. I think he just wanted to give him a good beating and scare him away from Mariko and the child. I think things just went bad on him."

"He may have killed Kawabata, and I think he was doing more than trying to scare my mom. He could have killed her. I will not give him the benefit of the doubt."

No one expected Ian to see clearly on this subject, so no one argued with him. He put a protective arm around his mother's shoulders, and they followed the crowd heading for the shrine.

Chapter Sixty-Seven

With much of her worries behind her, Bianca was looking forward to this final event of her trip. After today's festival, there remained only her goodbye party tomorrow evening, and then she would be flying home. Her time in Kyoto had passed so quickly, but she promised herself she would return soon.

The famous Fushimi Inari shrine in Kyoto with the tunnel of red *torii* gates was one of the most photographed images of Japan. Today was their annual purification ceremony.

They were lucky enough to find a spot immediately behind the cordon so that they were close enough to the event to feel a part of the ritual rather than a part of the crowd. Bianca watched in awe as the priests filed out in their white and purple robes and, with long torches, ignited three enormous bonfires at the center of the clearing. The fire pits were cloaked in evergreen branches with hundreds of wooden prayer sticks mounded on top.

Immediately, the pyres began to produce thick white clouds. The wind shifted and turned the vortex of smoke toward the crowd. Bianca's eyes teared, but she did not take her gaze off the sight.

Eventually, the smoke was replaced by flames, which ignited the sticks. The priests made a dramatic show of tossing more and more bundles of the prayer sticks into the flames; then they managed the fires with simple ladles of water as needed.

Bianca felt as if she were thrown back in time, witnessing this ritual as it had been practiced for hundreds of years.

The priests recited a soothing chant. Everyone had been given a paper with the chant so they could participate. Bianca wanted to follow along, but she was unable to read it. She simply listened and tried to mimic. She finally gave up, and just closed her eyes to feel the vibration of all the sounds around her. The voices, the bells, the gongs, the crackling of the fire. All enriched by heat radiating from the mounds.

A solitary gong caused her to open her eyes. Shrine maidens dressed in white and orange robes enacted a slow dance. She wished she understood it all—the ritual, the language, the chants, the symbols. But somehow the mystery of it was so enchanting she was almost glad it was unfathomable to her.

Once again, the blazing fire reminded her of how fragile this wooden city was. And how willingly the people of Kyoto embraced fire. They used it for their blessings, but they never forgot it was a threat as well.

Although so much of this day was lost to her, Bianca remembered reading how the white fox Inari was the god of prosperity and abundance, and that this particular Inari shrine in Kyoto was the head shrine of forty thousand smaller ones throughout the country. Hundreds of thousands of prayer sticks were sent here every year from all over Japan to be burned in the annual fires in the belief that the wishes would ascend to the heavens with the smoke and flames. Everyone chanted to extinguish sins and invite good fortune and to call Inari back from the fields to the mountain to rest after the harvest.

As the fires dwindled, Bianca and her friends left the main grounds and headed up to the red *torii* gates. Just before they reached the gates, Bianca saw the large stone foxes. Her first reaction was a cold shiver. But she needed to remember that these foxes were guardians, here to protect the shrine. Not the trickster foxes of her nightmares. Her fear and chill had to do with walking away from the bonfires and the late afternoon sun dipping into the horizon.

When she passed the foxes, Bianca was faced with two long tunnels of red gates. Her group headed to the right, where they paired up and started their walk. The early part of the ascent was disappointing as they shared the space with so many parishioners from the festival. But the longer they persisted up the mountain and through the tunnel of gates, the smaller the crowds until it was finally quiet.

Bianca found herself walking alongside Kenzo. She knew he was in his element. She had always found his presence soothing, and here he was, once again, quiet and meditative while the others behind them talked and talked.

"Bianca, I am sorry. I am not much company."

"Not at all. I appreciate the quiet. This is a good place to think. We certainly have plenty to think about."

They continued walking in silence. Now that the crowds had dissipated, she could truly see her surroundings. She admired red pillar after red pillar, each engraved in black. She stopped and ran her fingers over the deep markings on one.

"The *torii* gates along the trail are all donated by individuals and companies. The donor's name and the date of the donation are inscribed on the back of each gate. Some cost quite a lot of money. The smaller gates much less, of course."

"But there are so many. I feel we must have walked for a couple of hours already."

Kenzo checked his watch. "Yes, almost. They are called the *Senbon Torii*—a thousand gates. To hike the circuit is about two and a half miles in each direction, so it's not a surprise that it should take time to complete. Especially on the way up."

"We are so focused on the beautiful *torii* that I think we forget how lovely the surrounding nature is. Autumn is a perfect time to be in Kyoto and to do this walk."

"Yes, autumn is indeed the ideal time for this walk. At the beginning of autumn—at the equinox, we are reminded to stay balanced. As the day and night are balanced. To see things clearly. To not rush ahead to our futures or linger in our pasts, but to live in the present. We are practicing that right now. We are walking this path with no destination. It is good practice for us. We are just here. With no other purpose but to be here.

"But autumn is also about letting go. The falling leaves illustrate the beauty of letting go. It is not about death or dying. It is not meant to be a morbid thought. The leaves are not really dying. They are temporary, as we are. The leaves remind us of that. We must be open to the temporary nature of the world. Of ourselves. Embrace our evolution. The many versions of ourselves as we evolve. The lesson is letting go. Not just of things, but of wrongful ideas, of pride, jealousy. All these burdens that hold us back from experiencing joy."

Bianca agreed with Kenzo's assessment. "I am more in touch with the benefits of letting go after what we went through in Batavia this year. The storm really drove that home. And Richard's passing. Ian leaving to live here. And now he may stay." Bianca's voice cracked just enough to cause her to pause. But in that moment of forced silence, Bianca noticed that she was already starting to get accustomed to the idea that her son may remain in Japan. That change was good for him. For her.

"I am glad to hear that. I found that I lost touch with the concept of letting go over the past few years. I needed to come home to rediscover it. I—"

Bianca waited for him to continue. But he didn't. She wanted him to feel comfortable telling her what was on his mind, but she found him such a private person that she wasn't sure how much to press. "Kenzo, you can feel free to talk to me."

"I know. Bianca, you have been a very kind friend since you arrived in Batavia, but I think I have been the one to shut down and not invite others in. I have had many chapters in my life, not all of them to be proud of. I try not to have regrets, but of course…"

"Kenzo, we all have regrets. But as you have said, we need to live now and move beyond the past, and not get stuck on what the future holds. Regrets serve no purpose."

"Very true. The only benefit of a regret that I can see is to move someone to action, to try and repair some of the damage done." He took his hands, which had been clasped behind his back, and dug them deep into his pockets. "I came here to reconnect with family members. People I had left behind when life got difficult for me. I could not recover from the death of my wife. I was no good to anyone and I had to leave the memories behind. I have lived a lonely life as a result. But a life I believe I deserved and have learned to embrace. But I came home and found a loving granddaughter. Someone who does not hold any animosity toward me for leaving."

"Aki, she is truly a lovely girl. And if you want to know a secret, I think Ian thinks so as well."

"That is hardly a secret. Ian lights up whenever he sees her. And it seems the feeling is mutual." Kenzo picked up a red maple leaf and handed it to Bianca. "Her sister Natsumi is accepting of me but not as unconditionally as Aki. But she may still come around. Their mother on the other hand…"

"Your daughter?"

"Yes. Aoko is not so welcoming. She has not forgiven me entirely for leaving."

"Be patient. Give her time. She, too, needs to move out of the past, but soon enough, she will see how good it is for the girls to have you back in their lives. She will come around."

Bianca bent to pick up a yellow leaf and handed it to Kenzo, who accepted it with a small nod. "This talk reminds me of Irvin and how destructive a person he became. It was his inability to move on that must have hurt him so much. That turned him into a vengeful, dangerous person. Enough that Mariko could not remain with him. Irvin lived in the past, and he harbored resentment, fear, and envy, and he turned that outward. And look what that led to. He killed someone. Maybe two people."

"Yes. His is a sad story and a lesson for us all." They approached the opening at the end of the gates. Three hours had passed in no time.

"Now it is time for some *kitsune udon*."

"I'd love that. *Udon* is one of my favorite noodles. Why is the dish named after the foxes?"

"It has fried tofu on top in their honor. *Abura-age* is said to be their favorite food. Some say it is the pointy shape that resembles fox ears that gives it its name. So, every year after the festival, many indulge in a bowl."

"That sounds like just what I need today."

Rather than feeling tired, Bianca was refreshed. The ritual, the walk, the mystery of it all, and most of all, her talk with Kenzo, had helped her see things more clearly.

Chapter Sixty-Eight

Kyoto, Japan

Bianca put on a turtleneck and jeans, then ran a brush quickly through her hair. But she wasn't quite ready to head downstairs for the final night in her son's home. She settled on the edge of the bed to catch a calm moment before the swoop to the end of this trip.

She took an appraising look around the room. Her window overlooked the top of the maple pushing up from the garden, the golden afternoon light making some of the leaves shimmer like stained glass. The open luggage was mostly packed and neatly organized—ready for her to add the last few items tomorrow. She hated to leave behind the three purple cosmos stems that were in a glass of water on the nightstand. The uniquely delicate petals, almost transparent, would always be a reminder of this autumn visit to Kyoto. Finally, her gaze rested on Richard's photo. His dark eyes so familiar, she was sure they would blink at her.

"Thank you, Richard, for always being there for me. Even now. I know you are looking out for me. I miss you. But I am learning to move on. Thank you for that, too. Thank you for always loving me unconditionally. Always putting me first..." She whispered these words into the silent room.

She was interrupted by the distant sounds of the party. Everyone had gathered as they had when she first arrived. This would be her send-off.

She stood up, grabbed her scarf in case they moved into the garden, and headed downstairs.

After the food, the toasts, the mingling, they all settled down to listen. This time, Ian and Kenzo were going to play.

Bianca was pleased that the two of them had bonded. She was happy to see that Ian had father figures around. And it seemed that Ian and Kenzo would be spending more time together. Kenzo had decided to remain a few months to continue nurturing the relationship with his daughter and granddaughters. Bianca would miss him in Batavia, but she felt Kenzo was making the right decision.

She took her drink stirrer and mashed the lemon slice at the bottom of her glass. Out of the corner of her eye, she saw Aki, Kenzo's granddaughter, handing Ian and Kenzo their drinks to have beside them as they played.

Ian slung his guitar over his shoulder and started tuning up while Kenzo removed a trumpet from an old case. Aki had explained to Bianca that it had been at the family home since her grandfather had left all those years ago.

Bianca considered all musicians courageous for performing in front of an audience, and she wondered if time away from the trumpet had hurt Kenzo's playing skills.

She needn't have worried. Kenzo played as if his lips had never left the trumpet. Ian and Kenzo transitioned from one jazz standard to the next with few hitches. They seemed able to speak to each other with their instruments. And best of all, they both seemed happy. Happier than she had seen them since she had arrived in Kyoto.

After the music, Ian and Bianca sat together on the sofa, soaking in the last moments before sleep and then the airport tomorrow. Bianca did everything in her power to keep from crying. She focused her attention on the positive.

"That was quite a jam session. I can't say that I've seen you that animated before."

"Playing with Kenzo is truly something. He has a sound and an energy I haven't encountered before. I'm glad he will be around for a while. I'd like to keep this up. It's good for me. He's a real inspiration."

"Yes, he's special."

"I'm glad you have such wonderful friends at home. I worried about you in a new town, especially after Richard died."

"I know. I wasn't sure I could find my place there, but I have. As you have here. You have more than friends here, don't you? More like a family. It makes me happy." She opened her eyes wide in an effort to keep the tears right where they were, tucked close to the surface but not yet visible. They stung, but she kept them at bay. "Most of all, I am happy you are playing. Please keep it up."

"I'm going to do more than that. These events have taught me something. I will not be held down by the past. I've decided that I can continue writing music. Nothing can stop me from making more. Right? I had it in me to make the pieces that Irvin and J.C. stole. So I have it in me to make more."

"I'm proud of you. As Kenzo says, the well is full. You just have to keep drawing from it."

"*Kanpai!*" Their glasses and beer bottles clinked over the bar.

"To music," said Aki.

"To family," said Kenzo as he sent a smile Aki's way.

"To friends," said Ian.

"To chosen families," said Bianca.

They sipped and tapped their feet to the album Jiro had placed on the turntable.

"I was so impressed with your playing, Kenzo. I had no idea you were such an accomplished musician. How can you play so well after all these years?"

"I play in Batavia. This is my original trumpet. I have not played it in many years, and I missed it terribly, so I bought myself a new one. The trumpet and my turntable help prevent me from getting too lonely. I like the quiet, I like the hills, but sometimes I need music. Alone up there where no one can hear me, I am able to belt out whatever I want, whenever I want. It is liberating and good company."

Bianca tucked in closer to Kenzo. "Such a wonderful secret."

"We all have secrets, do we not?"

"That's true. I am glad to hear you have had your music all along. I often wondered about you spending so much time alone."

"It is my choice, and it is my preference. Now, I will stay here for a while and try to make up for some lost time with my family."

"That's a very good idea. But we will miss you back home."

"I will miss you too, but I will be back. Batavia is my home now."

"For now. But these things change, don't they?"

They both watched Ian and Aki huddled over a drink at the far end of the bar. They seemed so comfortable together—peaceful and completely absorbed in each other. It made Bianca happy to watch, but she knew that each one of these attachments made his return home less and less likely.

Chapter Sixty-Nine

Kyoto, Japan

The ride to the airport with Ian and Daniel had been full of awkward snippets of conversation. The impending goodbye filled the air, and they seemed to run out of things to say. They just couldn't pretend she wasn't going.

As much as she wanted to make these moments last, she was relieved to be out of the car and at the airport. This part was always painful. She needed it to be over.

Daniel rolled the largest suitcase ahead of them, searching for the check-in desk. Ian carried the medium-sized bag in one hand and had his other arm draped over her shoulder. That left her with just her backpack.

Daniel pointed the way. The line was short and efficient as usual, and before she knew it, she had arrived at the check-in, handed over her passport, and received a boarding pass.

Daniel tapped her on the shoulder. "Okay, Darlin'. It's time for me to say my goodbyes."

Bianca saw the emotion on his face, and she knew they had made a genuine connection during her visit. One she would like to investigate further. They had clicked.

She enjoyed his company. It was an easy relationship that was devoid of confusing complications. He was single. She was a widow who had finally reached a point of grieving properly and moving on. There was no guilt.

No complications. She also knew that these were safe emotions because she lived so many miles away.

He embraced her and it felt warm and comfortable, and she didn't want it to end. She also knew that when this hug was over, she would need to say goodbye to Ian. She had no idea how long it would be until they saw each other again.

She pulled away first. Daniel placed a small piece of folded paper in her hand. "I'd love it if you would write to me. I'll leave it up to you." Daniel looked at her for a moment longer, pecked her cheek, and walked away. He turned briefly. "I'll meet you at the car, mate. Cheers, Bianca." He threw her a kiss and turned back around.

She leaned into Ian's shoulder as they walked slowly through the terminal, delaying the inevitable.

When they arrived at the security checkpoint, she turned to him. She needed their goodbye to be quick. She couldn't drag this out. It would be too painful. But she knew him; he would want to linger until the last moment. No matter how much she would do for him, this she couldn't give him. If this goodbye took too long, she would break down.

"Ian, I have two things to say before I go. One—I know this place has a hold on you. It's very special, and I suspect that you—"

"Mom, I—"

"Let me finish. And I suspect that you have not decided whether to come home after graduation or not. I want you to know that I understand. I want you to know that you have my blessing to take whatever time you need out here. This is your life now, and you need to make choices for yourself. I'm fine. You need to enjoy all that this place has to offer you, and it offers a great deal."

Ian bent down and kissed the top of her head. "Thanks for understanding. It's been hard to talk about. I don't want to disappoint you. Or hurt you. But you're right. I feel like I'm only just beginning to understand what a special place this is. There is so much still to explore, and I feel very comfortable here. I have a deep connection I can't quite grasp."

"It suits you, Ian. I must say." She squeezed his waist a little tighter. "And so does Aki."

His face lit up and she knew she had struck a chord. "Yeah, She's special. I'm glad you got to meet her."

They indulged in a long hug. She sniffed his scarf, which held his scent. The same scent she remembered from hugs before he'd rush off to high school. Her eyes welled up, but she blinked them back the best she could. The last thing she wanted was for him to make choices based on her needs and not his own.

"Okay, it's that time."

He checked his watch. "But you have plenty of—"

"I know. But you know how I get nervous about the details of travel. I need to not worry about missing my flight. I won't enjoy the time. I'll just be watching the clock." She could only hold her tears at bay for so long.

She hugged him again and kissed his cheek. Then she took a long look at him, the stylish clothes, the curly hair that had gotten wild in the autumn wind, the constellation of three tiny beauty marks on the side of his face, and the dark, damp eyes that had never changed since childhood.

"Love you."

"Love you."

She turned around, her eyes scanning the terminal. Then she turned left. *Hidari.*

Chapter Seventy

Batavia-on-Hudson, N.Y.

Bianca warmed her hands on the mug of hot chocolate and extended her feet towards the bonfire. She truly felt she was home. This was real. Batavia was home, and these were her friends and even her family, she could say.

She had had a wonderful reunion with Shelby. Emily had placed him on the front windowsill in anticipation of her return. When she opened the door, Shelby never blinked. He meowed and gave her a piece of his mind, but once she picked him up, his purring could be heard across the room. She walked around with him on her shoulders for a few minutes.

Emily had put some basic provisions in the fridge so she could have a snack. First, she opened her suitcase for some green tea, intending to cling as long as possible to the rituals she had established in Kyoto.

When she opened her suitcase, she found Richard's photo on top, the last item she had packed away. She placed him back on the kitchen windowsill where he could watch her prepare tea. She didn't talk to him. There was no need. He knew where she was emotionally. She sipped and smiled at him, admiring the pressed cosmos she had placed in the corner of the frame before she left Kyoto.

But now in this bonfire circle, she looked around at her friends. Almost the entire village was there, some in front of the fire, others walking the bluff, some at tables playing checkers or eating from the buffet laid out so carefully in the bandstand.

Olivia had switched to maternity clothes and was starting to show. Ernie, Big Ben, Claire, the Dekkers, the Bauers. Eugene. They were all there. All her people. The ones she had come to rely on. Monica and Doctor Spenser were across the way. He was helping Monica get a marshmallow properly placed on her skewer. Olivia was talking to Ernie as they watched Tillie and Tengo frolicking. Two beautiful, happy animals.

The only one missing was Kenzo, and Bianca truly noticed his absence. She knew she would miss his serenity, his wisdom. But he was doing important things, and she was glad that he had found his family again.

Old Lester Quirke bumped her elbow as he passed her a bamboo skewer and a marshmallow.

"Could you help an old guy out? My arthritis isn't cooperating." He looked down at the ground where three marshmallows had already fallen.

She expertly skewered the fluffy pillows for him and handed them back. "Here you go."

"Thank you, dear. Now let's see. My dentures won't like this, but I love me a roasted marshmallow. You only live once. I'll worry about the consequences later. Are you going to partake?"

"No, I think I'll pass. Thanks for asking, Lester."

"Suit yourself. But for the life of me, I can't see how you can pass it up."

He reached out and turned the skewer slowly. Bianca watched the white confection turn golden and then charred around the front edges, and her mouth watered.

Lester nudged her again, and when she turned to him, he handed her a stick and a marshmallow. Her eyebrows peeked. "Food of the gods, aye? They are hard to resist, aren't they? It was just a matter of time."

She fixed hers up quickly and extended it toward the fire. She left it by the flame long enough to get good and charred; then she tried to eat the gooey treat without burning her tongue. When she turned to find something to clean her hands, Lester was gone, and Mike was standing above her.

"Can I join you?"

She motioned to the spot recently vacated by Lester. "Nice of Lester, wasn't it?"

"Very intuitive, that one."

He had his own marshmallow and handed her another.

"I wondered where you were." Bianca skewered the new marshmallow.

"I was at my office. The results were just handed down. You're the first I'm telling."

Bianca held her breath. "And?"

"And…" He shook his head. "I won. I don't know how, but I won."

"That's wonderful news!" She leaned over and hugged him, trying to avoid getting his jacket sticky. Another time, she would have felt self-conscious hugging him in public. The gossip always worried her. But she was past that now. She was happy for him and happy for herself. He wouldn't be leaving.

When she settled back in her seat, she noticed Claire staring. And then she noticed the others. Eugene called from across the flames. "Mike, what's the news? It looks like we should start celebrating!"

"Yep. I just got the call."

They all clapped. Most with enthusiasm.

"Thank you. I'm very grateful." He blushed and looked back at his now-burnt marshmallow. Bianca handed him her perfectly golden one with just the exact amount of char. "Here, as my congratulations."

"Thanks."

"So, this is great news." Bianca enjoyed watching Mike struggle with the gooey marshmallow.

"Bianca, it's only eleven votes. It's not exactly a mandate."

"Okay, so you can live with that. You are still sheriff, and you will make them proud. I know you will."

"I've got to get my head in the game. All this stuff with Maggie, the murders in town, and then the news about Sal and his past. I've allowed them to be distractions. I need to put my head in order."

"What about the investigation? Have they stopped bothering you?"

"I decided I don't care. I'm going to take your advice. I refuse to live in the past. It's a dangerous place that houses so many regrets. And I'm not banking on the future. If I learned anything from this election, it's that the future is not predictable. I'm just going to move forward and do my best. They can investigate me. I've got nothing to hide. I'm clean. It's their problem, not mine."

Bianca nervously fiddled with the marshmallow skewer and finally asked the question on her mind. "What about Sal? Have you decided what you want to do?"

"What happened to Sal is another story. I haven't come to terms with it yet. I have to decide what my role is there. Was he really corrupt? Was he killed? And who killed him? At first, I thought I owed him the answers, but now I am beginning to realize that it's a burden I am saddling on myself. No one expects it of me. And as much as I loved Sal, I may have loved a fiction of that person. Maybe the best thing to do for my sanity is to let the NYPD do its job, and I do mine. I have been reelected to this office, and I can't do it if my head's not in the game. That's how I almost lost this election and let this community down in the first place."

Bianca didn't answer right away. She knew Mike had been deeply burdened every day for years by what had happened to Sal and Mike's possible responsibility.

"Mike, that may be the best attitude. After spending time in Japan and doing a lot of thinking, I've decided that's the approach we need. To pay attention to today and to give ourselves second chances whenever we can." She thought about her disturbing dream and realized that at the end of her dream, she had been paralyzed. She couldn't move forward, and she couldn't move back because she needed to face her present. There was only the present. There was no yesterday and no tomorrow. It was only possible to live in the moment.

"But, there's something I need to know. You have to tell me."

"I told you, I knew nothing at all about what Sal did."

"I know that. I want to know what you named your hat." She motioned to his sheriff's hat resting on his leg.

He shook his head. "Oh no. Nope. You will never let me live it down."

"Oh, come on. You must tell me."

He shook his head.

"What if I guess?"

"Okay. If you guess, I'll confirm."

"Male or female?"

"I thought you were guessing."

"I am, but I need an idea of how you think about these things."

"Okay, okay. Male."

Bianca thought. And thought. "Comet?"

Mike shook his head.

"Flash? Phantom? No? So, not a superhero. How about Duke? Thunder?"

Mike shook his head, but his eyebrows shot up. She must be getting closer.

"Shane? Butch? Oh, I know! Black Stallion?"

"Nope." But she could tell she was almost there. She knew she'd get it. Then it hit her. She turned to him. "Silver!"

His face opened up in surprise, and she knew she had it. "Ha! I knew it!"

"Okay, okay. Calm down before people start asking. I admit it."

"That's a great name. 'Hi, ho, Silver, away! It should have been my first guess. You remind me of the Lone Ranger."

"Well, I'm honored because he was my boyhood hero." He smiled at her, and she was glad that they had shared this silly but intimate thing. What she hadn't told him was that she had a childhood crush on the Lone Ranger, and now, looking at him, she realized that he was handsome, just like the Lone Ranger. They smiled, and both blushed, then turned their gazes back to the fire.

Ernie was strumming his guitar. Bianca missed Ian, but she joined the song and found that being with them all here took the sting out of missing Ian. They held each other up.

Bianca found herself once again with the warmth of flames touching her face reminding her that friends could be family.

The bonfire had started to die down. The flames no longer furious but settling into embers. She watched the sparks float gently skyward until they were extinguished. Then her eyes found the moon, and she thought of Ian waking up to the sun.

A Note from the Author

I have taken liberties with the dates of some actual events. The Kurama and Fushimi Inari Festivals are held on October 22nd and November 8th respectively, but I collapsed the dates closer together to meet my narrative needs. Cormorant fishing ends in mid-September each year which would have been over by the time Bianca arrived.

Acknowledgements

Autumn Embers is a very personal story for me. Kyoto is a beautiful and inspiring city which also happens to be my son's home. I am grateful to so many people, but I'll try to be brief. I want to offer thanks:

To the Level Best Books community. It is a privilege to be a part of this warm and supportive group of talented writers. Special thanks to my editors Verena Rose, Shawn Reilly Simmons and Deb Well. I am grateful for all you do to make my writing dreams possible.

To my readers who have enjoyed visiting Batavia-on-Hudson and are trusting me to bring them along with Bianca to Kyoto, Japan. Thank you for your support.

To Elisa Tanaka for her enchanting cover art and map of Kyoto, and for being my cultural beta reader. Also, to Elisa for providing me with a first-hand account of the Kurama Fire Festival.

To the three amazing ladies of Sleuths & Sidekicks, Jen Collins Moore, Carol Pouliot, and Lida Sideris for the support and friendship an author needs while isolating during the birthing of a book.

To my colleagues at Writers in Kyoto and BooksonAsia.net—my inspiring writing community in Japan. I am so grateful for your guidance.

To Jann Williams and *Kyoto Journal* for your support and interest in my book.

To my incomparable beta readers, Sue Scheeren Watchko and Carol Pouliot. Thank you for your careful readings and insights once again.

To the talented authors who took precious time to read an advance copy and write an endorsement for *Autumn Embers*—Amy Chavez, Carol Goodman, Naomi Hirahara, Jen Collins Moore, Carol Pouliot, and Lida Sideris. I am deeply grateful.

To Jazz Spot Yamatoya for allowing me to include in my book your lovely and hospitable café and whisky bar.

To Bench & Mug Café, which, sadly is no longer located in Kyoto, but was one of my favorite quiet spots in the city and became the inspiration for the Bench & Mug in my Batavia-on-Hudson.

To my son's expat community and to his circle of Japanese friends who have welcomed him and made Kyoto home for him. You are his chosen family.

To Alessandro, my son, whose direction in life has always been an inspiration to me. And to Wakana, my lovely daughter-in-law, for bringing so much joy, for helping me with the Japanese language and for showing me around your city. I love you both.

To Mom and Dad, Delfina and Vincenzo Tersigni, for being who you are. I love you both. For my dad who always carried a little index card from my grade school teacher showing how I was reading above grade level. He was so proud that he carried it everywhere until it was tattered. To my mom, who has essentially become my unofficial publicist. It seems I have made them proud.

To Denis, as always. I love you.

About the Author

Tina deBellegarde's debut novel, *Winter Witness*, was nominated for an Agatha Award for Best First Novel. *Dead Man's Leap*, her second book in the Batavia-on-Hudson Mystery Series, was nominated for an Agatha Award for Best Contemporary Novel. Reviewers have called Tina "the Louise Penny of the Catskills." Tina also writes short stories and flash fiction. Her story "Tokyo Stranger," nominated for a Derringer Award, appears in the Mystery Writers of America anthology *When a Stranger Comes to Town*, edited by Michael Koryta. Tina co-chairs the Murderous March Conference and is a founding member of Sleuths and Sidekicks, where she blogs, tours virtually, and teaches writing workshops. She is a member of Writers in Kyoto and reviews books for BooksOnAsia.net. She lives in Catskill, New York with her husband Denis and their cat Shelby. She travels frequently to Japan to visit her son and daughter-in-law and to do research. Tina is currently working on a collection of interconnected short stories set in Japan. Visit her website for more: https://www.tinadebellegarde.com/

AUTHOR WEBSITE:

https://www.tinadebellegarde.com/

SOCIAL MEDIA HANDLES:

https://www.facebook.com/tinadebellegardeauthor/
https://www.facebook.com/tina.tersigni/
https://www.instagram.com/tdb_writes/
https://twitter.com/tdbwrites

Also by Tina deBellegarde

Winter Witness (Book 1, Batavia-on-Hudson Mystery Series)

275

Dead Man's Leap (Book 2, Batavia-on-Hudson Mystery Series)

www.ingramcontent.com/pod-product-compliance
Lightning Source LLC
Chambersburg PA
CBHW020400110726
47899CB00006B/1787